"Good day, General Raines. Once again, thanks for the cease-fire and the help in recovering the bodies."

Ben watched the Federal colonel make his way down the bank and step into a boat, then he turned to his team. "Well, I tried."

"They want a fight, Pops," Anna told him. "From President Osterman on down. We might as well make up our minds to give them one and get it over with."

"Problem is, Kiddo, once it starts for real it'll never be over."

"Get down, General!" a Rebel shouted. "The Feds just jerked down the white flag."

Ben and his team ducked for cover just in time. Gunfire raked the top of the bank where they'd been standing.

"Bastards!" Ben said, spitting out a mouth of dirt and grass.

"You really think this fight will last that long, Pops?" Anna asked.

"It'll probably last for years, Anna, in one form or another."

"And we'll win it?"

"Oh, we'll win the battles. I have no doubts about that. But the hatred will last for years and years. This civil war won't be like the first one, a hundred and fifty years ago. Many of those veterans shook hands and forgave one another. They posed together for pictures and paintings. Had parades. This is a brand new war, Anna—the USA's godless totalitarian government against the SUSA's small government offering maximum freedom for its citizens. We'll win the war, but to do it we're going to have to virtually destroy the states aligned with the USA. And that, my dear, is going to rip this country apart, so far apart it will leave a wound that might never heal."

BOOK YOUR PLACE ON OUR WEBSITE AND MAKE THE READING CONNECTION!

We've created a customized website just for our very special readers, where you can get the inside scoop on everything that's going on with Zebra, Pinnacle and Kensington books.

When you come online, you'll have the exciting opportunity to:

- View covers of upcoming books
- Read sample chapters
- Learn about our future publishing schedule (listed by publication month *and author*)
- Find out when your favorite authors will be visiting a city near you
- Search for and order backlist books from our online catalog
- Check out author bios and background information
- Send e-mail to your favorite authors
- Meet the Kensington staff online
- Join us in weekly chats with authors, readers and other guests
- Get writing guidelines
- AND MUCH MORE!

STANDOFF IN THE ASHES

William W. Johnstone

Pinnacle Books
Kensington Publishing Corp.

http://www.pinnaclebooks.com

PINNACLE BOOKS are published by

Kensington Publishing Corp.
850 Third Avenue
New York, NY 10022

First Printing: October, 1999
10 9 8 7 6 5 4 3 2 1

Printed in the United States of America

Book One

I have nothing to offer but blood, toil, sweat, and tears.

Winston Churchill

Prologue

If a war had not engulfed the entire world, plunging every nation into bloody chaos, the government of the United States would probably have collapsed, anyway. Personal income taxes had been going up for years, and the hardworking, law-abiding citizens were paying well over half their incomes to the government. The left wing of the Democratic party had taken over and passed massive gun-grab legislation, effectively disarming American citizens—except for the criminals, of course, and about three quarters of a million tough-minded Americans who didn't give a rat's ass what liberals said, thought, or did. Those Americans carefully sealed up their guns and buried them, along with cases of ammunition. When the collapse came, those Americans were able to defend themselves against the hundreds of roaming gangs of punks and thugs that popped up all over what had once been called the United States of America. The great nation would never again be accurately referred to by that name.

Slowly, a growing group of people began calling for a man named Ben Raines to lead them, but Ben didn't want any part of leadership. For months he disregarded the ever-increasing calls from people all over the nation. Finally, he could no longer ignore the pleas.

Months later, thousands of people made the journey to the northwest part of the country and formed their own nation of three states. It was called the Tri-States, and those who chose to live there based many of their laws on the Constitution of the United States, on the *original* interpretation of that most revered document. Basically, it was a commonsense approach to government, something that had been sadly lacking during the years when the liberals were in control of the old United States of America. After only a few months in their new nation, Ben knew that only about two out of every ten Americans could (or would, more to the point), live under a commonsense form of government. Under this form of government, everyone, to a great degree, controlled his own destiny. The Rebels, as residents of the Tri-States were named by the press, took wonderful care of the very old, the young, and those unable to care for themselves. If a person was able to work, he worked . . . like it or not. There were no free handouts for able-bodied people. If they didn't want to work, they got the hell out of the Tri-States—very quickly.

The first attempt at building a nation within a nation failed when the federal government grew powerful enough to launch a major campaign against the Tri-States. The original Tri-States was destroyed, and the Rebel army was decimated and scattered.

The federal government made one major mistake: they didn't kill Ben Raines.

Ben and the few Rebels left alive began rebuilding their army and then launched a very nasty guerrilla war against the federal government that lasted for months: hit hard, destroy, and run. It worked.

Before any type of settlement could be reached, a deadly plague struck the earth—a rat-borne outbreak, black death revisited.

When the deadly disease finally ran its course, anarchy reigned over what had once been America. Gangs of punks and warlords ruled from border to border, coast to coast. Ben and his Rebels began the long, slow job of clearing the nation of human slime and setting up a new Tri-States. This time they settled in the south—first in Louisiana, in an area they called Base Camp One—then spreading out in all directions as more and more people wanted to become citizens of the new nation called the Southern United States of America: SUSA.

Ben and the Rebels fought for several years, clearing the cities of the vicious gangs and growing larger and stronger while the SUSA spread out.

In only a few years, the Rebel army became the largest and most powerful army on the face of the earth . . . with the possible exception of China. No one knew much about what was going on in China, for that nation had sealed its borders and cut off nearly all communication with the outside world.

A few more years drifted by while the Rebels roamed the world at the request of the newly formed United Nations, kicking ass and stabilizing nations as best they could in the time allotted them.

Back home, the situation was worsening: outside the SUSA, the nation was turning socialistic with sickening speed. The old FBI was gone, and in its place was the FPPS, the Federal Prevention and Protective Service. Its' fancy title fooled no one. The FPPS was the nation's secret police, and they were everywhere, bully boys and thugs. Day-to-day activities of those living in the USA were highly restricted.

The new Liberal/Socialist government of President-for-life Claire Osterman and her second in command, Harlan Millard, was now firmly in control.

There were border guards stationed all along major crossings in every state, and now many of them had been moved south, to patrol the several thousand mile border of the SUSA.

A bloody civil war was shaping up between the USA and the SUSA. A bounty had been placed on the head of Ben Raines: a million dollars for his capture, dead or alive. Ben was accustomed to that. He'd had bounties—of one kind or another, from one group or another—on his head for years.

Anna, Ben's adopted daughter, had been kidnapped by the FPPS. She was to be tried as a traitor to the liberal/socialist government and executed. A highly irritated Ben knew the taking of Anna was to draw him out, for the FPPS was certain Ben would come after her . . . which he did, with blood in his eyes. That abortive move cost the FPPS several dozen agents, and accomplished nothing else for Ostermann and her henchman. It also further heightened the already monumental legend of Ben Raines . . . and made Claire Osterman and her government look like a pack of incompetent screwups.

It also brought the USA and the SUSA closer to an all-out bloody civil war.

Chapter One

"It doesn't have to be this way," Ben radioed the commanding general of the federal forces facing the Rebels across the wide expanse of land separating the two armies. No-man's-land was silent and deadly.

"I guess it does, General," the CG replied. "You don't give us any other choice."

"What is your name, General?"

"Does it matter?"

"I suppose not. But it won't take me ninety seconds to find out."

The Federal chuckled. "Berman, General Raines. Walter Berman."

"You regular army, Walt?"

"You know I'm not."

A very large percentage of Federals were mercenaries, drawn from all over the world. Many of the officers and enlisted personnel in the newly formed United States Army, Navy, and Marine Corps had bluntly told President

Osterman they would not fire on American citizens. The men and women in the regular armed forces of the USA who did elect to wage war against the SUSA had been shifted to other units, and were green and had never been combat-tested. All that was about to change . . . in a hurry.

"In it strictly for the money, hey, General?"

"It's a living. As a matter of fact, it's quite a good living."

Ben smiled grimly. True mercenaries never changed. "I suppose so, Walt. But aren't there enough wars around the world for you and your people to fight? Why come here and get involved in a conflict you can't win?"

Most of the world was involved in civil war, to one degree or another. Eyes in the Sky reported especially large troop buildups in Russia and China. Those two nations were about to have a go at one another.

"Oh, I think we can win, Ben. As a matter of fact, I don't have any doubts about the outcome."

"Neither do I," Ben responded softly. "And I think you're well aware of that."

There was no immediate response from Berman. Actually, Ben had not expected any.

"We'll see," Berman finally said.

"Don't waste your men," Ben warned him. "If you send them at us across this strip, they're going to die. And that is the only warning you're going to get from me."

"It's a long strip, Ben, and I'm not the only commander."

"I'm telling you. Personally. Like right now. The strip is the same any way you look at it. And that is something you already know."

"How can you be sure of that?"

"You'd be a piss-poor commander if you didn't know, that's why. And you didn't get to your status by being piss-poor at your job."

"Thank you, Ben. Yes, I know all about you Rebels and

your infamous strip of no-man's-land. But every barrier has its weak spots."

"Not this one. A couple of months back, yes. But not now."

There was a long pause from the Federal commander. "You're being very honest with the enemy, General," he finally said. "I don't know what to make of that."

"I don't consider you my enemy, Walt Berman. Not yet. When the first shot is fired or the first attempt is made to cross our boundaries, then you become my enemy. And from that moment on, there will be no quarter shown or mercy given. I want you to understand that."

"I am aware of your tactics. I've been studying you for years," Berman said.

"You must have been fighting in some very obscure wars, Walt. Or else working under a variety of names."

The mercenary general laughed. "One of the two. Look toward the east. It's becoming light."

"I know what time it is. Still time for you to take your people and find another war."

"Can't do that, Ben Raines. I've signed an agreement. And I always keep my word."

"I'll be certain that is chiseled on your headstone. Providing your body is found, that is."

"You are a cocky son of a bitch, aren't you?"

"No. Just very sure of myself."

"We'll see, won't we? Well, time for talking is over, General Raines. Too bad I can't wish you luck."

"Same here, General Berman."

Ben waited in silence for half a minute. Corrie said, "He's finished, Boss. I guess it's show time."

"I suppose so. Do they have anything in the sky anywhere, Corrie?"

"Nothing reported anywhere up and down the line."

"Hell, we know they have gunships. Where are they? Why don't they use them?"

"Don't they have airborne troops?" Cooper asked, standing off to Ben's left.

"They have remnants of one division," Ben told him. "Over half of the newly reorganized Eighty-second stood down. The rest have very limited access to air transport."

"Ground all the way, then," Anna remarked.

"For the most part," Ben said. "But they do have a lot of artillery. This is not going to be any cakewalk."

"It sure won't be for them," Corrie said. "Everything on this side is ready. We're sitting on go from the West Texas border all the way over to the Atlantic Ocean."

"But we're thin," Cooper said.

"So are they," Beth reminded him. "A lot thinner than we are. We've got civilian militias and home guards. Those are two very valuable assets we have that they don't."

"We're picking up movement on the other side," Corrie said. She paused for half a minute while the others waited. "The push is about to start. Ordering artillery to stand by."

"Fools," Ben said. "Stupid fools to pull a mass advance all at once, one several thousand miles long. They really must not know our strength. What kind of idiot is running the show over there?"

"Maybe it's your friend, Sugar Babe Osterman," Anna suggested. She looked at Ben, questions in her eyes.

Ben glanced at her, a frown on his face. "Kiddo, you just may have hit it right. She'd certainly be arrogant enough to attempt to do just that."

Artillery rounds began landing in the no-man's-zone as the Federals began attempting to cut a path through the minefield. Corrie cut her eyes to Ben.

Ben nodded his head. "Answer that, Corrie. Let's get this show on the road."

Then there was no more time for conversation as both sides began hurling artillery rounds. What talk there was had to be shouted over the crashing and roaring.

When the Federals stopped shelling in Ben's immediate sector, the Rebels knew the human push was only seconds away. The Rebels came out of their bunkers and holes and made ready their mortars, heavy machine guns, and Big Thumpers.

The zone fell silent, the Rebels holding their fire, allowing the first wave of Federals to begin slowly and carefully picking their way across the wide and deadly no-man's-strip.

Ben and his team waited on a ridge, in a carefully dug and fortified and camouflaged bunker just a few hundred meters south of the strip, and watched and waited.

"It's going to be a slaughter," Ben muttered. "They should have sent airborne troops in behind us last night." He shook his head. "They're doing everything wrong. Who the hell is giving the orders for this lash-up?"

"Federals advancing on Ike's sector, in half a dozen locations," Corrie reported.

"This just might turn out to be the shortest major assault in modern warfare," Ben muttered.

"Somebody who doesn't know what the hell they're doing has to be giving the orders," Cooper said.

"It must be Osterman and her dipshit advisors," Ben replied. "But those mercenary commanders won't put up with this for any length of time. They'll start acting on their own before very long."

"FO's all up and down the line reporting those are regular Federal troops leading this assault," Corrie said. "But they're spread very thin."

"I figured as much," Ben said softly. "Using them for cannon fodder." He sighed audibly. "Americans. Damn! What a waste of young men and women this is going to be. The merc commanders are saving their experienced troops for last. Then the real battles will start."

"Any change in orders?" Corrie asked. "Ike wants to know, Boss."

Ben did not hesitate with his response. "No, Corrie. No change at all. I can't do that. We can't afford to be charitable—we're not The Salvation Army. When they come into range, cut them down."

The sounds of dozens of mines being tripped filled the smoky air up and down Ben's sector. The faint cries of wounded quickly followed.

Ben's mortar crews began their work, sending some of the most lethal mortar rounds ever devised down the tubes. They 'thonked' out and up, and came down seconds later with devastating results. The mortars were a new version of the old 81mm mortar, and they packed a terrible punch with HE and WP rounds. In addition, Ben's scientists had perfected a new round that exploded in the air, about twenty-five feet off the ground, and carried dozens of hardened steel fletchettes. The killing and maiming power of that round was awesome.

The only possible problem was that an opposing force might have mortar-locating radar which could home in on the heavy base-plates. In this case, the Federals either did not have that technology or were not using it—probably the former, Ben thought.

Osterman had been spending very little money on military hardware. Her administration's latest war effort was on cans of hair spray, which were in the process of being totally banned because kids were inhaling the spray to get high. Very important project on which to spend taxpayer money—hair spray.

"First wave is retreating," Corrie reported, adding, "It's more like a rout."

"Maintain the fire," Ben ordered. "Adjust for range. Keep pouring it on."

Ten more minutes passed before Ben finally ordered his people to cease fire. "Get reports from all batt coms," he told Corrie.

"Receiving now, Boss. We kicked the shit out of them."

Ben lowered his binoculars and slowly nodded his head. For as far as he could see, left and right and in front of him, the strip called no-man's-land was littered with broken bodies. "We certainly did, Corrie. Radio General Berman. Tell him if he wants to risk his medics in a minefield we will hold our fire while he gathers his wounded."

"Right, Boss. New reports coming in fast. Let me get them down."

Ben rolled a cigarette and waited while Corrie took down all the information. He glanced around the bunker. His personal team was certainly relaxed enough. Anna was chomping on a fresh wad of bubble gum. Beth was munching on a candy bar. Cooper was sitting down reading a magazine. Jersey was staring out the slit in front of the bunker, watching the no-man's-land. They had all been through this more times than Ben cared to recall. Long, bloody, gut-wrenching years of combat, fighting for the right to be free in the SUSA.

"The Federals hit us in strength in half a dozen locations," Corrie reported. "They didn't gain an inch of SUSA ground. We were hit in much lesser force in about a dozen other locations. Same results. Prelims indicate the Federals lost, dead or wounded, approximately ten thousand personnel."

"Half a division," Ben said. "Young men and women wiped out just to satisfy that bitch Osterman. Jesus!"

"And it's just started," Cooper remarked.

Ben looked at his driver. "Yes. It's just begun." He looked briefly back at the no-man's strip of land. "Somebody get some coffee in here. It's going to be a long morning."

Claire Osterman stared in disbelief as the reports began landing on her desk in the New White House in Indiana. Thousands of troops dead or wounded. Not one inch of SUSA ground taken.

"Incredible," she muttered.

"Not really," said one of the senior advisors seated around her desk.

"What do you mean?" Claire 'Sugar Babe' Osterman demanded. She waved the sheaf of papers. "A bunch of ragtag, gun-happy, right-wingers just defeated thousands of professional soldiers."

"Claire," the longtime friend and advisor said patiently. He was one of only a few men and women who did not refer to her as Madam President when in semi-private or private conversation. "Ben Raines does not command a ragtag army. The Rebels are unquestionably the finest fighting force on earth. And you made a very big mistake by tangling with them."

Claire waved that away. "We've been over this before, Otis. I know your opinion. Enough, already."

Otis Warner stared at Claire for a moment. In all his years he had never known a person with such hatred as that which Claire Osterman held for Ben Raines. Not that some of it wasn't justified, Otis thought, for in his mind it certainly was. Ben Raines was a most unreasonable man when it came to the SUSA . . . among other matters. But Claire had a very bad habit of sometimes underestimating her foes.

Otis ignored her request to drop the subject. "Claire, let's try negotiating with President Jefferys. He is a very reasonable man. I think we could work something out."

Claire Osterman glared at her friend for several seconds. The others in the room suddenly had a very strong urge to be somewhere else. Claire was becoming angry, and when she lost her temper she sometimes flew into a towering rage. It was not a pretty sight.

Before Madam President could explode, Otis held up a hand. "Control yourself, Claire. Take a deep breath, have a sip of water. Just calm down and think about this. We're going to waste a lot of money fighting Ben Raines and the Rebels. If this war continues for one more day, we're going to be committed to seeing it through, no matter the cost or outcome. And it will be a protracted campaign, you can be assured of that. Are you certain that's what you want?"

Claire drummed her fingertips on the polished desktop for a moment. Then she sighed and shook her head. "We could bankrupt the nation . . . no, I certainly don't want that." She picked up some of the papers she had just been handed and muttered an obscenity under her breath. The defeat just handed the Federals was humiliating.

Then Claire's face hardened as the image and thought of a laughing Ben Raines entered her mind. "No," she said firmly, "I will not negotiate with the SUSA." She looked at Otis. "And that is final, old friend."

Otis Warner shrugged his shoulders. "So be it, Claire. Just don't ever think or say that I didn't try."

"Oh, I'm positive we shall be victorious in this war," another of Claire's 'advisors' piped up. Andy Shumburger had absolutely no business being a part of the national security team—he had difficulty walking and chewing gum at the same time—but he was a good party member who had led the fight to save the endangered blue-nosed, triple-titted, wiggle-wobble fish in his state. The facts that the fish was only approximately 1/16 of an inch long and no one had seen one in two hundred years didn't matter. A hundred and fifty families were thrown out of their homes and moved to another location, and two thousand jobs were lost when a building permit was refused a company who wanted to set up a factory in that particular location. The drive to save the mysterious wiggle-wobble fish cost the taxpayers about five million dollars, but the fish were saved. That made it all worthwhile—The Save the Wobble Fish Committee thought so, at least. If they could just see one, they would be sure. But if they didn't spot one in a few months the committee was already working on plans to erect a statue in memory of the wiggle-wobble fish . . . at taxpayer expense, of course.

Otis sighed and rolled his eyes at Andy's comment, but kept his silence.

The other advisors agreed with Andy. The USA under the direction of Madam President Claire Osterman and her party of Socialist Democrats would be victorious in the battle with Ben Raines and his terrible band of right-wing, gun-happy, redneck Rebels.

"Horseshit!" Otis muttered.

"I beg your pardon, Otis?" the advisor seated closest to him asked. "What did you say?"

"Nothing, Sam. Nothing at all." *But I am terribly afraid we are going to get our collective asses kicked very hard,* Otis thought. *Ben Raines and his Rebels have lost a few battles, but they have never lost a war, and they sure as hell aren't going to lose this one.*

"Otis, old friend," Claire said, leaning forward. "We are going to win in this fight with Raines. Remember this— we have the well-being of the nation and the good wishes of the people on our side. How can we lose?"

Very easily, Otis thought, but he smiled at Madam President and nodded in agreement.

"Let's go into the war room," Osterman said, standing up and moving around her massive desk. "We have to plan the next move for our military. I have an idea."

Otis sat for a few seconds longer before standing up and joining the group. *Even if we did allow the military to run this war, we'd still stand a good chance of losing it,* he thought, *but with a group of civilians calling every move losing is a certainty. This is madness.*

"Coming, Otis?" Claire called.

"Oh, yes," Otis said. He thought: *I wouldn't miss this for the world. A planning session guaranteed to lose a war.*

Chapter Two

Ben spoke with every batt com up and down the long front. The Rebels had suffered only a few casualties. The Federals had been thrown back and had taken heavy losses.

"They won't make this mistake again," Ben warned his people. "This move wasn't planned by any experienced military commander, you can bet on that. This lunacy was the brainchild of full-time civilians who never served any time in the military or spent a day in combat."

"Who the hell is running the Federals' operation, Ben?" asked Ike, Ben's longtime friend and second in command. "This frontal assault was totally dumb."

"Claire Osterman. I'd bet on that."

"I hope she keeps running it."

"She won't. The military won't put up with it."

"Ben, my intel people are telling me what we're facing is a mixed bag of regular USA troops and hired guns from all over the world."

"Yes. With more mercenary troops than American boys and girls."

"That makes me feel better about the heavy toll we just took on them."

"I know the feeling, Ike, but I can't help thinking about the Americans all tangled up in this." Ben sighed in frustration. "However . . . everybody has a choice, and they made theirs. We have to look at it in that light."

"That's the only way to look at it, Ben. When do we start sending our spec ops teams into federal territory and letting them raise some hell?"

"As soon as they start sending their teams into the SUSA, Ike. That's the way I'm going to play it."

"I kinda figured that would be your reply, partner. Suits me."

"All right. You take care, ole' buddy, and keep your powder dry."

"Same to you, Ben. Watch your ass. It's you the Feds want. Keep that in mind all the time."

"Will do."

Ben walked outside the bunker and stood in the late afternoon air, drinking coffee and smoking. After the Federal push early that morning there had not been another shot fired from either side, at least not in Ben's immediate sector. The Federals were dug in and keeping their heads down.

"Wonder what they'll throw at us next?" Jersey asked as the team walked out of the bunker to stand by Ben.

"That's a damn good question. They don't have much of an air force. We've got them out-gunned there probably ten to one. Our navy is small, but still much larger than what the Federals have. With Sugar Babe and her silly-assed, so-called advisors running the show out of the capital, a thousand miles away, there is no telling what might happen next."

"Hasn't been a mine go off in over an hour," Cooper said. "They must have picked up all the wounded they could get to."

"All the nations in the world that need some help getting stabilized," Anna remarked, "and the Federals pick a fight with us. Doesn't make any sense to me."

"It goes back years before the Great War, Anna. Long before you were born, long before any of you were born. America began a slow turn toward socialism. For whatever reasons, and they're many and complicated, it couldn't be stopped—or wouldn't be stopped, might be a better way to say it. Both of the two major political parties were to blame. I'll get some arguments on that point, but it's the truth. Those of us who wanted a return to small government and individual rights frightened big government, and weren't allowed to organize. You all know the story. You've heard me expound on it often enough."

"Yes, but you were there, Pops," Anna said. "You witnessed it firsthand. It's different than us reading about it in history books."

Before Ben could reply, a burst of gunfire erupted off to the west and spun them around.

"Infiltrators!" someone shouted, the call faint. "Coming up behind us."

Ben didn't have to order his team into cover. They were moving before the echo of the shouted alarm had faded away. Corrie was back in the bunker where the most sophisticated of her radio equipment was set up, the others spread out on the ground, behind cover.

A few seconds passed in silence. Then Corrie called, "At least platoon-sized, Boss. Maybe larger than that. They're good, too. Professional."

"How many locations are reporting this type of action?" Ben called.

"Several dozen, all up and down the line."

"Berman sacrificed green boys and girls as a diversion to HALO this bunch in," Ben said grimly. "Just before dawn today. Good move, Walt. Smart. But I'm going to kill you for that. Personally."

Something thudded on the ground in front of the rise of ground Ben was lying behind. "Grenade!" he shouted, then rolled backward a few yards down the slight mound of earth.

The grenade blew, and hot shrapnel hummed and whizzed over Ben's head.

Several CAR's yammered at once, and someone thrashed about in the bushes for a few seconds and then was still. Ben crawled back up to the crest of the rise and looked over the terrain in the light of late afternoon. The area was shrouded in shadows from the timber.

Ben caught a glimpse of something that just didn't quite fit in with the terrain and triggered off a burst of .223's from his CAR. Someone grunted in pain and then was still. Ben backed up just in time: the crest of the rise was lashed with gunfire, the lead kicking up dirt that showered him.

The team opened up with automatic fire and grenades. They kept it up for half a minute, tossing a dozen fire-frags, doing some fast magazine changes, and burning several hundred rounds of ammo. By that time a hundred more Rebels had moved in and surrounded the area.

"Give it up, people," Ben called from the ridge. "There is no percentage in dying. You will not be harmed in any way, and you will be treated with every courtesy accorded prisoners of war. You have my word on that."

"Who are you to be giving your word?" The question was thrown out of the brush.

"Ben Raines."

After a very short pause, the Federal said, "That's good enough for me. Coming out."

A dozen or so men stepped slowly out of the brush, hands in the air. They were immediately surrounded by two dozen Rebels. Another dozen fanned out and carefully searched the timber and brush around Ben's CP.

"All clear," a Rebel called after a few moments. "Ten dead. Four wounded."

"Get the medics in there," Ben ordered. "And ready some transportation to take them to the field hospital." Ben walked down the short incline and faced the Federals. "Who is in charge here?"

A burly man spoke up. "I am. Captain Broadhurst. Thank you for being so considerate to my wounded." He then gave his serial number and closed his mouth.

"That's good enough for me, Captain," Ben said. "You'll be escorted south to a POW camp. I assure you, neither you nor your men will be harmed."

"Thank you, sir." The captain saluted and Ben returned it. A moment later the Federals were being marched off, under heavy guard.

"We lost some people," Corrie said, walking up. "All up and down the line. But the Federal assault failed. They lost a lot of people, and we've collected several hundred prisoners. The assault didn't accomplish a thing."

"It showed us something about the caliber of men we're up against," Ben said. "And they're capable of doing just about anything to win."

"Almost like us," Anna said softly.

"Almost," Ben replied, after a few seconds pause. "But not quite. We still have some honor left. But can we maintain it if a civil war drags on?"

Ben paused and the others waited, looking at him. He did not reply, just turned and walked away.

"I don't think I have ever seen him this sad," Jersey said. "I don't like it."

"It's tearin' him up, that's for sure," Cooper said. "Worst I've ever seen."

"Not since Jerre's death, anyway," Beth said softly.

"Yeah," Cooper said. "You're right. God, I forgot about her."

"You can bet he hasn't," Jersey said. "And you can also bet he never will."

Before anyone could say anything else on the subject, Ben came out of the CP. "Get your gear together and let's roll, gang. We're changing sectors just to be on the safe side. This site may have been compromised."

In the big nine passenger SUV, Cooper asked, "Which way, Boss?"

"East, Coop. Toward the Bootheel of Missouri."

"Where do you want to stop for the night?" Corrie asked. "Which it will be in about an hour," she added.

Ben smiled at the not-too-subtle hint in Corrie's voice. "I don't know, Corrie. It isn't that far, and we'll be on Rebel roads. They're in good shape. We'll see."

They drove straight through to the end of the line, which surprised no one in Ben's team or his security people, who were always close by.

The officer in charge of the Rebels at the last outpost east in this sector, on the Arkansas/Missouri line, was not surprised to see Ben and his team unass themselves from the big wagon. He had been warned by other Rebels along the way that the War Eagle himself was on the prowl and might show up.

"How are things here, Captain?" Ben asked the commander of the small detachment of Rebels.

"Quiet, sir." He pointed east. "But the Federals are dug in tight just across the river."

Ben turned toward the St. Francis river. "How many?"

"Several companies, at least. This is the only bridge over

that river left intact in this area. They'd like to take it in one piece.''

"I bet they would. Is it wired to blow?"

"Yes, sir. The Combat Engineers did that some time back. I'm sure the Federals know it's wired. General? Do you think something is about to pop in this area?"

Ben shook his head. "I don't know what's going to happen, Captain. Or where."

"We know they've been moving in boats over there," the captain said, jerking a thumb toward the river.

"You ready for an assault?"

The young captain smiled. "Oh, yes, sir."

"Then let them come."

"You going to stay with us tonight, sir?"

"Thought I might. We'll stay out of your way. If the Federals attack, it's your show. Where do you want my people?"

"We're pretty thin, General. Anywhere will do, and we're glad to have you."

"We'll hold our own, Captain. We'll spread out to the south and dig in."

"Yes, sir."

"Carry on, Captain."

After the young officer had left, Jersey said, "You 'bout scared the shit out of him, Boss. Showin' up like we did."

"I used to know every officer in the Rebel army by their first name. Now I don't know but a handful. What is that young man's name?"

"Evans, Boss," Beth said. "He was a sergeant when we first hit Africa. By the time we pulled out of there, he was commanding a platoon."

"Thank you, Beth. I don't know what I'd do without you."

"I know what I'd like to do with her," Cooper said after Beth had walked out of earshot.

Ben smiled. "Get your mind off pussy, Coop."

"How does one do that, Boss? 'Specially when you're surrounded by good-lookin' women?"

Ben laughed. "I don't know, Coop. But do your best. I think the Federals are going to try to cross that little river tonight."

"They're fools if they do."

"Just more cannon fodder. Probing for weak spots. Let's get dug in. It just might get real interesting around here in a few hours."

Chapter Three

"They're really going to try it," Jersey whispered as the very faint sounds of boats sliding into the water reached the Rebels on the other side.

"More young American boys and girls being used as cannon fodder by their commanders," Ben said, disgust and sadness all mixed up in his voice.

"Federals probing at half a dozen other locations," Corrie said quietly.

A moment later the pop of flares was loud in the quiet night. The night became bright with artificial light. Then the carnage began as Rebels opened up with machine guns, Big Thumpers, and automatic rifle fire. Many of the Rebels had tears in their eyes as they opened fire on fellow Americans, but they had no choice in the matter. It all boiled down to kill-or-be-killed-time, and the Rebels were experts in staying alive.

The assault fell apart in only a few minutes, and the river turned red with blood. Bodies bobbed in the dark waters, and wounded Federals cried out in the night. The Rebels ceased their fire and waited.

"I don't think they'll try that again," Ben said.

"I really hope not," Jersey said, considerable emotion in her voice.

Ben worked his way down the bank and walked back to where Captain Evans was dug in. The captain greeted him somberly.

"Hard night, Captain," Ben said. "This isn't something that any of us wanted."

"No, sir. But we didn't start this war. All we wanted was to be left alone."

"Anyone in your command hit?"

"No, sir. Not a scratch. You would think they'd have softened us up some with mortars."

"I don't know what's in the minds of those commanders over there. But they do know they've got a hard row to hoe. Right now, I think people in the capital are calling the shots. But that won't last long."

"I figured a bunch of civilians were running things," Captain Evans replied. "The Federals have sure pulled some dumb stunts so far."

"How many Federals you think bought it this night?"

"At least three, four hundred dead, that many wounded."

"Hell of a price to pay for nothing."

"Yes, sir. It damn sure is."

Ben walked the camp, speaking to each Rebel he met. Some of them were badly shaken from having to fire on fellow Americans. The Federals were not punks and thugs. They were soldiers under orders to do a job. Ben wondered if the men of the North and South had felt the same way a hundred and fifty years back? Some of them, perhaps most of them, he concluded.

There were no more attempts to cross the little river that night. Ben and his team alternately slept and drank coffee and waited through the long darkness. When dawn finally cut the night with a silver and gold blade, the scene that greeted the Rebels was gruesome: dozens of swollen, bloated, and mangled bodies were caught in the brush on both sides of the river.

"Good God!" Cooper breathed.

"I'll damn sure second that," Jersey said. "We can't leave those Americans like that. It wouldn't be right."

Ben looked at her and nodded his head in agreement. "Captain," he said, "will you notify the Federal commander that we are requesting a cease-fire? We will assist them in retrieving the bodies of their comrades for proper burial."

"Yes, sir. Right away."

"Have someone rig a white flag just to be on the safe side."

"Yes, sir."

Rebels and Federals worked for an hour gathering up the dead. At first they worked in silence. Then some engaged in small conversation.

"Where you from, Reb?"

"Originally from Ohio, Fed."

"Then why are you fighting for the SUSA?"

"Because I want to live free, that's why. Why the hell are you fighting for a socialistic government that has its nose stuck in everything you do?"

"Your government doesn't do the same?"

"Hell, no!"

"That's not what I heard."

"You heard wrong."

"You got a cigarette?"

"Sure." The Rebel smiled. "But I thought smoking was illegal under your form of government?"

The young Federal grinned. "Yeah. I see what you mean."

"Take the pack. Just be careful. You might get caught and be court-martialed."

"Don't worry, Reb. I'll be careful."

On the bank, Ben and the Federal commander stood and talked quietly.

"Lousy way to make a living, isn't it, General Raines?"

"Sometimes, Colonel." Ben offered the Federal a bag of tobacco and rolling papers.

The colonel waved them off. "Thanks. I'd like to, but I can't let my men see me smoking."

Ben found that amusing, but carefully hid his smile. "Smoking isn't good for a person. We all know that. But as adults we have a right to choose."

"I suppose so, General," the colonel said noncommittally.

"How about just pulling your people back and we all live in peace, Colonel?"

"Can't do it, and you know it. A house divided won't stand."

"I see," Ben said slowly. "So we just go on killing each other?"

"Unless you want to surrender."

"You know that will never happen. So we continue to kill each other until there is no one left to kill on either side?"

"Looks like that's the only option left us."

"That's bullshit. There is no reason the USA and the SUSA can't peacefully coexist. Your nitwit President-for-Life, Claire Osterman, hates me. That's the bottom line. She's a goddamn socialist, and you know it."

"And you know perfectly well I can't say anything derogatory about my commander in chief."

"Good God, Colonel. You've got a brain. Why don't you use it?"

"I think this conversation is over. Thanks for your assistance in helping recover the bodies."

Ben sighed. "All right. Have it your way."

The colonel looked squarely at Ben. "I don't have a choice, General Raines. I swore an oath to uphold the union."

"So did thousands of others in uniform. But they elected to stay out of this fight."

"Traitors. Every goddamned one of them."

"You'd like to see them court-martialed?"

"You're damn right I would."

"I'm sorry you feel that way. Because I'd like to quit this mess before it really gets started."

The colonel looked at Ben and shook his head. "It won't happen. This nation must be made whole once again."

"Not as long as there is one Rebel left alive who can pick up a gun and fight. Not as long as the USA is governed by democrats/socialist."

"Very well. Good day, General Raines. Once again, thanks for the cease-fire and the help in recovering the bodies."

Ben watched the Federal colonel make his way down the bank and step into a boat. He turned to his team. "Well, I tried. Not much point in continuing to beat my head against a stone wall. But I probably will . . . for a while longer."

"They want a fight, Pops," Anna told him. "From President Osterman on down. We might as well make up our minds to give them one and get it over with."

"Problem is, Kiddo, once it starts for real it'll never be over."

"Get down, General!" a Rebel shouted. "The Feds just jerked down the white flag."

Ben and his team ducked for cover just in time. Gunfire raked the top of the bank where they'd been standing.

"Bastards!" Ben said, spitting out a mouth of dirt and grass he'd eaten as he hit the ground hard and bellied down. "Pour it on!" he shouted to the Rebels. "Give them a taste of everything we've got."

For ten minutes the Rebels hammered the Federal positions across the river with mortars, 40mm grenades, and machine gun fire. Then Ben called on the few artillery pieces this Rebel contingent had backing them up, and they began dropping in everything but the kitchen sink. That did it for what was left of the Federals on the east side of the river.

"They're pulling back, General," Captain Evans said. "The fools are retreating under heavy artillery fire."

"They won't be fools for long. In a few weeks, those left will be seasoned combat veterans."

"You really think this fight will last that long?"

"It'll probably last for years, Captain, in one form or another."

"And we'll win it?"

"Oh, we'll win the battles. I have no doubts about that. But the hatred will last for years and years. This civil war won't be like the first one, a hundred and fifty years ago. Many of those veterans shook hands and forgave one another. They posed together for pictures and paintings. Had parades. This is a brand new war, Anna—the USA's godless totalitarian government against the SUSA's small government offering maximum freedom for its citizens. We'll win the war, but to do it we're going to have to virtually destroy the states aligned with the USA. And that, my dear, is going to rip this country apart, so far apart it will leave a wound that might never heal."

* * *

Ben and team pulled out that afternoon, heading first south, then cutting back east, running along the Tennessee/Kentucky border.

"This has to be the longest front in history," Cooper remarked.

"Several thousand miles, Coop," Ben said. "And much of it undefended, except for spotter outposts every few miles, manned by volunteers from the home guard. All in all, it's a hell of a way to run a war."

Ben turned in the captain's chair to look at Corrie. "Anything coming over the air?"

"Nothing of any importance, Boss. Just Rebel chatter."

Ben smiled. "Warning the boys and girls I'm on the way, hey?"

Corrie laughed. "Something like that."

Ben glanced at his watch. "I'm getting hungry, gang. Coop, find us a spot to chow down."

That was often easier said than done. In addition to Ben's security detail—a full platoon, which was always with him—a full company from Ben's old original battalion, including tanks, traveled with him.

"Spotter plane looking at us, Boss," Corrie said.

"Ours?"

"Negative. It's Federal."

"Let them look." Ben dug out a map. "We're only a few miles from the Kentucky line. Probably making the Feds nervous, wondering what we're up to."

"The ruins of Clarksville just up ahead, Boss," Cooper said. "We can pull over there and eat."

"Sounds good. Where is the nearest Rebel contingent of any size, Corrie?"

"Thirty miles to the east. Part of our 501. Want me to bump them?"

"They know we're here. Find us a place to eat, Coop. Let's give those in that spotter plane a thrill."

The convoy pulled over at Coop's signal, and guards were posted. Field rats were opened and the Rebels ate and relaxed for a time.

"These new field rations aren't half bad, Boss," Beth remarked after swallowing a mouthful of hash. "You must have read the scientists the riot act."

Ben chuckled. "You might say I told them if the new rats weren't eatable, I would stick them up their ass."

"That would certainly get my attention," Coop said.

Ben looked up, studying the sky. The spotter plane was heading back north. "We just might get some sky visitors in a few minutes. Let's be sure we're ready for them."

Corrie spoke briefly into her headset, then returned her attention to her lunch.

The Rebels used several types of SAMs, but the two most widely used were the much newer and greatly modified versions of the Stinger and the Armburst. Ben's scientists had improved on each weapon, including range and warhead. The Stinger had more range, but the Armburst could be fired inside a closed space with no danger from backblast. The Armburst was used quite often in Rebel ambushes.

The Rebels finished their lunch and disposed of the wrappers and containers, then waited for the action to start . . . and they all felt it was coming.

"Choppers!" a Rebel yelled. "Coming straight in from the north."

Ben lifted his binoculars and counted a dozen gunships, coming in low and fast. "Get to cover, gang. The shit's about to hit the fan—big time!"

The gunships came in with everything they had, hammering and yowling. The Rebels lifted their shoulder-fired launchers and cut loose. Five gunships exploded in midair, showering the ground with hundreds of pieces of hot metal and various body parts. One huge propeller went cartwheeling end over end across the ground and out into a field, digging up dirt until it finally came to rest.

One gunship made the mistake of coming straight in, readying its rockets to destroy a Rebel Main Battle Tank. The gunner in the MBT had been tracking the chopper. He got off one lucky round from her main gun, and the 155 HE round literally blew the gunship into a million pieces. Nothing bigger than a matchbox was left. The tiny pieces began dropping to the ground, clinking as they bounced off Rebel vehicles.

"Damn!" Ben breathed in awe after witnessing the horrific explosion. "That doesn't happen very often."

With half their force destroyed, the gunships began quickly backing off just as a Rebel Scout radioed frantically back to Corrie.

"Ground troops coming at us hard!" she yelled to Ben. "About six thousand meters away."

"How many?" Ben yelled over the sounds of battle.

"A whole shitpot full was what he said."

Ben had to smile at the report. "Tell him to get out of there."

"His feet were working as he radioed in."

"I bet they were. OK. It's too late to make a run for it. You've radioed for air support?"

"Affirmative. But there is none anywhere in this area."

"Then we'll handle it ourselves."

Ben did not have to give any orders concerning positioning of troops or equipment for the upcoming fight. His people knew exactly what to do, and did it quickly. Tanks were repositioned, machine gun and mortar pits were quickly dug. Cans of ammunition were handed out from supply trucks. Troops got into position. The Rebels waited.

"Federals have stopped their advance," Corrie reported. "Approximately three thousand meters away."

"Give them some mortars. HE and fragmentation."

"Scouts have stopped on some high ground. They'll act as FO."

"Good enough."

The mortar crews began dropping in the rounds. Corrie called out the corrections in elevation as soon as the FO's radioed them in.

"That's it." She spoke into her headset. "You're right on target. Pour it on."

A few heartbeats later Corrie said, "They're advancing. Two thousand meters. Several hundred in strength."

Ben looked skyward. The gunships were gone. "Whoever's running this show doesn't know shit from Shinola," he muttered. "This kind of luck can't hold for us."

He held up a hand. "Cease firing," he ordered. "Let them come."

"Cease firing?" Corrie questioned, not sure she correctly understood.

"Cease firing," Ben repeated.

"What the hell happens now?" Cooper muttered under his breath.

Ben heard the muttered question and smiled. "We meet them eyeball to eyeball."

Cooper flushed. The Boss wasn't supposed to have heard that.

"Ready all Big Thumpers and machine guns," Ben ordered. "Everybody on full auto. Tell the tank commanders to level all main guns."

Corrie cut her eyes to Ben for a second. He met her gaze. "Do it," Ben said.

"Yes, sir," she said, then radioed the orders.

"Jesus Christ!" Beth whispered. "Those Feds are running into a wall of steel and lead."

"We'll be here a friggin' week pickin' up all the pieces," Jersey said.

"One thousand meters," Corrie said.

"Can those types of tanks fire their main guns point-blank?" Anna asked, awe in her voice.

"I think they have to do some adjusting," Cooper answered. "Or something. Hell, what do I know about tanks?"

"Same as you know about anything else," Jersey said, not about to let the opportunity pass by. "Nothing."

"Aw, now, my pretty cactus flower," Cooper replied. "Despite it all, you know your love for me runs as deep as a river."

Jersey made several gagging sounds. "Excuse me while I puke."

"Five hundred meters," Corrie said.

Ben waited, his face expressionless.

A Rebel's words drifted to Ben and team. "Christ's sake, there they are, crossing that field."

"I'll court-martial the first person who fires without my order," Ben said, raising his voice.

"Four hundred meters," Corrie said.

"Must be six or seven hundred of them," another Rebel said. "Damn near a full battalion."

"Like ducks all in a row," the Rebel next to him replied. "This is wild."

"Three hundred meters." Corrie called it out. Again she looked at Ben.

"I can't believe the Federal commanders are this stupid," Ben muttered. He stood and watched the slow, steady advance of the Federal troops across the green and yellow-speckled meadow.

"The sun is in their eyes," Anna observed. "Hell, maybe they can't see us."

"But they know we're here," Beth said. "They just keep on coming. They're not even trying to hunt any cover. This is crazy!"

"Two hundred meters," Corrie counted down.

The Federal troops broke into a slow trot and began yelling. The yells were a mixture of bravado and profanity, the profanity directed at the Rebels and the SUSA.

"That is going to make it a lot easier," Jersey said.

"Damn sure is," Beth said.

"Goddamn bunch of communists," Cooper said. He was only slightly wrong in his political applications.

"One hundred and fifty meters," Corrie said nervously, again cutting her eyes to Ben.

"Almost," Ben said. "Get ready."

"We been ready," Cooper muttered. "Are we gonna invite them in for coffee?" He was careful this time to make sure Ben didn't hear his remarks.

Ben lifted the old M-14 he had taken from the rear of the big wagon and jacked in a round. The Rebels lying close to where he was standing smiled. The old Thunder Lizard was one hell of a weapon. On full auto it was a son of a bitch to hold.

"One hundred meters," Corrie said. "Damn, Boss!"

"Fire!" Ben yelled.

The meadow across the road turned into a killing field as the Rebels cut loose with everything at their disposal.

Chapter Four

It was carnage. Nothing else would describe the scene in the meadow. The Federals walked right into a hot wall of death. There was no escape.

Ben kept up the nearly point-blank barrage for three long minutes. When he finally ordered a cease-fire, the silence seemed almost audible.

Out in the meadow, only a few yards from the two-lane road, there was little movement and only a few moans of pain.

"Son of a bitch!" Jersey breathed, standing up and looking out at the bloody meadow.

"Small group of Federals hightailing it to the north," Beth said, looking over the scene through binoculars. "Some of them have thrown away their weapons. Or lost them."

"Check the field for survivors," Ben ordered.

"I don't see how anyone could have survived that," Anna remarked.

"Corrie, have you found the Federals' frequency?"

"Negative, Boss. Still looking."

"Well, get on some band and tell whoever is listening to come get what is left of their battalion. And to come under a flag of truce or they'll be in deep shit."

"Medics reporting a lot of badly wounded out there," a doctor told Ben a few minutes later. "You want to set up a field hospital, General?"

Ben hesitated only a few seconds. "Yes, we might as well. Let's try to save as many as possible."

"We shoot them, then patch them up," Cooper said. "I just wonder if they'd do the same for us."

No one replied, but all who heard it had their doubts if the Federals would care if any Rebel lived or died.

"I have one of the Federals' frequencies, Boss," Corrie told Ben. "I have given them your message."

"And?"

"They say thanks, and they're on the way. Dust-offs will be coming in very soon."

"Advise them I will shoot down any gunship I see."

"Will do." A moment later: "Message received, and they will comply."

"Good enough."

"Home guard on the horn, Boss. Says they discovered how the Federals got across our no-man's-strip. They've found where the choppers have been landing just inside our territory. Looks as though they've been bringing in a platoon at a time."

"That clears up that little mystery. Corrie, tell the cooks to set up a tent and make a lot of coffee. We're going to be here for quite a while."

"OK, Boss."

In less than fifteen minutes after Corrie touched base with the Federals, the sounds of a dozen big choppers reached the Rebels. They were guided in, and teams of doctors and medics jumped out and were escorted across the road and into the meadow, where Rebel medics and several doctors were working.

A three-star general in BDUs strolled up to Ben and saluted smartly. "General Raines? I'm General Maxwell. Call me Max, if you will."

"OK, Max. I'm Ben."

"Thank you for your kindness in helping my people."

"No problem. I can truthfully say I wish to hell they had stayed on their side of the line."

General Maxwell did not respond to that comment. "Is that coffee I smell?"

"Sure is. Fresh brewed. Care for a cup?"

"Love one."

Over mugs of steaming coffee, the two generals looked at one another, saying nothing.

Ben finally broke the uncomfortable silence. "Get used to heavy casualties tangling with us, Max. We've been doing this all over the world."

Max smiled. "It'll change when the White House bows out of trying to run things. Not that I'm telling you anything you haven't already deduced."

"Yes. I reached that conclusion early on. But nothing is going to change. We're fighting for our homeland."

"We'll see, Ben. The gods of war are fickle." He took a sip of coffee. "Good coffee."

"Smoke if you like. In the SUSA we don't try to run every aspect of adults' lives."

That stung the Federal general. Finally he managed a small smile. "It's for the people's good."

"Horseshit. It's totalitarianism, pure and simple. In the SUSA, probably ninety-five percent of the drivers wear seatbelts. But there are no laws forcing them to do so. It's just common sense."

Max looked out at the meadow. "Those were green

troops commanded by inexperienced officers. We know that you know there are thousands of mercenary troops waiting for the green light to move in.''

"Mercenaries die just like anyone else, Max. And I know you know that I could end this in fifteen minutes if I chose to do so.''

"And I know you know that we have limited nuclear capabilities.''

"Then let's just blow each other into cinders and let the survivors start all over. They couldn't possibly fuck it up any worse than the last two generations have.''

General Maxwell smiled. "You're damn sure right about that last bit. But you won't use nucs, and neither will we.''

"Nucs aren't the only thing I have,'' Ben said.

"So you can win more or less humanely? All right. Do it. Turn loose your germ warheads. Kill hundreds or thousands of children and elderly.'' He shook his head. "You'd do that only as a very last resort . . . if you could bring yourself to do it even then. And I have my doubts about that. No, for a while, at least, this is going to be a soldier's war, on the ground. But we have millions more to draw from, General Raines. Eventually, attrition will take its toll on you.''

"You have it all thought out, don't you?''

"Maybe. Just . . . maybe.''

"I'll ask you the same question I've asked other Federal officers—why do you—''

Maxwell held up a hand. "I know what you're going to ask, Ben. And the answer is, because average Americans are just not smart enough to adequately look after themselves. Somebody has to do it for them. Oh, there's much more to it, but that's it in a nutshell.''

Ben stared at Maxwell for a moment. The Federal had a definite twinkle in his eyes. "Bullshit, Max!''

Maxwell laughed. "Of course it is. It's power. That's all

any restrictive form of government is—power to a select few. You make the masses more or less content, give them plenty of milk while those at the top enjoy the cream."

"Well, I'll be damned! Somebody finally told me the truth."

"And you don't enjoy the cream, Ben? Come on! Of course you do. You want a position in government? It can be arranged. You want to command a division of crack troops. OK. It's yours. Just toss in the towel and come on over to our side."

Ben carefully placed his mug on the camp table and stood up. "Conversation is over, General Maxwell. I can't say it was nice talking with you."

"Don't be a fool. Sit back down, man, and listen to me. I'm offering you a place at the table. Relax and partake."

"I see," Ben said slowly. He sat down. "Osterman thinks she's running the show, right? She's a figurehead. You people are the power behind the throne."

Maxwell smiled and shrugged his shoulders. He refused to speak.

"You people made a deal with a gang of mercenaries. You're getting rid of a bunch of idealistic green Federal troops who are one hundred percent behind Osterman. As soon as they're gone, there will be nothing to stop you. But you're forgetting those commanders who stood their troops down and refused to get mixed up in this fracas. What about them?"

"They will be dealt with. We don't worry about them."

"What is to prevent me from going public with this information?"

"Who would believe you Ben? You rank right up there as one of the most hated men on the continent." Maxwell chuckled. "So go right on with this fight. You're doing us a favor, really. Kill off our green troops while you suffer casualties as well. You see, there is no way for you to win.

If you're smart, you'll join us. Think about it. You don't have to die needlessly. We have a place for you."

"Forget it. No way I will join you."

"It's up to you, Ben."

"You people were setting all this up while I was in Africa. That's why white mercenaries were so scarce over there. You people had most of them under contract . . . or were working on doing just that."

"Very good. But I really wish you hadn't gotten rid of Bruno. He was doing the world a favor by getting rid of millions of niggers. My one regret is I wish he had finished what he started. He would have if you hadn't been so goddamn persistently successful."

"Once again, the Rebels are going to be all that stands between freedom and . . ." —Ben shook his head— ". . . God only knows what form of government you people have in mind. I don't even know what to call the government now in power . . . not really. It's the worst mess I've ever seen."

Maxwell grinned. "It is screwed up, isn't it? A liberal with a hard socialist bent can fuck up an anvil. But we'll fix it once in power."

"Fix it? Fix it into what?"

"Oh, get rid of all the sexual perverts, run the greasers back to Mexico, do something with the niggers, put the ladies back into the home and the kitchen where they belong, then whip the country back into shape."

Ben shook his head. "You're dreaming, Max. None of that is going to happen. You really will have a civil war on your hands if you try that crap."

"We won't try it all at once. It'll be done gradually, over a period of time. If you're still alive, you'll see it happen, I promise you. Now, if you wish, go ahead, call a press conference and tell the world all I told you. I don't care, because no one will believe you."

Ben knew that Maxwell was telling the truth about that. No one outside of the SUSA would believe him. "No, I won't do that. No point in it."

General Maxwell rose from the bench. "Think about what I told you. Think about my offer. It's yours if you want it. But if you persist in making war, the offer will be withdrawn."

"You can withdraw it now. Win, lose, or draw, my answer is no."

"I'm sorry to hear that. You would have been an asset." He lifted his mug and drained it. "Thanks for the coffee."

"Anytime."

Ben sat and watched the general walk back across the road, rejoining his own troops. "Interesting, but not surprising," Ben muttered. He sighed and looked down at his own coffee mug. "The second civil war," he said. "Compliments of all you assholes back in the nineteen sixties, seventies, and eighties who just couldn't keep your goddamn hands off the Constitution and the Bill of Rights. You just had to screw up a good thing. I hope you're all alive and witnessing this. And I hope you choke on it!"

Chapter Five

Ben moved his column eastward, staying just inside SUSA territory, along the Tennessee Kentucky border, until he linked up with part of his 501 Brigade, the day after the near total wipe-out of Federals in the once peaceful meadow.

"Somebody on the other side is finally getting smart, General," a batt com said to Ben. "They're massing troops instead of having everybody spread out thin as paper."

"We've been getting intel all day confirming that. What's your take on it?"

"I think they're getting ready for one hell of a push."

"All along the front?"

The colonel didn't hesitate. "Yes, sir. I'd bet they're going to slam into us at a dozen points."

"I feel the same way." Ben moved to a wall map in the CP. "The Federals are concentrating at these points." He pointed to a dozen locations, from South Texas to the Virginia coast. "But according to our Eyes in the Sky only

five push points have artillery and armor to back them.
I'm betting those will be the places where we'd better
concentrate our air strikes. I've already talked with Ike
about this, and he concurs. On these seven other locations,
and that includes our immediate area, we're probably
going to lose some ground. That's all right. We'll fall back
gradually, let the Feds think we're on the run while we do
an end-around and box their asses in. Then we'll teach
them something about Rebel warfare, Sneaky Pete style.''

The colonel grinned. ''Now you're talking, General.
Down and dirty and close-in.''

Ben alternately walked and rode the front lines with the
colonel, shuffling and repositioning some troops until the
lines were as strong as he could make them. He made
certain every company commander and exec knew the
bug-out plans, and exactly where they were to go and what
they were to do when that order came down the line.

Ben decided to take his team and security people on
east about fifty miles, to beef up a small detachment of
Rebels and home guard stationed there. They made the
run and were in camp by late afternoon.

''We're glad to see you, General,'' the captain in command of the Rebel company greeted Ben. ''In more ways
than one. We're out-gunned about five to one by the Feds
just over that ridge there.'' He pointed. ''Across the strip.
And they're receiving reinforcements every few hours.''

''Armor?''

''Not much. We're about even on that score, a little
ahead on artillery . . . for now, that is.''

''The big push is going to be to our west about fifty
miles. But that doesn't mean we're not going to take some
shoving here. If we can't hold without significant losses,
we'll fall back a few miles and hope they follow.''

The captain grinned. ''Down and dirty time, General?''

''You bet. Eyeball to eyeball and junkyard mean. I want

every Claymore you've got ready to be picked up when we bug out. If the Feds are stupid enough to follow, we'll have some nasty surprises waiting for them.''

"Yes, sir!"

Ben unfolded a map. "We'll all head southeast, toward this crossing of the Cumberland River, then we'll blow the bridge. That will delay them for several hours and give us time to regroup."

"I'll make sure everyone knows."

"I'll put my people over to the east. That appears to be your weakest point."

"Yes, sir. Only one platoon of home guard over there, and some of those ole' boys are getting a little long in the tooth for this type of work."

Ben nodded his head as he hid a smile. Those 'ole' boys' the young captain was talking about were rough as a cob, and mean as a rattlesnake when they got pissed off. The Tennessee 'boys' would damn sure hold more than their own when it came down to the nut cuttin'. Many of them had been part of civilian militia units before the Great War and the collapse.

Ben and his people didn't have long to wait before the Federals launched their offensive. They had just finished eating evening chow, with two hours of daylight left, when a Scout who was stationed on the ridge overlooking the no-man's-land radioed in.

"Gunships coming in from the north. A lot of them."

"They'll be troop carriers all mixed in with those Cobras and Apaches," Ben warned.

"Choppers coming in from the west and east," spotters radioed. "They're doing end-arounds, and coming in fast. Several dozen already on the ground and spilling troops on our side of the strip."

Artillery began dropping in, and the Federals were dead bang on target. One round landed off to Ben's right, and the concussion put him on the ground and sent him rolling. He was unhurt but knocked flat on his butt.

"Shit!" he hollered, crab-crawling over the ground toward the bunker. Before he reached the bunker, he saw Cooper turn several somersaults in the air from an incoming. Coop crawled to his knees and shook his head. He appeared to be unhurt.

Ben never made the bunker. Shrapnel was whistling and howling all around him. He found a depression in the ground and crawled in. Unless a round landed right on top of him he would be relatively safe, for the depression was about three feet deep.

The Feds were really pouring on the rounds, forcing the Rebels to keep their heads down while they advanced toward Rebel positions.

Ben jerked his small handy-talkie out of the pouch and started giving orders. "All tank commanders, get the hell out of this area. Back it up. Get out of range. We'll need you later. Move it!"

"The Feds are going to be all over us in a few minutes, Boss!" Corrie radioed.

"General!" the CO of the outpost yelled into his radio. "Airborne troops landing at locations we talked about west and east of us."

"Any sign of paratroopers dropping in on us here?"

"Negative, Boss. We're just getting the shit pounded out of us, that's all."

"You're telling me?"

"Feds landing more troops by chopper," the Scout on the ridge broke in. "Already several hundred on the ground. I'm out of here."

"OK," Ben radioed. "Time to bug out, folks. Grab what you can, and get gone. If we stay here we're dead meat."

Ben pulled his rucksack to him and slipped the strap over one shoulder. He gripped his CAR and waited until there was a very short lull in the shelling. He left cover in a rush, running for about twenty-five yards before he heard incoming. He hit the ground belly down and stayed put until another lull came, then heaved himself up and ran another few yards. This was repeated half a dozen times until he reached a stand of thick timber. He rested for a couple of minutes, catching his breath, then took off running once again.

He saw a dozen other Rebels, dark shapes in the thick timber running hard out for safety and a dozen more dead and mangled on the ground. He did not stop. Behind him, the shelling had intensified. He had been correct in ordering the bug-out. The outpost was being destroyed by the Federal shelling.

He did not connect with his team. He had no idea where they were. He knew only they had bugged out several minutes before he did.

Ben headed southeast through the timber until he came to a clearing. Deciding not to cross it, he stayed at the edge of the timber and worked his way around the meadow. Then he climbed to the top of one of the rolling hills and scanned the area through binoculars. The outpost had been destroyed, smashed into nothing. One Rebel tank was burning off to the west.

"Shit!" Ben muttered, casing his binoculars. He moved on.

Then he heard the gunships coming in low and fast from the north. Ben ducked into some brush, squatted down, and waited until they had passed.

He counted a dozen gunships, the latest version of the old Apache. The Rebels had hundreds of them, and obviously the Federals had their share, too. The Apache gunship packed more firepower than many World War Two attack bombers.

Ben cautiously slipped from cover and once more headed southeast. The gunships had been heading due south.

He walked for about half a mile, then again scanned the area. "Damn!" he muttered, spotting teams of Federals slowly working their way south. They were stretched out for as far as Ben could see.

Ben looked more closely. The teams were not moving the way green troops would; they moved as though they knew exactly what they were doing and had done it many times before. They held their weapons relaxed, but ready. Their trigger fingers were on trigger guards, not on the triggers. They appeared to be doing everything right.

"The Federals put the first team in," Ben muttered. "Now it gets interesting."

Ben heard gunfire off to the west. Some Rebels were mixing it up with the Feds. But Ben's Rebels were badly outnumbered in this fight, and fighting troops just about as experienced. This particular contingent of Rebels was in for a very bad time of it.

And so am I, Ben thought, *if I don't move my butt and get the hell out of here!*

Ben rose from a kneeling position and turned just as a Fed was walking up behind him. The man had been tracking him, and for a few seconds his eyes were on the ground.

Ben jumped him before he could get off a round, and the two of them rolled on the ground for a few seconds. Ben was a good twenty years older, but taller and heavier. He was also the far more experienced gutter fighter.

The Fed got in one good punch to the side of Ben's head that brightened his world for a few seconds. Ben got a better grip on the merc and jammed his stiffened fingers into the man's eyes and put a hard knee into his crotch. As the Fed convulsed in pain, Ben bent the man's head back and gave him the knife edge of his right hand to the throat. Ben felt it all give way, and the man's mouth suddenly filled with blood as the mercenary began gasping in vain for breath. Ben rolled off the Fed as he convulsed on the ground. He left the man's weapons, took his bandoleer filled with .223 magazines, tore his rucksack from him, and left him dying on the ground. Then he hauled his ass away from there.

As he walked, Ben looked inside the rucksack. Several containers of field rats, three grenades, and two pairs of clean socks. He could use the food and the grenades, and the socks looked as though they would fit him.

Ben continued moving southeast at a good pace. He figured his team and the majority of the troops who were stationed at the outpost were a good thirty minutes ahead of him. Maybe more than that, for they were younger and could move a lot faster for a longer time.

Ben was not an old man, wouldn't be for a while, but he damn sure was no spring chicken. He had to rest often to conserve his legs.

The men of the Tennessee Home Guard had plans of their own as to where to bug out, and Ben had not made any attempt to countermand those plans. They had a better chance of survival than anyone else. This was their country.

Walking up a hill, Ben paused for another look around. It was not at all encouraging. Federals appeared to be all around him. Somehow they had gotten in front of him and cut off his planned escape route.

"All right," Ben whispered to the wind as dusk began closing in all around him. "So I'll head straight east. At least for a while." He knew that not too many miles ahead of him, straight east, he would be blocked by lakes and

the Cumberland River. He had no choice in the matter—
it was the only direction left open to him.

Ben checked his compass heading and started walking.
With the exception of a few bruises from being knocked
down a couple of times by incoming shell concussion, he
felt pretty good.

He walked for half an hour, then paused to rest and
check his handy-talkie. There was no chatter coming
through. He was either out of range, or the damn thing
was busted.

Just as he was about to get up and resume his trek Ben
heard voices coming from his right, which was south. He
perked up and listened.

"We've got to take him alive. The bastard's worth a
million bucks."

"I'm not sure that reward applies to us," a second man
said.

"It does. I got that straight before we left. Military or
civilian, whoever brings him in gets a million."

"Good enough. But how the hell can you be sure he's
heading in this direction?"

"He's got no choice. He damn sure can't go north.
South and west are blocked off. This is the only way open
to him."

"Not for long," a third voice spoke. "The river is only
a few miles away."

"That's what I mean. He's cut off. All we have to do is
be patient."

"And wait right here?"

"Why not? We're ahead of him. The last sighting proved
that. The bastard is not a young man. He can't cover a lot
of ground in a hurry. North is thick brush and ravines.
South is our people. We've got him. It's just a matter of
time."

Ben did not want to fire and risk giving away his position.

Besides, he wasn't sure all three were close enough together for one burst to take them all out. Hell, he wasn't even sure of their exact location.

Too many ifs.

Ben waited in the brush. It was almost as thick as the darkness that had fallen.

Finally he heard the sounds of the Federals moving away, toward the east. Ben waited for a few more minutes, then left cover and headed first south for several hundred yards, then gradually cut east. He moved slowly and carefully, stopping every few meters to listen to the night.

And hour later he could smell and sense the river.

Ben stopped and slipped down into a wash and rested. The Cumberland was no small creek; he'd never get across it without a boat. If he stayed put he'd eventually get captured or killed in a shoot-out. If he headed in any direction, the odds were a little bit better, but not all that much.

"Oh, the hell with it," Ben muttered. He climbed out of the wash and began making his way south.

Several times during the next hour he spotted Federal patrols in time to avoid contact. However, luck has a nasty habit of running out if one starts to depend on it, and Ben knew that only too well.

Before long he would need rest and a few hours sleep, but he knew there was little chance for either. Any place suitable for rest and sleep would be carefully looked at by the Feds. Ben would just have to keep going and hope for the best.

Something came out of the brush and hit him hard, knocking him sprawling. Ben lost his grip on the CAR and rolled away, just as his attacker took a vicious kick at his head. Ben grabbed the man's boot and twisted just as hard as his position would allow.

The man grunted in pain and fell backward, landing hard on his butt. That was all the opportunity Ben needed.

He pulled his boot knife and struck hard with it. The blade drove deep into the man's thigh, and the attacker yelped in pain. Ben jerked the blade out and struck again, this time higher up. The blade sliced deep into the man's belly and Ben twisted upward, feeling the sharp blade cut into and through vital organs. Ben clamped one big hand on the man's throat and squeezed, cutting off any scream.

Ben held on as the Fed twisted and thrashed on the ground. Horrible choking sounds made their way out of the tortured throat. Ben squeezed even harder and drove the knife deep into the man's chest. The Fed convulsed once, and then was still as life swiftly left him.

Ben released his grip and pulled out his knife. Shaky from the sudden expense of energy, he crawled to his knees and rested there, the dead man cooling on the ground.

Ben wiped the blade clean on the dead man's pants leg and sheathed it. He found his CAR and wiped the dust from it, then took two grenades from the dead man and several full magazines of .223's. There was nothing else on the man that Ben could use. He rested for a few more minutes and then moved out, heading south.

Ben had heard the very faint sounds of a lot of gunfire since leaving the Rebel outpost. The Feds and the Rebels had locked horns a number of times. He had no way of knowing which side had been victorious, but he had a bad feeling in the pit of his stomach that it was not his Rebels.

He continued walking.

Ben caught a few hours sleep from about 3:00 A.M. until six. Then he was on the move once more. It had been a restless sleep, for the sounds of helicopters had awakened him a dozen times. Just as daylight was spreading over the land, he climbed a low hill and took a look around. What he saw was not at all encouraging.

He was surrounded. There appeared to be no way out for him, and the Federal troops all seemed to be facing in his direction. They had him pinpointed.

Ben backed up and looked around, finding some good size rocks and several small logs. He tugged and rolled the rocks and logs into a makeshift barricade, occasionally looking around. The Feds were all moving in his direction.

Ben took his handy-talkie from the pouch and keyed the mic. "This is the Eagle. Anybody listening?"

Corrie's familiar voice touched his ear. "Right here, Boss."

"Are you secure, Corrie?"

"Ten-four, Boss. We're in Rebel territory and holding."

"Can you tape this?"

"Affirmative, Boss. Taping."

"Tell Ike he's in charge of it all. I've had it. I've got maybe three or four hundred Feds moving in on me, and probably more on the way. I'm not sure exactly where I am. For the Rebels to try any type of rescue would be nothing but a suicide mission. Don't try it. Understood?"

"Affirmative, Boss."

"I'm going to give them one hell of a fight, but there is no way I can win. You copy all that?"

After a short pause, Corrie said in a choked voice, "Affirmative, Boss."

"I'm not going to be taken alive. Not if I can help it. And I don't have time to get maudlin here. The SUSA forever. Let that be your battle cry. Understood?"

"Ten-four, Boss."

"Is the team all right?"

"Affirmative."

"Anna?"

"She's OK, Boss. None of us were hit."

"Not much else to say, Gang. The Feds are at the base of the hill and moving in on me. The SUSA forever. Forever!"

Corrie was crying. "Affirmative, Boss."

"Good luck to you all. Eagle out."

Chapter Six

Ben chunked a grenade over the edge of the hill and smiled when it exploded.

The Feds opened fire from all sides, the lead howling and ricocheting all around him.

"Come and get me, you miserable socialistic assholes," Ben muttered. "But, goddamn you all, when you do I'll take some of you with me."

Several Feds on the north side of the hill charged Ben's position. When they reached the crest they were met with half a magazine of .223 rounds. Scratch four Feds.

After half an hour of give and take, the Federal fire abruptly ceased.

"Now what?" Ben said to the cloudy sky and the increasing winds.

A shout reached Ben. "General Raines! This is General Berman. Give this up, Raines. You can't get off that hill. There is no escape for you."

"Berman, you mercenary prick!" Ben said. He took a deep breath and shouted, "Come and get me!"

"Don't be a fool, Ben!" Berman shouted. "Give it up."

"So Madam President Osterman can hang me? I'd rather go out with a bullet right here on this hill."

"Well, that's not going to happen. We're going to take you alive, I promise you that. You might be banged up some, but I can guarantee you will be alive. Think about that before we begin the assault."

Tear gas or pepper gas, Ben thought. *That's what they're going to use.*

And a gas mask was something Ben did not have.

Ben wriggled around in his small shelter and took a quick look in all directions. He sighed as he ducked back down. Must be at least three hundred Feds surrounding the small hill.

No thoughts of surrender entered Ben's mind. The Feds might overpower him, but it would be only after a fight.

Then Ben heard the unmistakable pop of a gas canister launcher. "Here we go," he muttered.

He quickly wet a handkerchief and placed it over his face just as the canister hit the top of the hill and the gas began spreading. After that there must have been a dozen more pops in a very brief time. The air became choked with fumes, and in a few seconds Ben was unable to see.

"Shit!" he coughed out just as he heard bootsteps running toward him. Something slammed into the front of his head, and Ben's world turned to darkness.

When he awakened he found himself cuffed and chained, the metal bonds around his wrists and ankles. He did not have to open his eyes to know he was on the floor of a plane, a big prop job—four engine, Ben figured, from the sound of it. C-130, probably.

He did not know how long he'd been out, but it seemed as though it had been hours. He concluded the blow on the head had been followed by some sort of chemical injection to ensure his staying unconscious.

He cracked his eyelids and was not surprised to find boots filling his vision—a long row of them. Berman was taking no chances. Ben was under heavy guard. He felt his left shirtsleeve jerked up, and the lash of a needle. Seconds later, he was once again enveloped in darkness.

When he woke again, it was quiet. Daylight was streaming through a window set high up off the floor. Ben moved his hands and feet. The chains were gone. He tried to sit up, but did not have the strength to make it. He moved his head and blinked his eyes. Well, at least he could do that much.

Then he realized he was in a bed.

He shook his head, and that hurt! He summoned all his strength and managed to sit up, his feet on the floor. His bare feet. No boots, no socks. He looked down at his legs. His BDUs were gone. He was dressed in pajamas. Green ones.

Sitting on the side of the bed, he looked around the room. One window, too far off the floor for him to see out of. A very sturdy looking door—closed, and locked, Ben figured. A metal, three drawer dresser set against one wall. A sink, also metal. A commode, metal.

Sure as hell not a luxury hotel.

He inspected the walls and ceiling. Bare. No mirrors and no camera to monitor his moves.

Ben decided to try to stand. He failed the first try and fell back on the bed, made it on the second try. He stood for a moment, swaying until he got his balance. Then he tried to walk, and fell down hard on the floor.

Ben lay on the cold tile for a moment, silently cussing.

He forced himself to his knees, then managed to get to his feet and stay there. Damn, but he was weak.

He took a couple of hesitant steps and did not fall. "Wonderful," Ben muttered. "I am certainly making progress."

He walked back to the bed and sat down, resting for a couple of minutes. During that time he again visually inspected his surroundings, looking for anything he might use as a weapon. There was nothing.

He walked over to the sink and turned on the cold water. Bathing his face several times, he felt better. Then he cupped his hands and drank deeply.

He stared at the window longingly, wishing he could see out, get some idea where he was. He gave that up. Might as well wish for . . . what? Well, at least he was still alive, and not dangling from the end of a rope. That would come soon enough. Osterman would probably personally tighten the noose herself, smiling all the while. Miserable bitch!

Ben began slowly walking around and around the interior of the small room, feeling his strength slowly return. He still didn't feel like running any foot races, but he was getting better.

And hungry. Damn, but he was hungry. Then he knew he was getting better, thinking about food. He instinctively glanced down at his watch—or where it used to be. It was gone, of course.

He drank some more water and felt better, glanced upward out the high-set window. The sun didn't seem as bright, but it was high in the heavens. Not as strong, rather than not as bright. Ben suddenly got the impression he was a long way from Tennessee.

North! The word jumped into his brain. He was far north. Somehow he was sure of that.

Ben heard a key clink in the lock. He turned just as

the door opened. Several men stood there, one of them General Walt Berman.

"You do get around, don't you?" Ben said.

Berman smiled. "Yes, I do. How do you feel?"

"I'm not a hundred percent yet. But getting there."

"Hungry?"

"Yes, I am."

"Well, we brought you a tray of food. It's nothing fancy, but it is good food. And we eat the same thing, by the way."

"Thanks."

"Think nothing of it."

"Where am I being held?"

Berman stared at him for a few seconds, then shrugged. "I can't see where that would hurt anything, Ben. You damn sure can't get out. You're in upstate New York. This facility used to be a state hospital for the insane. Insane probably isn't a politically correct term, but I'm not much into that liberal crap."

"What time is it?"

"About noon. Lunchtime. Here is your food. Enjoy the meal."

A tray was brought in, placed on the dresser. The guard carefully backed out. Berman gave Ben a mock salute and closed the door.

Ben heard the lock click with a very secure sound.

He carried his tray over to the bunk and looked at the food. Thick portions of ham (already cut up into bite-size pieces), generous helpings of mashed sweet potatoes and corn (in separate compartments), two slices of bread, two pats of butter (probably oleo) a piece of apple pie, a large mug of coffee, two packets of sugar, a packet of instant creamer.

"Not bad," Ben muttered, picking up the plastic fork and digging in.

The food was good, and Ben ate every bite and then drank the coffee. He wished he had a cigarette to go with it. "Wonder if I'll get a smoke before they hang me," he muttered.

Ben took the tray and walked over to the door. He tapped on it. "I'm finished. You want the tray?"

"Back away from the door," a man ordered. "I'll lower the flap in the center of the door."

Ben backed away. "I'm back. Still holding the tray."

The flap banged open. "Put the tray on the flap."

"You got a cigarette?" Ben asked, placing the tray on the metal flap.

"Sure. I'll have to light it for you."

"No problem. I appreciate it."

"Back up, away from the door."

Ben again backed up, and watched as a lighted cigarette was placed on the flap.

"OK. Pick it up."

Ben snagged the smoke and backed up. "Thanks, buddy."

Ben sat on the floor, his back to a wall, and smoked the cigarette. He enjoyed every puff. While he smoked he visually inspected the ceiling and walls. He could detect no sign of hidden cameras or microphones. There was no mirror in the room, so that let out a two-way.

Ben got up and tried to move the bunk. It was securely bolted to the floor, and so was the dresser. The bolts were shiny new.

He tried one with his fingers. "Well, you can forget that," he muttered, after straining and only succeeding in skinning his fingers.

He wondered when his interrogation would start. He did not have long to wonder.

About a half hour after lunch, the door swung open—outward. Ben made a mental note of that. The hall seemed to be filled with men. None of them were armed, but they all carried the old style police nightsticks.

"All right, General," one said. "Time for your meeting with General Berman."

"I'm all aquiver with anticipation."

The man laughed. "No need to be. We don't go in for physical torture. That's been old hat for years, and you know it."

"The woman you're working for would, and enjoy every moment of it."

"Woman? Oh! President Osterman." The man frowned. "No, she wouldn't. She's a wonderful person. I met her once when I was still in my teens, and she was trying to get this country back on its feet. I read the weekly motivation letters that come from her office." He pointed his club at Ben. "Don't you say anything bad about Mrs. Osterman. I won't stand for that."

So it's a mixed bag of mercenaries and Federal troops here, Ben thought. *And all those rumors I've been hearing for several years about the USA are true. Kids are getting a healthy dose of brainwashing in public schools. Well, hell, we're doing the same thing in the SUSA. The only difference is we're telling the kids the truth.*

"Let's go, General," the young man said.

"Do I get some slippers?" Ben asked. "I wouldn't want to catch my death of cold."

The young man—probably twenty-five years old, Ben guessed—hesitated. "Yes, I suppose so. Get him some hospital slippers," he ordered.

The slippers were floppy on his feet, but they felt good against the cold floor. Ben was taken to an elevator and down one floor to the main floor. The hospital, Ben noted from the elevator control panel, had two floors and a basement. He would certainly keep that information in mind.

Ben was taken to an office in the center of a long hall. At the far end were double doors. Sunlight streamed through the glass. Ben pretended not to notice the path to freedom.

General Berman waved him to a chair in front of his desk and tossed a package of cigarettes on the desk and a lighter. "Smoke, Ben?"

"Thanks." Ben got a smoke and lit up. "Got any coffee, General?"

Berman laughed. "Coffee drinking man, hey? Me, too. Sure. I'll have a pot sent in for us. How was lunch?"

"Very good. Surprisingly so."

"We all eat the same thing, as I told you. No point in not enjoying some small creature comforts while we're here, right? Well, Ben, let's get to it, shall we? Good. You won't be here for very long. I have to tell you that. Three, four days at the most, I imagine, and then, if you haven't agreed to some demands, you'll be sent to the capital for a public trial. Now . . . you really don't want that, do you?"

"It doesn't hold much appeal for me, no."

"I'm sure it doesn't. Ah! Here's the coffee." A man placed a tray on the desk with a pot of coffee, two cups, sugar and cream in containers. "How do you take yours, Ben?"

"Black with a little sugar will do."

"Same here. Years in the field sort of makes cream impossible, doesn't it?"

"Yes, it does. What demands?"

"Just a few. If you agree to them, your life will be spared. You have President Osterman's word on that."

"Her *word?*"

Berman smiled. "Her word."

"I wouldn't trust that bitch if she swore it in the middle of a bible factory."

"Just hear me out, Ben. What's the harm in that?"

"The bottom line is, my life is spared and I get to spend the rest of my life in prison, right?"

"That's about the size of it. But in as much comfort as possible. Not in a cell. A . . . well, sort of apartment, you might say."

"Probably on a military base, in solitary confinement for the rest of my life."

"That's about the size of it."

Ben shook his head and smiled. "No deal. I'll take the rope."

"Ben—"

"Forget it. Hanging me will mean the civil war will continue forever. My death will be a rallying cry. The war will never stop." Ben leaned forward. "As long as there is one Rebel alive, the war will go on and on and on. As long as the Tri-States philosophy of government is remembered, passed down from generation to generation, the war will, in some form, continue. Try me and hang me, Walt. I will make no deals in exchange for my life. None."

The mercenary general stared at Ben for a moment. Then he smiled and shook his head. "I told both Osterman and Millard you would never go for the deal. They were sure you would."

"Now what?"

"I don't know. I'll contact Osterman's office and tell them it's no deal. After that?" He shrugged and spread his hands. "It might get rough."

"At your hands?"

"No." The general's answer was quick and firm. "I have never gone in for that sort of thing. But someone else is going to replace me. In a few hours. There is always that to consider."

Ben entertained thoughts of telling Walt about his conversation with General Maxwell, then thought better of it. He had a hunch the mercenary knew all about it and was a part of it. "You think roughing me up will change my mind?"

"Of course not. If anything, it will only serve to strengthen your resolve. I personally don't think it will come to that. However ... who knows? These damned young and dedicated followers of Osterman are capable of doing anything. I don't like them, and don't trust them."

"You've got several here at the hospital."

"Don't I know it. Bradford, the shithead that escorted you here a few minutes ago, is one of the worst. Totally brainwashed. That creepy jerk is dangerous."

Ben laughed at the expression on the general's face. "I gather he's not one of your favorite people."

"You can bet on that. Ben, my people and I are being pulled out of here tonight. Then you'll be solely in the hands and at the mercy of Osterman's goons. I won't be here to help you. Think about that. One soldier to another, flip-flop a little, make them think you're going to agree to the terms I offered. Buy a little time. How about it?"

"I'll give that some thought."

"Good. Do that. Save yourself some grief at least for a while."

"And after they get tired of waiting?"

"It probably will get rough. I won't lie to you."

Ben took a sip of the very good coffee and lit another cigarette. "Why the concern on your part, Walt?"

"I don't like physical torture. Now, I'll hunt you and shoot you in open warfare, do my best to beat you, kill you. But that's war. That's the risk you run. I might use chemicals on a person. I have used chemicals to get the truth. But not physical torture."

Ben lifted his coffee cup in a salute and smiled. Walt did the same. The two middle-aged soldiers understood each other very well.

Ben tossed the cigarette pack back on the desk, and

Walt picked it up and tossed it back to him. "Tuck those away." He fiddled around in a desk drawer and tossed Ben a box of matches. "Hide them. Hell, you might get a chance to sneak a smoke, who knows?"

Ben sensed the meeting was over. "I didn't like you at first, Walt. Still don't know if I can really trust you. But I find myself wishing we were both on the same side."

"I know the feeling all too well." Walt stuck out a hand and Ben shook it. "Good luck to you, Rebel."

"Good luck to you, mercenary." Ben laughed. "But not too much luck in this war."

Chapter Seven

Suppertime passed, and no one brought Ben a tray. He sat on his bunk and watched the summer light gradually slip into darkness. He would have liked to smoke, but decided he'd better not. He tucked the pack of smokes and box of matches under the bedding on the bunk.

About an hour after dark, the cell door swung open. Bradford stood there, backed up by six guards. Ben sat on the bunk and stared at the young man.

"General Berman is gone," Bradford announced. "I'm in charge now."

"Congratulations," Ben told him. "When do I get something to eat?"

"After we talk . . . maybe."

"Maybe?"

"You might not feel like eating." Bradford smiled after saying that, and it was not a pleasant smile.

"I don't feel like talking right now."

"Perhaps I can change your mind." Bradford slapped a fist into an open palm.

"Somehow I doubt it, punk." Ben spat the words at him. "I have absolutely nothing to say to you."

"Get him out of there!" Bradford ordered.

The next hour or so wasn't all that pleasant, but Ben had received rougher treatment in his life. Bradford seemed more interested in spouting dogma from Osterman's philosophy of government than in punching Ben around, but the craphead still managed to get in some good licks.

When Ben was dragged, literally, back to his cell, his mouth was busted, his head ached, his nose was bleeding, and his stomach hurt from being used as a punching bag, but he hadn't said a word or uttered a sound of protest or pain.

The guards threw him into his cell. Ben landed hard on the floor. He lay there until the door was closed and locked, then crawled to his hands and knees and managed to make it to the sink. Still sitting on the floor, Ben turned on the water and began bathing his busted and bruised face. There was no washcloth, so he had to use his hands. The cold water revived him, and he crawled over to his bunk and stretched out. That helped to relieve the pain in his stomach muscles.

There was no hope for sleep—Ben hurt too much for that. He could and did while away some very interesting moments thinking of ways to kill that damned dickhead Bradford at the earliest opportunity, and those damned guards, too. Ben knew he was in for a very rough time until he could find a way to break loose from the damned nuthouse. He was going to start planning that, right now.

Ben finally drifted off into a pain-filled sleep.

He was jerked awake by a very rude hand and rolled onto the floor. There, he was kicked in the back and the stomach half a dozen times by men wearing boots. The last kick he received was on the back of the head, and that dropped him into merciful unconsciousness.

Ben awakened on the cold floor of his cell. He hurt all over. One of the men had apparently stomped on his left hand, and it was swollen to about twice its normal size. He could only open one eye; the other was swollen shut. The back of his head was caked with dried blood. He managed, with a great deal of effort, to pull himself over to the sink and, using his right hand, turn on the water. He got more water on the floor than on his face the first try, but the cold wetness felt good on the hot face.

Hot! Ben thought. *I'm running a fever. If I don't get off this floor and into that bunk with some cover on me I'll be looking at pneumonia. And I sure as hell don't need that.*

He managed to get into the bunk and pull the blanket over him. The pain was like needles sticking into his body. Sleep finally came, and with it, some relief from the pain.

"Get up, you son of a bitch!" Bradford yelled at him. "Here's your breakfast."

Ben heard a tray being placed on the floor and the door closing. Suppressing a groan, he threw off the blanket and managed to sit up. He sat on the side of the bunk for a moment until his head stopped spinning and he could make his legs follow the command from his brain. Then he slowly made his way over to the tray on the floor.

Ben managed to squat down without falling over on his face and pick up the tray and get back to the bunk without spilling anything or dropping the whole damn thing. He sat on the bunk and looked at his breakfast.

The contents of the tray did not look at all appetizing. It contained a thick glob of oatmeal, two greasy looking sausage patties, a slop of some terrible looking scrambled eggs, a couple pieces of bread, and a mug of coffee.

Ben ate every bite, and could have eaten more.

He wanted to smoke a cigarette but decided against it. Now was not the time.

He set the tray on the floor, stretched back out on the bunk, and promptly went back to sleep. He slept for several hours. When he awakened he felt much better, thought he might live, after all—at least for the time being. He sat up and looked around the room. The tray was gone. Someone had picked it up and left without waking him up. He had slept the sleep of the physically exhausted.

As Ben stood up, he thought that much of the pain was gone. He took a couple of steps and discovered he was wrong. His bruised muscles protested every movement. He tried to ignore the pain and began walking around the room, getting some of the kinks out.

One thing he knew for certain: if he had to take many more beatings like the one he'd received hours before, there might be permanent damage. His body just could not take more kicking episodes.

He found his slippers and sat down on the bunk to put them on. He sat for a moment, feeling the material of the slippers. They seemed to be made of some sort of mixture of paper and cloth. He felt under the thin mattress and found the box of matches Berman had given him.

"Might work," Ben muttered. "I've got to give this some more thought."

But how much time did he have to think about it? That, he didn't know.

And just how would he pull it off?

He didn't know that, either, but he did have a tiny germ of an idea.

He put the matches back under the mattress and started thinking about freedom and how he might attain it. He didn't quite know exactly how he was going to do that, only that he must. He had to, or he would die.

Ben awakened on the floor of his cell. His captors had come for him before noon, long before any escape plans had been thought of or thought out, and hammered on him again and again. He had lost consciousness several times, each time to be brought back into painful reality by having buckets of water tossed on him . . . at least Ben *thought* it was water, he wasn't sure.

During the beatings, in which a number of the younger guards under Bradford's command took part, Ben was called a number of things.

"Goddamn fascist!" was the favorite, it seemed.

"Right-wing dictator!" was a close second.

There were other names, but they usually didn't register through the fog of pain in Ben's body.

All during the hours of torment, Ben thought that if he survived this he had to get out, had to get free. The guards were going to cripple him, he was sure of that, sure that was their intention, and just as sure that they had been ordered to do that. By whom, he didn't know, but he hoped that one day—if he succeeded in escaping—he would find out.

Whatever he was going to do, no matter how bad he felt he was going to have to do it soon . . . immediately. One more beating like the one he had just suffered, and something in his body would give way or break.

Ben dug out the box of matches and made sure they were the strike-anywhere type. He put them in his shirt pocket. Then he began shredding the ends of his slippers to provide a better ignition point. He worked quickly but carefully. His mind was made up: he was going to make his break, or attempt it, the next time the guards came calling. If they killed him during his try . . . well, so be it. A quick death would be better than a slow, prolonged one.

Ben began walking stiffly around and around his cell, very slowly at first. Then, gradually, he increased his steps. He forced his mind to accept the pain until at least part of the stiffness left his legs. Then he rested and caught his breath. Before his muscles could cool down, he was up and walking again. He repeated this process several times, until he began to feel better—winded and hurting some, but better.

An hour passed, with Ben occasionally getting up and working his bruised legs just to keep them from stiffening up.

Then he heard a noise in the hall. He took a couple of single matches from his pocket and got up from the bunk, holding the shredded slippers in his left hand, the matches in his right. He walked over to the steel door, considering just how he was going to play this.

Something heavy rapped on the door—a billy club, Ben imagined. "Hey, General Tough Boy!" a voice called. "You still alive, old man?"

"Yes," Ben said with a theatrical groan. He hoped the groan sounded authentic.

"That's good, you old fart. Bradford wants to talk to you again." That was followed by laughter.

"Yeah, talk," another man said. "You bet."

"You feel up to it?" the first man questioned.

"Do I have a choice?"

More laughter. "Nope, none at all."

"All right."

"Stand away from the door, General Asshole."

I'm going to ram that billy club down your throat, you miserable punk, Ben thought. "OK," he whispered. "I'm standing back." Ben lit the slippers and they began to burn brightly. The key slid into the lock and clicked. Ben smiled.

When the door began to slowly open toward the hall, Ben slammed into it with everything he had. The edge of the steel door struck the first guard in the face and knocked him backward, blood pouring from his broken nose and smashed lips.

Ben moved swiftly out the door and into the hall and stuck the burning slippers into the second guard's face, jamming the flame into the man's eyes.

The guard dropped his billy club and opened his mouth to scream. Ben jammed the burning slippers into the man's mouth, reached down and scooped up the billy club and whacked him hard in the center of the forehead.

Ben turned and smashed the first guard on the top of the head with the club, then hit him again for insurance. He turned and hit the second guard on the side of the head just as hard as he could. The odor of burning flesh was strong in the hallway. The slippers were still smoking in the man's mouth.

Ben dragged the men, one at a time, into the cell. The first guard was about Ben's size. Ben swiftly undressed the Fed down to his underwear and pulled on his uniform. The shirt was just a tad too small, and the waist of the britches a bit too large.

Ben went through the pockets of both men, taking everything they had: billfolds, keys, pocket knives. He then straightened up and savagely smashed the club down on the heads of the guards one by one. They weren't dead when he finished, but they would be out of commission for a long time.

Ben quickly tried on a pair of boots that looked as though they might fit him. They were a half size too big, even with the two pairs of socks taken from the feet of both unconscious guards, but they would have to do.

He stepped out into the hall and locked the cell door,

then stood for a moment, silently savoring his freedom. Then he took a deep breath and moved up the hallway.

He was looking for the gun room. When he found it, he would show these young socialists that an old dog could still bite.

Chapter Eight

Ben walked up the hallway, carrying one of the nightsticks he'd taken from the guards. His boots echoed off
the tile. He met no one. He paused at the elevator, then
decided not to chance it. He took the stairs down to the
first floor and cautiously pushed open the door, peeking
out.

The hall was deserted, but he could hear rock music
coming from somewhere far down the long hall—a song
he was not familiar with. Ben made it a point never to
listen to rock music, so he was probably unfamiliar with
ninety-nine percent of it. He had not paid any attention
to rock music since years before the collapse and the Great
War.

He stepped out into the hall, looking at the double
doors which led to the outside. They were chained shut.

He walked slowly down the hall toward the sounds of

the music. It was coming out of the open door to an office. Ben stood for a moment, pressed up against the wall just outside the open door. He listened for the sounds of voices. Nothing.

Got to do it, Ben thought, *can't stand out here until I'm discovered.*

He looked into the office. One man sitting at a desk, his back to Ben. Ben recognized him as one of those who had taken great delight in beating the crap out of him.

Your turn now, Ben thought, silently stepping into the office and easing up behind the guard.

The man sensed movement behind him and turned. His mouth opened in shock as he recognized Ben. Ben popped him on the noggin with the club and the guard went night-night.

Ben tied him up with the man's belt and a length of electrical cord which he jerked out of a wall socket, then gagged him with his own handkerchief. The guard had been carrying a sidearm in a holster and Ben took that, along with the two full magazines from the guard's belt pouch.

Ben checked the 9mm. Full up. He jacked a round into the slot and quickly checked the office for anything else he might use. Nothing. He fanned the unconscious man's pockets and took his keys and wallet, then took a jacket from a wall hook and slipped out of the office.

He wanted to find Bradford. He had a present for that son of a bitch.

He walked the long hall, looking into each darkened room with an open door. Nothing. When he came to a room with a closed door, he tried the doorknob. Locked.

He fumbled with several of the keys he'd taken from the guards until one opened the door. Ben smiled as he looked inside. The armory.

When he again stepped out into the hall, Ben was armed with a CAR and had a rucksack filled with spare magazines and a couple hundred rounds of .223's. He also had half a dozen grenades hooked onto the web belt he'd found in the room.

"Now then, you assholes," Ben muttered. "Let's just see how tough you are."

Ben walked the hall, moving slowly and cautiously. He heard the faint sounds of voices coming from somewhere far down the hall. The CAR was set on full auto. Ben did not realize it, but he was walking along with a smile on his bruised face, curving his swollen lips.

Two guards stepped out of a room. They stood for several seconds, not believing what they were seeing. That was the last thing they saw on this earth. Ben gave them half a mag of .223's. The guards went down. One flopped for a few seconds, then was still.

"What the hell is happening out there!" The voice came from the room the guards had just exited.

"Retribution," Ben muttered, waiting in the hall.

The man stuck his head out of the room. "Oh, shit!" he said.

"Right," Ben said, and squeezed the trigger.

Scratch another of Osterman's faithful followers.

Ben walked the hall from end to end. There was no one else to be found . . . at least not on that floor.

Ben searched the bodies of the dead and removed everything in their pockets, stowing it in another rucksack he found in the second office. He stacked all the weapons and ammo he could find in a utility room near the chained entrance. He would go out those doors when the time came.

Ben looked at his left hand. It was still swollen, but much of the swelling was gone. Ben again flexed the fingers on that hand. They worked, albeit stiffly, and there was no sign of anything broken.

He glanced at the nice watch he'd taken from one of the now expired guards. Five o'clock. It would be dark soon. Good. Ben liked the night.

He found the steps leading to the basement and cautiously walked down. He stood for a moment, looking at the heavy steel. Memories of his beatings were returning to him . . . very unpleasant reminiscences. He recalled that there were other prisoners being held in cells in the basement, and he guessed the basement area was soundproofed.

Wouldn't do to have screams reverberating throughout the nuthouse.

Ben tried the door. It was not locked, but it was very heavy. He could hear an angry voice shouting something. He could not make out the words, but he was sure it was Bradford doing the shouting. That was one voice Ben was not likely to forget for a long, long time.

"You damned, right-wing whore!" The words came to Ben more clearly as he made his way up the hall. It *was* Bradford. "Confess."

The sound of a woman's voice drifted to Ben, but he could not make out any of the words.

"Whore!" Bradford shouted. "Filthy whore of the militia!"

This time Ben could understand the woman's reply. "Fuck you, you goofy bastard!"

Ben smiled. He liked this woman already. She damn sure had Bradford pegged accurately.

"Let's toss her in with the hardcases," someone suggested. "Let them gang-bang her. We'll watch until she confesses."

"No," Bradford said firmly. "That wouldn't be punishment. Hell, she'd enjoy that. She's a militia whore. She was a survivalist, remember."

"I bet she wouldn't enjoy . . ."

A generator kicked in about that time, and Ben couldn't understand all the words.

Laughter drifted to Ben as the generator, or whatever it was—air-conditioning unit, perhaps—settled down to a low hum.

"Bet she sure wouldn't enjoy that, for a fact."

"I'd like to watch it!"

More laughter.

Ben worked closer. He didn't have to wonder what the perverted bastards were laughing about. He felt he knew exactly what it was.

He edged closer and peered into a large room. A naked woman was strung up by the wrists, dangling from an eye-hook set in the ceiling. Her bare feet were just touching the floor. She had angry red welts on her belly and thighs and buttocks. Bradford stood beside her, holding a thick leather belt. He looked as though he was enjoying inflicting torture on the woman.

He probably was, Ben thought. *The sadistic son of a bitch.* Ben's first thoughts about Bradford were certainly proving correct: he had pegged him as being twisted.

The woman was blonde, with short-cropped hair, and looked to be in her mid to late thirties. Ben could not help but take in her nakedness since she was dangling without a stitch on. *Very lovely woman,* he concluded.

Ben stepped into the room and cut the legs out from under Bradford with a short burst from his CAR. Then he turned the muzzles toward the other two and forever put an end to their perversion.

Leaving Bradford groaning and twisting on the floor,

Ben cut the woman's bonds with a knife he'd taken from one of the guards and gently eased her down.

Still holding her so she would not fall, Ben said, "Can you stand alone?"

"I don't know. Hang onto me a moment longer. Who are you? Are you from the New York Militia?"

"No. Are there still others being held here?"

"Yes, but I don't know who they are. They're in the process of being reindoctrinated."

"This country's really gone to hell, hasn't it? Reindoctrination centers. Jesus. Are there more like this one?"

"All over the USA. I think I can walk now. My clothes are over there on the floor in the corner. That damn Bradford made me strip while he and his shitty buddies watched."

"That doesn't surprise me one little bit. What's your name?"

"Lara. L-a-r-a."

"OK, Lara. Ready to give it a try?"

"Yes."

Ben turned her loose and the woman walked—with as much dignity as possible, considering her state of undress—over to a corner and began pulling on her clothes.

Ben turned to Bradford. "You are one miserable son of a bitch, Bradford."

"I'm hurt bad, General. You've got to help me."

"General?" Lara paused in her dressing.

"I'm Ben Raines."

Lara's eyes widened, and she leaned against a table for support. "My God!" she breathed. "Yes. Of course you are. I recognize you now. Your face is so bruised and beat up—"

"Ah, Lara, would you mind continuing dressing? Finish slipping on that bra, maybe? It's a bit disconcerting talking with you while your, ah, you know, are, ah, exposed."

Lara blushed from her toes to her nose, and quickly slipped on her bra.

"Thank you," Ben said drily. He turned his attention toward Bradford. "Fuck you, punk."

"You can't leave me like this!" Bradford protested. "My legs are broken."

"Good," Lara said. "I hope you die, you rotten bastard."

"Filthy degenerate militia whore!" Bradford spat the words at her.

"You're calling *her* degenerate, you twisted son of a bitch?" Ben asked. "My, my."

Lara smiled, but it was a smile that held no humor. "Some of the things they've done to women in here are unspeakable, General. And to men. They've castrated some militia members. Lobotomized others. All in the name of democracy, of course."

"Sure. Back before the collapse and the Great War, some of us who didn't have our heads up our asses used to call what Osterman and her ilk advocated cultural Nazism."

"I've read a few of your writings, General, but to be found with anything you wrote in one's possession now could mean death. It's classified as subversive and highly traitorous."

"I've heard." He smiled. "Well, I've never claimed to be a literary threat to the memory of John Steinbeck. Tell you what—call me Ben, please. OK, Lara. Search those bodies and take everything on them . . . everything. Then we'll see about the other prisoners."

"What about me?" Bradford moaned.

Ben shot him.

He looked at Lara. She shrugged. "I was going to do that if you didn't, Gen—Ben. That bastard has ruined the lives of several hundred people."

"At first he seemed like sort of a good guy."

"He always does . . . did. He told me before the torture

started that if I'd go down on him he'd see to it that I didn't get sent to a reindoctrination camp. I told him I'd rather eat a live tarantula."

Ben laughed at that, but that hurt his bruised and swollen face. "They talked about putting you in with some prisoners."

"The real hardcases. Criminal types. That would have been . . . unpleasant."

"I would imagine. OK. Check the others. I'll search Bradford."

"What about the other guards?"

"What others? I've either killed or put out of commission every guard I found."

"How many?"

"About half a dozen."

"Six more, then."

"We'll worry about them as soon as we're finished here."

Lara got nervous about that. "We could be trapped down here, Ben."

"No, we won't. There's a door at the end of the hall. I saw it. It has to lead out of here. If it's locked, we can blow it open."

Bradford had a wad of cash on him—as had all the others—and several government credit cards.

"These guys must have just gotten paid," Lara said, stuffing the money in her jeans pocket—which, Ben had observed, she filled out quite handsomely.

Ben hid a smile, thinking, *I must be getting better.* "We can use the money. It's a long way to our lines."

"That's where we're going?"

"You have a better idea? I'm certainly open to suggestions."

"The Feds scattered our militia movement." She grimaced. "Those they didn't kill or capture. And after this,"—she waved a hand at the bodies of the guards—

"they'll kill us on sight. The Rebel lines sound good to me."

Ben nodded his head. "OK. Get that rucksack over there on the table and put all the sidearms and spare mags in it. And their personal possessions." He looked around at the dead guards. "The boots on that guy," Ben said, pointing, "look about my size. The ones I have on are too big. Give me a minute."

"OK. You get them," Lara said quickly. "I'll stand guard. Those half a dozen others still on the loose worry me. Don't they worry you at all?"

"Not all that much," Ben said, bending down and quickly unlacing and jerking the boots off the dead man. "The Rebels are always outnumbered. It's something we've all gotten accustomed to."

"You have no idea how inventive these people can be when it comes to torture. They were just getting started on me." She shuddered in remembrance. "To be honest, I was hoping for a quick death."

Ben was trying on the boots. They were a perfect fit with only one pair of socks. He finished lacing them and then stuffed the spare socks in his pocket. "Put that out of your mind. Concentrate on staying alive. Let's check on those other prisoners . . . ready?"

"As I'll ever be." She picked up the rucksack.

"Let's do it, then. As the old line reads, We've miles to go."

"Who wrote that?"

"Damned if I can remember." He grinned at her. "My tastes usually ran to, 'A bunch of the boys were whooping it up in the Malamute Saloon . . .' "

A door slammed somewhere in the lower floor.

"Company," Ben said. "Now the fun begins."

"Fun?"

"Killing Osterman's goons."

"Tommy?" a voice called.

"Tommy Bradford," Lara whispered.

Ben smiled. "Right here!" he called. He lifted the muzzle of his CAR.

The bootsteps drew closer.

Chapter Nine

The guard stuck his head into the interrogation chamber and Ben shot him in the center of the forehead. The man's M-16 clattered on the concrete floor. Ben hauled the body into the room, which now was beginning to stink of death.

"Get his rifle and spare mags," Ben told Lara. "And search him for money and keys."

Seconds later, Ben and Lara stepped out into the hall. Ben locked the door behind them. "Let's find those other prisoners," he said. "And I want to find the records room of this damn place. I'm going to destroy every file here."

"We've still got a few guards to deal with," Lara reminded him.

"I haven't forgotten them. I just make a point never to sweat the small shit."

She smiled at him. Her teeth were very white and even. "Do you ever get excited about anything, Ben?"

"Rarely, with one exception."

"And that is?"

Ben cut his eyes to her and grinned. "You really want me to tell you?"

She laughed and shook her head. "I think I can accurately guess."

The first cell they came to, set down a separate wing of the basement, held two men. Ben unlocked the door and said, "I don't care what you've done to get locked in this funny farm. It's time for a fresh start. When you hear an explosion, that will be your cue to leave. If I see you before then, I'll shoot you without hesitation. Understood?"

Ben made the same little speech to every man in every cell, some of whom were in bad shape from beatings. They all understood.

"Ben Raines," one of the men whispered to his cellmate. "That's Ben Raines! Pass the word down the line."

Ben and Lara went up the stairs to the ground floor and promptly ran into two of the remaining guards. Lara finished them without changing expression.

"I just don't like those people," she said.

"Gee, I would never have guessed," Ben said. "Come on, let's finish it and get the hell gone from here. We've got to find that records room."

They ran into no more guards during their search. When they found the records room it was filled with filing cabinets stuffed with hundreds of records on New York State individuals who did not share Madam President Osterman's views on government. Ben spilled them all on the floor, all over the room, and set them on fire. He smashed the computers, printers, and monitors while Lara stood watch in the hall.

Ben smashed out the windows so oxygen could feed the flames and stepped out of the room, closing the door. "The fire will be contained in that room for quite a while," he said. "Let's prowl some more."

Ben found another room filled with computers. He

destroyed them, except for a couple of laptops which he discovered contained modems. He stowed them in carrying cases along with floppies and electrical hookups. "We might be able to use these," he explained. "We'll check them out later."

"Let's get the hell gone from this place, Ben," Lara said nervously.

"You getting a little edgy?" Ben asked with a smile.

"Damn right I am. Those guards might have to check in with somebody every so often."

"Good point."

She sighed. "They don't call in on time, and this place is likely to be crawling with Feds."

"OK. Let's see about some transportation. We'll find us a car or a pickup and then we'll get the gear I stowed by the entrance, blow those chained doors open, and we'll be gone."

Ben found an almost new, full-size pickup truck with a full tank of gas and a full reserve tank.

"Won't they know what vehicle we're in?" Lara questioned.

"They might be able to figure it out in a day or two. But not immediately."

"Why?"

"Watch."

Ben lined up the remaining vehicles and removed the gas caps. Then he tossed a grenade against the chained doors and blew them open so the freed prisoners could get gone. Then he stood back and shot holes in the gas tanks of each vehicle.

"Pull that pickup over here and get ready to get the hell gone when I jump in. We're not going to have but a couple of seconds, at the most."

"OK, Ben," Lara said, eyeballing the two grenades Ben held, one in each hand. The pins had been pulled and he was carefully holding the spoons down. She had already concluded that being around Ben Raines was nothing less than exciting . . . and decidedly unpredictable.

Freed prisoners began exiting the nuthouse. "Get the hell away from the parking lot!" Ben yelled at them. "This whole damn area is about to blow. Move, damnit!"

The freed prisoners scattered in all directions.

Ben waved at Lara. She pulled the truck alongside him and Ben opened the door. He popped the spoons and chunked the grenades under the cars; they splashed in the gathering pools of gas.

"Go!" Ben yelled.

Lara pulled away. Three seconds later the grenades blew and the entire parking lot lit up like a major volcanic eruption. The concussion waves of the explosion rocked the pickup truck. Lara hit the highway and picked up speed.

"Where the hell are we, Lara?"

"Northeast New York State. About forty miles south of the Canadian Border. Vermont is only a few miles to the east. You want to try for Canada?"

"No. They have troubles of their own. Let's head for the Adirondacks. Do your people have food and clothing cached in there?"

"You bet we do. Everything we'll need to stay alive and make one hell of a fight of it if we're cornered. I was going to suggest we head there."

"You're driving, Lara. You know this country. I don't. How far is it?"

"The way the roads are, plus the roads we'll have to take once we leave the hard surface highways, five or six hours at least. Probably longer. That is, if we don't get caught. And that may be one big *if.*"

"Not as big as you might think. By the time the Feds get everything sorted out, three or four or more hours will have passed. By then we should be close to wherever the hell it is you're taking us."

She laughed. "Deep in the brush, Ben. This truck has four-wheel drive on demand. That's good. 'Cause we are sure going to need it."

"You know they'll come after me, in force. They won't stop looking for me. They will never stop searching for me. And anyone who helps me is subject to be hanged. You might consider telling me to hit the road."

"You've got to be kidding! I'm not about to dump you out on your own. Listen, you can put new life into a movement that has almost been wiped out by the Feds. And believe me when I tell you that we have no informants in our bunch. We've gone as high-tech as finances will allow. We have polygraph and PSE equipment, and everyone, *everyone*, gets tested occasionally, with no notice given beforehand."

"Good move. Did you find any Federal plants after the first test?"

"Unfortunately, yes, we did. We were hoping we wouldn't, but we found two."

"What did you do with them?"

"We shot them and buried their bodies deep. Then we changed meeting places, and still do every now and then."

"How many people can you muster?"

"About fifty. And we're all hard-core, Ben. We can do it all, from machine guns to C-4. And we have it all. I gather you have something in mind?"

"Maybe. Just maybe. I think perhaps getting back to Rebel lines would be taking a big chance . . . odds of us making it are slim, and getting slimmer, the more I think about it. I think that perhaps I might be more useful organizing local units to fight. What do you think?"

"I agree. We've got to take back our country town by town."

"Lara, none of you are involved in the killing of abortion clinic doctors, are you?"

"Oh, no. Personally, I'm pro-choice. I've never had anything to do with those types who advocate violence to stop abortion. We've got some people in our group who are opposed to abortion, but not so much they support the bombing of clinics and the killing of doctors."

"And not racist?"

"Oh, no. Not at all."

"You're certain of all that?"

"One hundred percent certain, Ben. My group is racially mixed, and has just one goal in mind—to restore this nation to a constitutional form of government." She smiled. "Along the lines of the SUSA."

They rode in silence for a few miles, passing through one small town that appeared to be deserted. Ben questioned Lara about that.

"A number of the smaller towns in this area are deserted, or very nearly so. There simply is nothing to keep them going ... economically speaking. Tourism is gone, and will probably remain that way for years to come. People just don't have the money to spare."

"Osterman's government has raised taxes?"

"Are you kidding?"

"No. I've been out of the country, Lara. I really don't know what's been happening."

"Taxes are nearly sixty percent now. And will go higher if Osterman has her way. The liberal/socialist/democrats have so damn many programs to support."

"But the people are being taken care of from cradle to grave, right?" Ben asked with a smile.

"That is one way of looking at it," Lara said after a few seconds pause. "If you close one eye and have impaired vision in the other."

Before Ben could respond the bright lights of a vehicle

illuminated the cab of the truck as a car suddenly appeared behind them, pulling in close.

"I don't like this," Lara said.

"Let's see what he does next," Ben suggested. "Before we do something stupid."

The driver of the car behind them cut on his red and blue warning lights.

"State cop," Lara said, disgust in her voice. "We sure didn't get very far."

"Haven't they been federalized up here in the USA?" Ben asked.

"Yes."

"Then they adhere to Osterman's policies, right?"

"As far as I know. Why?"

"Then he's dead," Ben said flatly. "There is no fence-straddling in this war. No one sits on the sidelines. You are either one hundred percent for us, or one hundred percent against us."

"That's the way it's going to be, Ben?"

"That's it. That's the way it's got to be. You in or out?"

"I'm in," she replied without hesitation. "All the way. It's what I've been telling my group for months."

"We'll talk about the foot-draggers in your group later. Keep driving. Let's see what he does."

What he did was cut on his siren. The whooping and whining seemed to fill the night.

"Pull over, Lara."

"How do we play this?" she asked.

"That's entirely up to the cop behind us."

Lara pulled over and stopped on the side of the road, leaving the motor running.

A man's voice coming over a loudspeaker cut the night. "Get out of the truck, both of you. And keep your hands where I can see them."

"When I get out, I'm going to shoot out his headlights," Ben told her. "You get to the front of the truck, pronto."

"All right."

"We'll get out together. That way his attention will be split. On three."

Ben counted to three, and he and Lara opened their doors and stepped out together. He dropped into a crouch and brought up the 9mm. He blew out both headlights, then shot out the warning lights. The night suddenly became a lot darker. He jumped into the ditch that ran along the shoulder of the road.

"I'm down in front," she called in a stage whisper.

"Stay there. And get ready to return his fire."

Ben shouted, "Get out of your unit! Do it if you want to live. Right now."

"You're in a lot of trouble, mister!" the state cop shouted. His voice sounded very young; maybe twenty-two years old, at the most.

"Just a kid," Lara said.

"If he isn't careful he isn't going to get any older," Ben responded.

Ben was slowly working his way up the ditch and then up the slight bank, coming in behind the state police car. He stayed low, to avoid being seen in the glow of the taillights. He could see the silhouete of the policeman sitting in the front seat. Ben suddenly raised up and said, "Keep your hands on the steering wheel, buddy. Or die where you sit. It's all up to you."

"Don't shoot, mister. I'm doing what you tell me to do."

"Turn off the taillights, then sit right where you are."

The cop did as ordered.

"Get back in the truck, Lara. And lead us out and down the first gravel road we come to." Ben got in the passenger side of the squad car.

The young cop's eyes widened as the interior lights came on and he got a look at Ben's battered face. "What the hell happened to you, mister?"

"It's a long story. Follow the truck and don't do anything cute. And don't say a word until I tell you to."

Fifteen minutes later, after spending ten minutes on a winding gravel road, Lara pulled over. The cop pulled in behind her.

Laura walked back to the car. "There's a dirt road just ahead that leads off to the right," she said. "Looks like it runs into a stand of timber."

"All right," Ben said. "Wait here for us. Drive down that road, boy," he told the cop.

"I know that road. It doesn't go anywhere. I'll get mired up to the axles!"

"That's the general idea, boy."

A hundred yards later, the car was sunk up to the frame in the mud.

"Strip," Ben said.

"I beg your pardon?"

"Take off your clothes. Right down to the skin. Do it!"

Ben handcuffed the naked man to the steering wheel. He then destroyed the radio with several 9mm slugs. Ben bundled up the cop's clothing and boots and fought the door until he got it open. The car was mired up that deep.

"Man," the young cop hollered. "Are you going to leave me here? Like this?"

"That's right."

"But this isn't decent!"

"You work for Osterman, and talk about decency? You're a real comedian, aren't you?"

Ben stepped away from the car.

"Wait! I know who you are now. You're General Ben Raines. You damn traitor!"

Ben paused and looked into the car. "You're calling

me a traitor? How many freedom loving people have you arrested and stuck in reindoctrination camps?"

"It was for their own good."

"Boy, you have really been brainwashed, haven't you? You're just about a hopeless case."

Lara tapped on the horn, urging Ben to hurry up. "Got to go, boy."

"This is embarrassing!"

"But you're alive."

The young cop thought about that for a few seconds. "You killed all those fine officers over at the hospital, didn't you?"

"You call that house of torture a hospital? Do you really know what goes on over there? Take a look at my face, boy. What do you think happened to it? You think I fell out of bed and landed on my head?"

"I'm sure you resisted being placed under arrest," the naked socialist/democrat insisted. "The officers were fighting to protect themselves. You certainly can't blame them for doing that. That is a fine facility where you were being held. I knew Officer Bradford. He is . . . was, a fine officer. He'll be buried with full honors."

"Incredible," Ben muttered, and turned to start slogging through the mud back to the gravel road.

"I won't forget this treatment, Ben Raines," the young cop hollered. "What you've done to me is unforgivable. It's . . . it's perverted. That's what it is."

Ben shook his head and slogged on through the mud back to the road. He got in the pickup. "Let's get the hell out of here."

"You left him alive?"

"Sure. It'll be hours before anyone finds him."

Lara's eyes were full of amusement as she looked at the bundle of clothes Ben laid on the floor of the truck. "You left him naked?"

"As the day he was born."

Lara chuckled as she headed back toward the highway. "Ben Raines on how to win friends and influence people."

"He'll have a story to tell his grandchildren."

"Would you tell that story to your grandchildren?"

Ben laughed. "Hell, no!"

Chapter Ten

About an hour later, Lara cut off the main highway onto a secondary road. "I know where I am, Ben. Don't worry."

"You're driving."

She glanced down at the instrument panel. "This thing sure gets good gas mileage. The needle has barely moved."

"Yeah. I like it, too. Rides very well. But we've got to get rid of it soon as we can. That cop radioed in, and unless he was a complete fool he gave dispatch the license number and description."

"I was thinking about that, looking for something to steal. Haven't seen anything yet."

"Nor have I. People must lock up their vehicles at night."

"Oh, they do. You know that car theft is no longer a felony in the USA?"

"It isn't? What the hell is it, then?"

"Oh, just a misdemeanor, if you're below a certain age."

Lara smiled and glanced at Ben. "It isn't the thief's fault, you know?"

"Oh, shit!" Ben muttered. "Not that crap."

" 'Fraid so. It's society's fault, never the individual's."

"Let me guess—the coach wouldn't let the punk play, so he vented his rage on an uncaring society by stealing."

"Or worse. Yes, that's right. Or the prettiest girl in school wouldn't date him."

"Or the kid next door had a new bike."

She laughed. "Or they were poor."

"Or his mother was frightened by a goat. Yes, I know. It's all a crock of crap. It always has been. We've practically done away with crime in the SUSA simply by teaching right and wrong in public schools . . . starting at a very early age. For the few who are born bad, we have long prison terms, if they're not killed by property owners while attempting to steal."

"And you've done it all in a very short time."

"In less than a decade. Through education and strict law enforcement. That's all it takes. Plus a little help from home, if it's available."

"And if it isn't available?"

"That's where society does come into play. Through sponsor programs and one on one buddy systems. Those are big in the SUSA. People aren't required to take part, and they aren't criticized if they don't do so. That's not the way it is in the SUSA. Stick your mouth into someone else's business down there and the nosey person is very likely to get a fat lip. It's just that people care about each other in the SUSA."

Lara smiled. "That sounds very much like an oxymoron."

Ben returned the smile. "I guess it does, at that. But that's the way it works, and the people like it that way."

"And the liberals hate it because it does work."

"Exactly." Ben caught a glimpse of a battered old road sign. "How big is this town we're coming to?"

"It's deserted. Used to be a tourist town. Quite a few lakes around here, but nobody's lived here since shortly after the Great War and the collapse."

"Let's find a place to pull over and stretch our legs and answer a call of nature."

"I'll certainly go for the latter. Your legs stiffening up on you?"

"A little. I'm a bruise from my head to my toes. Bastards really worked on me."

"They will never work on anyone else," Lara commented drily.

"Amen to that." Ben looked around as they pulled into the edge of town. "Nice looking little town."

"Used to be. When I was little, my dad used to bring the family here on vacation. We'd fish and swim, and hike and cook out every day. There were ranges where kids could learn archery, and others where gun safety classes were taught. That's where I first got interested in shooting."

"Any of your family still living?"

"No," Lara said softly. "My dad was a member of a militia group. This was several years before the Great War and the collapse. I was gone, in college. One night the Feds raided our house looking for illegal weapons. Well, there weren't any. I don't believe anyone in the entire group had any illegal weapons. My dad was a strong believer in the right of privacy, due process, the right to own and bear arms, the Constitution in general. Dad fought the Feds that night—unarmed, in his pajamas. One of the Feds hit him with the butt of a rifle. Fractured his skull. Dad died a few days later. He never regained consciousness.

Of course, since Dad was an open member of a militia—
he never denied it—the press painted him as a right-wing
nut. He was anything but. No illegal weapons were found
in the house, naturally. There were never any illegal guns
there. The government never did apologize for killing my
father. My mother and two younger brothers then became
very active in the militia movement. So did I. My mother
died shortly after the Great War. My brothers were both
killed by the Feds two years ago."

"Who reported your father had illegal weapons in the
house?"

"A noesy neighbor. A democrat/socialist left-winger all
the way. When the collapse came, a gang of roaming thugs
hit what was left of our town, on a rampage. My brothers
and I fought them off, away from our house. Killed several
of them . . . using guns my father had buried just before
the gun ban and national confiscation went into effect."

"And the neighbor? What happened to him . . . or her?"

"Him. Mister Warner. That gang of rampaging punks
killed him."

"Could you have prevented it?"

"Sure. At least I think so. But we didn't. My brothers
and I just looked at each other and shrugged. I remember
Warner calling out for us to help him. I also remember
the tirades Warner would throw about guns and how everyone who owned a gun was a right-winger, especially anyone
who belonged to the Republican Party. I remember how
he never even came over to apologize for being at least
partly responsible for my father's death. I also remember
thinking with sort of a grim satisfaction 'To hell with that
left-wing bastard.' I'm sure God will punish me for that.
But I don't think the punishment will be too severe. I seem
to recall from bible lessons that God liked His warriors."

Lara turned down a road and drove for several miles,
the road running alongside a pretty lake. "Some old tourist

cabins out this way. It's a fairly isolated place. But there is more than one way out."

Lara pulled in behind a row of log cabins and parked in a garage that looked as though it had seen better days . . . which Ben was sure it had. Behind them were dense woods. The truck could not be seen from the road or from the air.

"I brought several blankets from the storeroom of the nuthouse," Ben said, getting out and stretching. His joints popped and creaked, and his muscles screamed silently.

Lara looked at him. "You sound like the Tin Man in need of a good oiling."

Ben laughed and nodded his head. Damned if his neck didn't creak with the movement. "At this moment, I certainly feel like him, too."

Lara lit a small candle Ben had taken from the storeroom of the nuthouse and looked at the back room of the cabin. Then she looked at Ben in the flickering light.

"Oh, crap, no way!" Ben said, looking around him. Then they both started laughing.

The place was ankle-deep in trash.

"Let's just sleep outside," Lara suggested. "The temperature is mild."

"That will sure beat the hell out of trying to clean up this mess."

The two of them slept outside, on the ground. Ben was very tired, still a long way from full recovery from the beatings he'd taken, and he slept deeply and straight through until after dawn.

When he awakened he was still stiff, but some of the soreness was gone. He stretched and groaned and looked over at Lara. She was still sleeping.

Then Ben heard the faint sounds of vehicles, and the sound was growing louder. He reached over and shook her.

"Wake up, Lara. We've got company coming. Sounds like several vehicles."

There was a large bruise on the side of her face and a mouse under one eye from the savage beating at the hands and fists of Bradford, marks Ben had noticed during the night. *The whipping she took from the heavy belt must be painful,* Ben thought. Lara had yet to utter a single complaint. *Tough lady,* Ben concluded.

She sat up and rubbed her face, rubbed it very gently, Ben noticed. "I hear them. But there is no way they could have tracked us."

"No. It's just an all-out search. I'll bet you they're spread out all over the state. I told you this is how it would be."

"I wonder if the Feds have upped that million dollar reward on you."

"Possibly. But I'd guess this is just part of a massive search for us. Let's get inside that cabin and get ready to make a fight of it."

They grabbed their blankets and rifles and headed for the cabin. Ben looked back at the weed-filled yard. There was no trace of tire tracks from their pulling in hours back.

"Take the back of the cabin," Ben told her. "I'll take the front. If they spot the truck, open fire."

"We don't have a chance in here, Ben. They'll blow this cabin apart."

"Yeah. I know. You have a better plan?"

She grinned at him, then shook her head. "I wish."

Ben paused for a second, then walked over and kissed her. "Good luck."

She smiled. "Is that a promise of things to come?"

"Damn right."

"You sure you can handle me?"

"I can try."

She laughed softly and pushed him toward the front of the old cabin. "I can hardly wait."

The command reached them: "Check out those old cabins over there!"

"Here we go," Ben said.

Chapter Eleven

Ben had his CAR on full auto, and he had watched Lara do the same with her weapon. They each had taken two 9mm pistols from their rucksacks and they were loaded up full and ready to bang. Each had several grenades within arm's reach. The Feds might kill them, but they would pay a terrible price before that happened.

Ben peeped out through what was left of the broken and very dirty panes. Four vehicles. One HumVee, one big nine-passenger wagon, and two Ford Broncos. He figured between fifteen and twenty people.

Ben counted seven people all strung out along the road in front of the cabins. The rest were working their way behind the row of cabins. Only a few seconds were left before they would spot the pickup parked under the open-ended carport.

"Get ready to start the music," Ben called in a stage whisper.

"What the hell was that?" one of the Feds asked, stopping along the side of the road.

"What?" another asked.

"I heard somebody say something."

"Probably somebody in the back."

"Hey!" The shout came from behind the cabins.

Ben lifted his CAR.

"What?"

"There's a pickup truck back here. Parked under the carport."

He never said anything else. Lara opened up with her CAR, and a half second later Ben did the same. The men and women who made up this small contingent of Osterman's army went down like pins in a bowling alley.

Sixty rounds later, Ben and Lara ejected empties and rammed home full mags.

One Fed made a run for the HumVee. Ben cut him down. Another started running for the big wagon. Lara stitched him, turning him around and around twice, and he dropped lifeless to the ground and did not move.

"Goddamn you!" a woman shouted from the outside. "Damn you all. You filthy, right-wing militia scum!"

"Fuck you!" Lara shouted.

Ben smiled and decided to stay out of this fight. It was getting very interesting.

"I knew it had to be militia!" the woman Fed shouted. "You cowardly, back-shooting Republican whore!"

Ben chuckled. His breath blew out gunsmoke.

Lara's CAR stuttered. There was no reply of any kind from the Fed in the yard.

"Have you ladies concluded your conversation?" Ben called.

"I just ended it," Lara said. "The bitch isn't moving."

"I would certainly say it was over," Ben muttered.

"Help me!" a man called from the back of the cabin.

Ben waited to see what Lara would do. He did not have to wait long. Her CAR clattered, and there were no more cries for help from the outside.

"One tough lady," Ben muttered. "I'm glad she isn't my enemy."

"You object to taking no prisoners in this war, Ben?" Lara called.

"He picked his side, Lara. He knew what he was doing."

"That's the way I see it. Is anyone moving out front?"

"No. No one."

"Same back here. I count nine people down."

"Seven here."

"I figure maybe one or two more."

"Yeah. That's the way I see it." Lowering his voice to a stage whisper, Ben said, "I want those two Broncos. They look new to me. If at all possible, keep your fire away from them . . . OK?"

"OK. You know that the big vehicles like the Broncos, Blazers, and Dodge Rams are made only for the government now. No one else is allowed to have them . . . well, some selected civilians, of course."

"Of course. That's the way socialism works. A Russian philosopher summed up a socialistic form of government this way—What's mine is mine, and what's yours is negotiable."

Just then a man made a wild run for the vehicles. Ben stopped his running in mid-stride.

"You get him, Ben?"

"I got him."

Ben and Lara waited for a long five minutes, Lara finally saying, "I think that's it."

"All right. Keep a sharp eye out in the back. I'm going straight out the front."

"OK."

Ben opened the front and quickly stepped to one side,

staying inside the cabin. No shots split the early morning. He stepped out onto the porch. Bodies lay sprawled in the front and on both sides of the cabin. Ben could not believe they were all dead, but none were moving or showing any other signs of life.

Ben stood for a moment, his eyes shifting from body to body. "Lucked out again," he muttered. Raising his voice, Ben called, "It's clear out here, Lara."

"Same back here."

"I'm going from body to body to make sure. Moving out now."

"Same here. Moving now."

Ben found two that were still alive, but they were not long for this world. All those in front of the cabin had taken bursts in the chest and belly.

"One left alive back here," Lara called. "But he's badly wounded. He's not gonna be alive long."

Ben walked around the cabin. "Let's hide the big wagon and the Hummer under carports. We'll put the bodies in a cabin. Somebody will find them . . . eventually."

The vehicles were hidden. After anything they might be able to use had been taken, Ben and Lara began picking up weapons and stripping the bodies of ammo and grenades. Lara took the boots off the dead woman and found they were a perfect fit. She changed into a set of BDUs she found in a vehicle and laced up the boots.

They found several cases of field rats and sleeping bags in the big wagon, more ammo and grenades in the Hummer. Field radios and cans of water in one of the Broncos. 40mm grenades for the Bloop Tubes under the standard sized M-16's in the other Bronco.

"Here is a fuel transfer kit," Ben said. "Complete with pump that operates off the cigarette lighter or dashboard power point. We'll top off both tanks in the Broncos and then get the hell gone from here."

"We take both vehicles?"

"Yes. We'll get out of here and stop a few miles down the road. You can show me on a map exactly where you have in mind to take us. That's in case we get separated."

"I checked the spares on both Broncos. They're new and aired up."

"Good thinking. What are we missing? Anything?"

"I can't think of a thing."

"OK. I'll top the gas tanks while you walk around . . ." He paused.

"What's the matter?"

"Did you take the wallets from the bodies?"

She grimaced. "No. I'll do that while you're topping the tanks."

Fifteen minutes later, everything had been done.

"Let's get out of here, Ben," Lara said. "I didn't see anyone radio in, but we don't know for sure they didn't."

"You're right about that. You ready?"

"Let's roll."

"Take the lead. I'll be right behind you."

The Broncos were almost new, and handled well. Ben was feeling much better. The day had dawned bright and sunny, and the temperature was pleasant. They now had enough field rats to last them several weeks. They had sleeping bags and blankets, and a portable water purification system. Things were definitely looking up.

Of course, all that could change around the next curve in the road.

And it did.

Ben saw Lara's brake lights flash on and he hit the brakes in the middle of the curve.

She stuck her head out the window and yelled, "Road-block up ahead. I don't think they saw us. It's at an intersection, and there are several cars and trucks ahead of us . . . coming from the other direction."

Ben didn't know what direction she was referring to, not that it really mattered. He jerked the Bronco into reverse and began backing up, then turned around and waited for Lara. She pulled ahead of him and they both headed back in the direction they'd just come. A mile later, Lara pulled over and stopped. Ben pulled up alongside her.

"I think I know another way, Ben. But I won't make any promises."

"We've got to do something. We damn sure can't stay here. Lead us out of here."

A couple of miles later, Lara turned off on a gravel road, Ben right behind her. They drove for fifteen minutes, making several twists and turns and road changes, before she pulled into the driveway of a long-deserted house. They both got out.

"I think I'm lost," she admitted.

Ben smiled at her. "You *think?*"

"OK. I'll admit it. I don't know where in the hell we are."

"Well, this road has to lead somewhere, even if it's to a dead end. Are we in the park yet?"

"Oh, hell, we've *been* in the park for a long time. Ever since we left the hospital. The park is almost six million acres. About half of it wilderness. We're almost in the center of it. If I can lead us out of this maze, we'll be only a few miles from real wilderness, and home free."

"Which way?"

Lara looked at the sun and then pointed. "That way. But the road leading off in that direction sure doesn't look very promising to me."

"Beats getting captured and tortured, or shot to death, doesn't it?"

"You do have a point. OK, Ben. Let's go. We can't get any more lost than we are right now."

"I wouldn't bet on that. Let's don't get separated. Take it slow."

"Will do."

Luck returned to the pair. Fifteen minutes later, they pulled onto a hard-surfaced road and Lara stopped and walked back to Ben.

"I'm pretty sure I know about where we are, Ben. If I'm right, a few miles down this road and we'll take a blacktop off to our right. That'll be to the northwest. Well, more west than north. If I'm right, we're home free."

"Then get us out of here. I'm right behind you."

Lara was right on target: a few miles later a potholed road led off to the right. She turned off on it, and Ben followed. Almost as soon as they did, Ben felt swallowed up by the silent majesty of the wilderness. Hills thick with timber lay on both sides of the road. Off to Ben's left, which was south, several very respectable mountains—Ben figured at least twenty-five hundred feet high—jutted up not too far away. There were deep ravines on both sides of the road.

They crossed a lake, over a bridge that Ben figured had only a few more years left before spans of it collapsed. Then, a few miles farther on, they entered what was left of a tiny village. Lara drove on to the road's end and pulled over.

"Another tourist town that died a number of years ago," she explained as Ben leaned against a Bronco and lit a cigarette. "No one has lived here for years. As you can see, punks and looters have just about destroyed the place."

"The government has no plans to rebuild?"

"No."

"That seems odd to me."

"The park is filled with empty villages just like this one. Nobody can afford a vacation anymore. Well, let me amend that. The majority can't afford anything resembling a real vacation."

Ben's smile was sad. "The left-wing liberals' dream of utopia has finally arrived. No one has more than anyone else . . . except for those in power and their friends. But the government takes care of everyone from cradle to grave. Right?"

"That's about the size of it, but in reality no one really has proper health care. Unless they are absolutely life-threatening, major operations have a waiting period of one to three years. There just aren't enough doctors and hospitals for all the people who want care . . . and not enough money, really. Not for adequate care."

"With all the taxes on you people, where the hell is the money going?" Ben paused and grimaced. "As if I didn't know."

"Government programs—"

"Naturally. How silly of me to ask."

"Programs the likes of which you have never seen," Lara continued. "The government is taking care of drug addicts and drunks. They're taking care of the so-called home-less—which in this time of thousands and thousands of homes just sitting empty is ridiculous. They're taking care of the whiners and the crybabies and the thieves and punks, and God only knows who and what else. The government has made work programs . . . sort of."

"You want to explain that?"

"No one is forced to work in this society. If they don't work, the government will take care of them. Ten times worse than before the Great War."

Lara fished in her shirt pocket and came out with a crumpled pack of cigarettes. She lit up.

"Where'd you get those?"

"Off one of the dead Feds. He had a whole carton in his rucksack." She grinned. "Bootleg cigarettes are a booming business in the USA, Ben. As is bootleg booze from Canada, and from moonshiners."

"But the government puts smokers in jail!"

"If they catch them, yes. But not the first time. The first time is just a warning. Same with drinkers and people who eat forbidden food."

"Forbidden food? Oh . . . you mean like fried foods, and snacks that aren't considered healthful?"

"That's right."

Ben started laughing. He couldn't help it. He recalled an episode of an old TV program about disc jockeys, one of them fearful of the 'phone cops.'

"What is so funny?" Lara demanded.

"This crazy form of government now in power. It really doesn't have a name. In some ways it's unique. The bottom line is totalitarian . . . but on the fringes, all around the edges, it's something else."

"It sucks!"

Ben started laughing once again. Even though the laughing hurt his bruised ribs, the expression on Lara's face was priceless.

"Damn, Ben!" Lara stamped a boot and stood facing him, hands on her hips.

That broke Ben up even more. God knows, he needed a good laugh, and now he was getting one. He finally managed to contain his laughter, and held up a hand. "I'm sorry. I wasn't laughing at you . . . more at the situation, I suppose."

"You had me worried there for a few moments."

Ben wiped his eyes and said, "Let's tuck these vehicles out of sight and prowl this little village. While we're doing that, you can tell me how we're going to travel the final miles to our destination."

They found parts of a garage and lean-to still standing to hide the Broncos, and then began walking what was left of the silent village. There was nothing left of any value that immediately met the eye. Punks and thugs and other people who could best be described as human trash had picked over the town many times, leaving nothing of value behind them.

"How many times have you seen this?" Lara asked, waving a hand at the looted buildings.

"More than I care to remember, over the long years," Ben replied. "It began within hours, perhaps moments, after the fall of government. When I recovered from the illness, it had already spread all over the nation."*

"I remember it well. I was just out of college, and home for a few weeks before I started a new job. I stepped out of the house one morning, looked around, and thought the air smelled funny. Then I don't remember anything else for a couple of days. Sure didn't take long for the whole damn world to fall apart," she added softly.

"No, it sure as hell didn't."

Ben cocked his head to one side and listened for a few seconds. "We've got company coming, Lara. Let's find us a good ambush spot. And do it quickly."

"Damn! You take the woods to the left. I'll take the right. That's about the best I can do on the spur of the moment."

"See you later, darlin'," Ben drawled, and took off for the timber.

*Out Of The Ashes

Chapter Twelve

Ben made it to the edge of a building and bellied down in some brush. He smiled when he saw the first vehicle approach—a beat-up old pickup truck. For a fact, the visitors were not soldiers or the police.

The second vehicle was a car of nearly ancient vintage, and the third vehicle was a Jeep that looked as though it might be from the World War Two era.

Three people in the pickup, four in the car, three in the Jeep.

"Only five to one odds," Ben muttered. "Things are definitely looking up."

The three-car caravan stopped, and eight men and two women got out to stand and stretch in the street. The women looked as rough as the men.

They were all armed with rifles or shotguns, and Ben suspected that under their jackets they all carried pistols. These did not appear to be average law-abiding citizen types. Ben suspected they were bounty hunters, probably sanctioned by the government.

"He ain't here, Red," one of the men said, his voice carrying clearly to Ben.

"You don't know that for a fact, Johnny."

"Son of a bitch could be anywhere," one of the women said. "Maybe hooked up with one of the survivalist or militia groups around here."

"Hell, most of them are busted up and scattered," another of the men said. "Or dead or in prison."

"For a fact," another man piped up. "We don't have to worry none about those people anymore."

"Don't make a mistake and sell Ben Raines short," the man called Johnny said, taking a slow look around him. "Bastard's got more lives than a sack full of cats, and more luck than anybody I know."

"And that whore with him," the other woman in the bunch. "Don't forget about her. She's a top leader in the militia movement. She won't be no piece of cake."

"No," another man said with a laugh. "You're right about that, Jean. Just a prime piece!"

"Get your mind off pussy, Mack," the woman said.

"Why?" Mack questioned.

"Knock it off!" Johnny ordered. "There's a reward out for the woman, too. And don't forget, if we take them alive they're worth more."

"Oh, I intend to take Lara Walden alive," Mack said. "I got plans for her."

Both women looked disgustedly at him, but said nothing.

"You really want to screw some militia whore?" a man asked. "She's probably got some horrible disease."

Mack looked at him. "Jeff, you've got shit for brains, you know that?"

"Why?" Jeff demanded. "How come you to say something like that, Mack?"

"Because you're stupid, that's why. Isn't that right, Pete? He's dumb as a post, isn't he?"

"That's enough!" Johnny said. "Good God. Knock it off. If you want to fuck that whore, Mack, fine with me. But first we've got to take them alive. So let's start looking and knock off all the jabber."

"I agree," Jean said.

"Who the hell asked you?" Mack challenged.

Ben lifted his CAR and gave the knot of bounty hunters half a magazine. A second later, Lara opened fire from across the street. Four bounty hunters went down, spinning and jerking from the impact of .223 rounds. The others hit the ground and scrambled behind their vehicles for cover.

"Harry!" Johnny yelled. "See if you can get to the grenades in the Jeep."

The man called Harry jumped up and tried to make the Jeep. Ben and Lara's CARs spat together, and Harry went down in a bloody heap.

"Any other bright ideas?" Jean called.

Johnny said nothing.

"They're on both sides of the street," Sally said, her voice carrying clearly to Ben and Lara. "And we can't move."

"I say we give it up," Pete called. "It's better than stayin' here and dyin.' "

"And if we do, you think Ben Raines is just gonna let us go?" Johnny asked. "Don't be a fool. That man's as coldblooded as a damn snake."

"Johnny's right," Sally said. "We've got to fight our way out of here."

"OK," Jeff said. "I'll sure go along with Sally on that. But how do we do it?"

No one had a ready reply to that question. Ben and Lara waited, neither of them making a sound.

"Help me!" one of the wounded men called. "My belly's on fire. I'm hurt bad. Help me."

"He's gut-shot," Jeff said. "I seen him take the slugs. We can't do nothin' for him."

"You bastards!" the wounded man groaned. "You're just gonna let me die, ain't you?"

"Can't none of us get to you, Cal," Sally called. "I'm sorry. But that's the way it is."

"We would if we could," Jean added. "You know that."

"All right," Cal moaned. "But try to kill that son of a bitch who shot me, will you?"

"You bet we will," Jean called. "You can count on that."

Both Ben and Lara held their fire as they listened to the conversation.

"Red, you're closest. How 'bout Benny?" Johnny called.

"He's dead. I seen him take a round in the head like to have blowed one side of his head clean off. It was an awful thing to see."

Ben could see part of what he thought was a man lying behind a truck tire. He lifted his CAR and gave the man a quick squirt of lead.

"Oh, Sweet Jesus!" the man hollered. Then he was still.

"Mack?" Jean called. "Mack! Answer me."

"He can't, not now or ever," Jeff called. "That burst of lead took him in the top of the shoulder and must have traveled on to his heart or something. He hollered once, and then was still and quiet. He's gone."

"Shit!" Johnny said. "Raines? You hear me, Raines? Is that you?"

Ben said nothing.

"You on the other side of the street!" Johnny yelled. "Whoever you are. Answer me."

Lara said nothing.

"Goddamn 'em to hell," Johnny cussed.

"It's Raines and the whore," Sally said. "Has to be. Who else could it be?"

"Goddamn militia people, is who," Jeff said. "Those bastards hate us, you know that."

"Or survivalists," Red opined.

"Listen to me!" Johnny yelled. "You people shooting at us. Let's talk about a deal here. How about it?"

Neither Ben nor Lara replied.

"They ain't gonna deal, Johnny," Jean said. "They got us cold, and they know it."

"Where the hell is Red? Red?" Johnny called. "Red! You answer me, now. Red!"

Red could not utter a sound, now or ever again. He was dying with two bullets to the head. One of them had shattered his jaw. The other had struck him in the back of the head and mangled his brain.

"Red's layin' in a pool of blood," Pete called. "I can just make him out from where I am. He ain't movin', don't look like to me."

"Bastards have pretty well cut us down," Johnny said, his words just audible.

"Hey, you Rebels!" Sally yelled, startling those around her. "Talk to us. What do you want to let us live?"

Silence from both sides of the street.

"You sons of bitches!" Sally squalled. "Back-shooting, cowardly scum."

"That kind of talk ain't likely to help us none, Sally," Jeff cautioned the woman.

"To hell with it, Jeff," Sally came right back. "If we're gonna live, we've got to fight our way out of this mess. They won't deal."

"I'm sure open to suggestion," Jean called.

"Pete?" Johnny called. "What the hell are you doing?"

"I think he's praying," Sally called.

"That'll be a first for him," Jeff said.

"Don't knock it," Jean said. "If I thought it would do any good, I'd be trying it, too."

Ben carefully worked his way up to his knees and pulled a grenade from his battle harness. It was going to be a long toss, but he thought he could do it. If nothing else, it would damn sure get their attention.

He pulled the pin, and with a grunt of effort chucked the pineapple. It landed just in front of the Jeep and then slowly rolled under it.

"Shit!" Jeff squalled. "It's a grenade!"

The grenade blew, and the old Jeep disintegrated into many pieces. Two seconds after the grenade exploded, the gas tank went up with a roaring swooshing sound.

Ben and Lara watched as the burning body of the bounty hunter called Jeff was lifted into the air and dumped about twenty feet from the blazing Jeep. Sally jumped up screaming, her clothing on fire, her hair a burning torch, engulfing her entire head. Lara shot her, to put her out of her misery.

Pete jumped up and made a run for it, away from the inferno in the center of the street. Ben chopped him down with one burst, and Pete ended his life kicking and screaming in the middle of trash and litter.

"Goddamn you both to the hellfires!" Jean screamed. She jumped up, yelling and cussing. Firing her rifle from the hip, she advanced toward Lara's side of the street.

Lara shot her. Jean sat down in the street, still firing her rifle and cussing. Lara finished her with another burst. Jean toppled over, and was quiet.

Ben chucked another grenade into the blazing mess. It must have landed directly at Johnny's feet. When it blew, bits and pieces of the last bounty hunter in this group went flying out of the smoke and fire.

The old deserted town grew quiet except for the snapping and cracking of the flames, which were now slowly burning down into nothing.

Ben stood up from behind cover and watched as Lara stood up. "Let's find something to smother the flames and smoke," Ben called. "If those tires start burning, the smoke will be sure to attract unwanted company."

"Entrenching tools in the Broncos," she said. "We'll toss dirt on the flames."

"Let's get to it. I don't feel like another war today."

"Personally, I'd like to have a bath."

"There's a creek right over there," Ben said, pointing. "If you're not bashful."

"What do I have left that you haven't seen?"

"Not a thing, Lara."

She smiled at him.

Chapter Thirteen

The fires were eventually doused with shovels of dirt and with water carried from the creek in collapsible canvas camp buckets. When they finished, both Ben and Lara were filthy from the ash and soot.

"Bath time," Lara said. "God, do I need one."

"Take it, and take your time, enjoy yourself. I'll stand guard and then you can keep a lookout while I bathe."

"Wonder if this soap we got from the nuthouse will lather."

"One way to find out."

Lara looked toward the creek. "That water is going to be cold."

"We have two choices—we can stink, or we can shiver for a little while and be clean."

"You do have a way with words, Ben. Be back in a few minutes."

"I'll be here."

There was no need to hurry. There had not been much

smoke, and what there had been apparently had not drawn anyone's attention. No planes or choppers appeared in the sky, and no ground troops made an appearance.

While Lara took her time in the cold waters of the creek—Ben occasionally heard a shriek from her—he dragged the bodies out of the street and dumped them into a ravine behind a row of decrepit old stores. He then shoved dirt over them, covering them as best he could. The animals would eventually get to the bodies, but that was nature's way, and there was nothing else Ben felt like doing with the bounty hunters.

At Lara's call that she was finished, Ben wandered down to the creek. "Your turn, Ben. But let me warn you—that water is *cold!*"

Very lovely woman, Ben thought, watching Lara dry her hair with a clean shirt. "You feel better?"

"One hundred percent. And the soap does lather."

Ben didn't linger in the creek as long as Lara, but he got his body clean and washed his hair, then dressed in clean BDU's while waiting for his underwear to dry in the sun.

"Is there underwear in the supplies you have cached?" he asked Lara.

"You bet."

"The one thing we forgot to get back at the nuthouse."

"Believe me, I know. Mine is still drying over there on a rock."

Ben and Lara spent the next hour prowling the ruins of the town. They found a couple of old fishing rods and reels and some assorted tackle. Lara showed Ben the faint track of an old logging road that led off into the timber and another track that led to a nearby lake.

"How far is the lake?" Ben asked.

"About five miles."

"Should be jumping with fish."

"Oh, yes."

"Let's put this town behind us, then. What do you say?"

"I'm for it. After we pull the vehicles down this old road a few hundred feet, we can toss some brush over the entrance here. It might fool anyone who comes looking."

"You don't think the Federals will?"

"It's doubtful, Ben. Feds that come into the wilderness don't generally come back out . . . if you know what I mean."

Ben knew. The freedom fighters in the USA had gone underground, and were waging a guerrilla type of war. They were in control of a lot of the wilderness areas. "How about troops from Fort Drum?"

She shook her head. "Nothing there anymore. The military has all been shifted down to the border with your nation."

Ben nodded his head. "And they'll stay down there, too. Before this war is over, every man and woman Osterman can draft into service will be along our borders."

"She still has the thousands of mercenaries under contract," Lara reminded him.

"As long as the money holds out, they'll stay. But how much is that costing the taxpayers? Several millions of dollars a day, I'm sure . . . probably more than that. When the money runs out, the mercenaries will leave. The currency in the SUSA is the strongest in the world. The USA's dollar is weak, with no hope of getting stronger. We have trade agreements with many of the world's nations. This is not their fight, and they'll stay out of it. Many of them have signed agreements to that effect. This is strictly a civil war between Americans, Lara. And until the socialist/democrats up here in the USA learn to compromise and live and let live, this civil war will drag on forever."

"Can the SUSA stall long enough for the money to run out?"

Ben shook his head. "No. Not stall. Hold out, yes. And we will. We'll lose some territory and then regain it. Ground will pass back and forth several times before the worst of it is over."

"And the SUSA will be victorious?"

"We'll win the fight. Victorious? I guess that will depend on the individual's point of view."

"I . . . think I know what you mean."

"We'll talk more about it. I've got a few ideas about this civil war that we need to discuss. Right now, let's get out of here. Head for the lake."

"Damp underwear and all, hey?"

Laughing, they headed for the Broncos, Ben pausing long enough to grab his still slightly damp drawers from a rock.

The road out to the lake had not been used in a long time, and the going was very slow. The road, never a hard surface road, had long since grown over, and several times they had to break new ground through the brush because of trees that had fallen and were blocking the road.

"Forget about hiding our tracks," Ben said.

"The Feds don't come into the wilderness, Ben, as I said. Once we get past the lake, there are booby traps all over the place. Too many Federal patrols, have been caught in here, too many times."

"That means you know the way, though?"

"Oh, you bet I do. That was one of the reasons Bradford was torturing me, trying to get me to tell him the way to our camps."

"What about spotter planes and choppers? Don't they ever fly over?"

"Not anymore. Not since the war began with the SUSA.

Even when they did, they didn't get too low." She smiled at him. "We have shoulder-fired missiles."

"How much farther to the lake?"

"Just about a mile. We'll get there in plenty of time to catch a mess of fish for supper."

"If they're biting."

"Oh, they always hit a lure. Lake hasn't been fished in a long time."

"Lead on, Lara."

They broiled fish for supper, and they were delicious. They finished washing up just as night was casting its darkness over the land, creating silver shadows over the lake. A light cooling wind was blowing.

"Peaceful time," Ben said, looking out over the quiet lake. "It's lovely."

"Yes, it is. I remember when it was always like this," Lara replied, a wistful quality in her voice. "I sometimes wonder if those times will ever come again."

"Oh . . . someday. Maybe not in my lifetime, but certainly in yours."

"You're not that old, Ben."

"Maybe not. But I sure feel like it often enough."

"Years of war will do that. I've been fighting the socialists ever since they came in power. Hiding and living out in the wilderness. Before that it was the gangs of punks and warlords all over the nation. I know a little something about it."

"I'm sure you do, Lara. Freedom never comes cheaply, does it?"

"Nothing worth having ever does. Especially freedom. We took it for granted for too long, I think."

"Yes, we did. And we forgot how damn sneaky the left wing can be, especially when the print and broadcast media was overflowing with those types, aligning with them in sometimes not too subtle ways.'' Ben paused for only a few seconds as his ears picked up very faint sounds not normally associated with the forest. ''I think we've got company, Lara.''

''Yes. I figured they would come in before long. Relax. Those are my people.''

''How can you be so sure?''

''The way they move. We've had to become expert in the woods, Ben. We had no choice in the matter. It was either that, or die.''

''They're good. They were right on top of us before I heard one of them.''

''That would be Jimmy Smathers. He's just a kid, just learning. They brought him along this time because they knew it was us.''

''How old is this boy?''

''Seventeen.''

''Hello, the camp!'' The voice came out of the gathering darkness.

''Come on in, Chuck,'' Lara called. ''And meet General Ben Raines.''

There was a long silent pause. ''General *who* did you say, Lara?''

''Ben Raines. He was a prisoner there in the nuthouse with me. Hadn't a been for him, I'd be dead right now . . . or wishing I was. Come on in.''

Ben stood up and heard someone say, ''Jesus Christ, Chuck. It's really him.''

Shadows in the gloom suddenly became human as men and women began stepping out into the clearing. Ben counted seven men and four women. Lara stood up and put her arms around one older man—just a few years younger than Ben, he guessed. ''Good to see you, honey,'' the man said. "We've been worried about you, but didn't know for sure where those damn Feds had taken you."

"I'm all right, 'cept for a few bumps and bruises. Ben, this is the commander of our militia unit, Chuck Harris. Chuck, General Ben Raines."

Ben shook the man's hand, then was introduced all the way around. There was Dave, Ed, Marty, Dan, Louis, and Jimmy. Then he was introduced to the women: Nora, Lou, Belle, and Val.

They were all armed with M-16's and 9mm sidearms. They all had grenades hooked onto their battle harnesses and carried half a dozen extra magazines for the M-16's and two for the sidearms.

After a few minutes of small talk, most of it about how Ben and Lara got away from the hospital, Lara fixed another pot of coffee and Ben said, "Let's get down to it, people. We have a civil war to fight, and I need you all on the side of the SUSA. What about it?"

Without a heartbeat of hesitation, Chuck said, "You've got it, General. You tell us what you want, we'll do it."

"I don't want elderly people or children harmed . . . if at all possible. That's the first thing. If an adult works for Osterman's government they're the enemy, and I don't give a damn what happens to them."

Chuck and the others smiled and nodded their heads. Chuck said, "That is exactly how we feel about it, General. Of course, I felt that way about the people who worked for the IRS—to name just one agency of the government— back before the collapse and the Great War."

Ben laughed. "I know a lot of people who felt the same way. Now then, supplies. I can get us supplied by air drop. It'll be the long way around, but I can get it done. What do you need?"

"Medical supplies, for a start," Chuck said quickly. "All kinds. How about if I make out a list?"

"Great. Can you get me a radio hookup?"

"No problem. I'll have it set up for you tomorrow at our base camp."

"Good enough. Have the list ready for me, and we'll get things moving."

"Coffee's ready," Lara announced. "The first pot, that is. It'll take about three pots for this crowd."

"I'll fix the second one," Dave said.

"General," Nora said. "The only news we get worth a damn is on shortwave. The other news is all bullshit . . ."

Everyone laughed at that. Ben knew that for the past couple of years the news in the USA had been controlled by the government. It had been somewhat lopsided and biased before the collapse and the Great War. Ben, along with millions of other people who did not have their heads up their asses had believed for years the press was controlled by the left wing. Now that was a fact. The news now was pure crap.

"How is the war going down along your borders?" Nora asked. "The press up here is reporting great victories for the Federals. I just don't believe that."

"Well," Ben said. "There certainly had been no great victories on either side a few days ago. I haven't heard a newscast since I was taken prisoner several days ago, but I doubt seriously the Feds have made any significant advances into Rebel territory. I'll know for sure tomorrow when I talk to my people."

"Then you'll be going back?" Dan asked.

Ben smiled. "This war has gotten very personal for me, very quickly. I think we need an advisor up here." He chuckled. "And since I am the commanding general of the Rebel Army, I can pick any person I want for the job. So, I pick me."

Chapter Fourteen

"Anybody awake down there?" Ben spoke calmly into the mic. "This is the Eagle."

"General!" The communications tech yelled the word so loudly that the speaker distorted it. "Where the hell are you? Ah ... I mean, sir."

Ben threw back his head and laughed at the tech's excitement. "Patch me through to President Jefferys, please."

"Right away, sir. Hang on."

There was about half a minute of silence, then Cecil's voice came booming out of the speaker. "Ben! Thank God, you're alive."

"I have a few bruises, ole' buddy, but soon it'll be payback for the Eagle."

"How do you want to be picked up, Ben?"

"I don't, Cec."

Another short pause, then: "You, ah, want to run that by me again, Ben?"

"I'm staying right here. I'm going to be working with a militia group from this end."

"I suppose there is no point in my trying to dissuade you, is there?"

"None at all."

"All right. Then I won't try."

"But I do need supplies, Cec, and it's going to have to be a precision drop, at night."

"We can handle that. Give me the coordinates and what you need."

"Better tape this. The list is long."

"OK. You want any help up there? Your team, I mean."

"As much as I'd like to see them, no. They'll understand, I'm sure of that. Maybe later, after we get cranked up and running smoothly, I'll call in some people. But not now."

"OK, Ben. It's your show. Tape is rolling. Go."

"How are your people going to get all that up here without being spotted and shot out of the sky?" Chuck asked after Ben had finished speaking with Cecil.

"They'll come up under heavy fighter escort. Tankers will be up to refuel them when needed. They'll fly over the Atlantic until cutting west over Canada. The Canadians won't bother my people. The Canadian government might not like us using their air space for this purpose, but they won't attack my planes. They'll make their drop here and then head back the same way."

"I've notified my people all over the park to be on the alert for stray 'chutes."

"Good enough. Now all we have to do is wait."

"You turned down your president's offer to send troops in, General. Why?"

"Because we don't need them for the type of war I plan to wage up here, Chuck."

"We can handle it?"

"Easily. You'll see."

"Civilians are going to get hurt, aren't they?"

"Probably. But those who get hurt will be supporters of Osterman and her government. It's as I said before—people are either with us, or they're against us. There are no fence-straddlers or so-called moderates. Moderates, in my opinion, don't stand for anything. They're wishy-washy."

Chuck smiled at that. "You're as hard as people say you are, General."

"My people and I—millions of us—have fought for years for the right to live in peace, under our own form of government. Governments all over the world have recognized us and signed trade agreements with us. Some nations have even adopted our way of governing. The Tri-States philosophy works. We've proved it. It won't work for everybody. It wasn't meant to. But we've shown that we can live in peaceful coexistence with our neighbors. And we'll fight for our way of life, Chuck. If any government threatens us, we'll get mad dog mean and down and dirty to preserve that way of life. You all—all your people—know our system. It's so simple a form of government, so workable, it scares the shit out of liberals. But I'm preaching to the choir here, Chuck. You know all this."

"Yes, I know. We all do," the leader of the local militia agreed. The group of men and women he headed was a mixture of militia and survivalist people. "But I'm asked often if it would work outside the SUSA. Alongside and with other forms of government?"

"No. Not fully. Besides, we never planned that it would. We don't try to force our way of life on anyone else. All we want is to be able to live under our own government and be left alone. We've proven we can. Time and again." Ben sighed and shook his head. "Frankly, we're running out of patience with those who want to destroy us. If other governments want to play kick ass, we'll damn sure play it with them.''

"President Osterman sure plans to kick our ass."

"She'll never succeed, Chuck. All she'll succeed in doing is ripping North America apart."

"Let's play worst case scenario, General. What happens if the Feds do get the upper hand, and you sense we've lost the war?"

When Ben looked at Chuck, the militia leader felt as if an icy knife had been plunged deep into his guts. He had never seen eyes so cold and mean. "I'll destroy North America," Ben said, his words causing another chill to wriggle snake-like through Chuck's body. "I'll turn loose every goddamn germ-warhead missile I have and stand there during their flight and curse into the fires of Hell every fucking liberal socialist/democrat that ever took a breath."

The militia members and Ben loafed around for the next two days. Ben rested, bathed his bruised body in hot water (which Lara heated in a huge iron pot over an open fire for him), ate well, and slept a lot. He was at about ninety percent recovery at mid-morning of the third day in the militia camp when more of Chuck's people began coming in. They would assist in the retrieving and the distribution of the supplies to be dropped in late that night.

Ben was introduced all around, and many of the new people were in open awe of the man. It was a feeling that Ben had never liked, and had never gotten used to, but he knew there was nothing he could do about it . . . except live with it.

Several hours before dark, the entire camp began moving out toward a long and wide valley several miles away, hoping the supplies would be dropped there.

The planes would come in low, guided in by Chuck's people forming two wide lines of light provided by powerful flashlights.

"No wind," Ben remarked as they arrived in the valley. "Let's hope it stays that way. My people will put the supplies right on target, but it'll be a hell of a lot easier for them if there is no wind."

"Will this supply drop run you people short down in the SUSA?" Jimmy asked.

Ben smiled, as did others within earshot. "No, son," Ben replied. "Not at all. We have enough supplies stored to run us about twenty years."

"Twenty years!" the young man blurted.

Ben laughed. "At least twenty years, my friend. We believe in staying prepared. We have dozens of crews down in the SUSA that do nothing but build and stock and restock supplies from underground storage areas. We seldom throw away anything that can be used. We have millions of tons of everything you could possibly name, from commodes to panty hose and from dried beans to powdered milk."

"Good God," Jimmy breathed.

Ben smiled again as the young man walked off, shaking his head. He checked his watch. He had deliberately given Chuck and the others the wrong time for the drop. The drop would not be made at 2000 hours. It would be at 2020 hours.

During one of the conversations with Cecil, down at Base Camp One, Cecil had dropped a one-word warning to Ben, several times. That one word told Ben that the militia movement had been recently infiltrated, and warned him to be very careful. A little bit of double talk between the two men had altered the time for the supply drop.

Ben felt certain that if the Feds—or some other group— were going to strike, it would be right before the drop was made, for the traitor would know the procedure. There would be no radio contact between the ground and the planes; the signal would be by strobe lights.

Ben was 99.09% certain the infiltrator was not Lara. She was still carrying the marks of the beating she'd received from Bradford. That sure as hell had not been faked. Nor had her killing of the guards or the ambushes.

Nor did he believe the traitor was Chuck.

Ben had not been able to ask Cecil how he knew about the infiltrator in this particular militia group, but the Rebels had people in place all over the USA, planted there months and even years before.

At 1930 hours, Ben motioned Lara and Chuck off to one side and told them what was taking place. Both were shocked speechless for a few seconds.

"That can't be, General!" Chuck protested. "My people were just polygraphed a couple of months ago. They all passed the tests without a hitch."

"Then perhaps the contact was made after the last test," Ben told him. "The Feds lucked out, that's all. We might never know why one of your people was turned, but it happens. It's happened with my people . . . more than once."

"Ed Morris," Lara said softly.

"What?" Chuck challenged. "That can't be, Lara. I've known Ed all my life!"

"Why do you suspect him?" Ben asked.

"His kid," Lara replied. "His boy was just accepted at a very prestigious university . . . full scholorship paid for by the government. You remember, Chuck, we wondered about it."

"Yeah," the militia leader said. "No kid of a known militia member—a man on the run—was ever accepted by any high tone school like that. Ed said it was because of his son's grades. But other kids with high scores—whose parents are Osterman supporters—have been rejected. It just didn't sound right to me,"—he looked at Lara—"us. But we had no reason to doubt Ed. Until now," he added softly. "Damn! But it's hard to believe."

"It might not be Ed," Ben cautioned. "We'll just have to wait and see. I'm betting they'll make their move just minutes before the drop. I'll fake a radio message and announce that the planes are on schedule. If they make their move, we'll have plenty of time to handle it and get ready for the actual drop."

"And if we take the traitor alive?" Lara asked.

"There will be very advanced drugs included in this drop," Ben said, "several generations advanced from sodium pentothal. We'll find out who the traitor's contact is, and deal with them later."

"That I'll be looking forward to," said Chuck. "With a great deal of anticipation."

"You know," said Lara, "Ed and that new fellow in Chris's unit, Nolan, are real buddy buddy. They talk a lot when the two units are together. And Ed said he didn't know the guy before he joined up."

Chuck nodded in the darkness. "Yeah. That's right. He sure did." Chuck sighed. "So we'll watch both of them."

"Who gave this Nolan person the polygraph?" Ben asked.

"Why . . . damned if I know," Chuck admitted.

"I can find out in about one minute," Lara said. "I trust Bob Odell with my life. He's saved it several times over the years. I'll ask him. Be right back."

She was back in a couple of minutes. Even in the gloom

Ben could tell her face was grim. "Ed administered the polygraph to Nolan. Or says he did, anyway."

"Well, I'll be damned!" Chuck said.

"It still isn't conclusive proof," Ben said. "But we'll keep an eye on them. And pass the word to only those in your group you know you can trust—men and women with no families or kin on the outside. I'll make the announcement in a few minutes that the planes are on the way."

"Then the shit hits the fan," Lara said.

Ben smiled. "My, my, darling. You do have such a way with words. You have the soul of a poet."

Lara smiled sweetly and flipped Ben the bird.

Chapter Fifteen

A couple of minutes after Ben made the announcement he noticed that both Ed and Nolan were gone. "Down!" he called first to Chuck and Lara. Then Ben yelled, "Everybody get down. We've been set up. It's a trap."

The night became pocked with flashes as the turncoats aligned with Ed and Nolan opened fire on the men and women they had called friends for years.

Ben saw several of Chuck's group buckle and go down under the gunfire. Chuck's immediate group had been warned that something was up, though, and they hit the ground at the first shouted warning.

Ben leveled his CAR at unfriendly flashes coming from the edge of the clearing and gave them half a mag. He couldn't tell if he hit anything, but the firing abruptly ceased.

"Rotten bastards!" Belle yelled, on her knees and firing into the pockmarked timber and brush around the clearing.

On his belly behind part of a rotted log, Ben checked

the luminous hands of the expensive watch he'd taken from one of the guards back at the funny farm. The planes would be making their drops in twelve minutes.

"Abort it! Abort it!" someone yelled from the darkness of the timber. "Get out of here!"

Chuck's group had already pinpointed the locations of many of the turncoats, and they had worked close. They now increased the fire and began tossing grenades. Suddenly the situation changed, and Chuck's people were on the offensive. The turncoats panicked and began running. Chuck's militia cut them down.

The fire from the timber abated, then ceased altogether. Ben yelled, "Throw up security lines around the clearing. Then take a head count and find out who turned. Alert your people in the park."

Chuck began yelling orders. Ben again checked his watch. When Chuck finished, Ben called, "Planes here in seven minutes. Form up the light lines."

Chuck walked up, cussing. "Dirty traitorous sons of bitches! I'll have every damned one of them shot."

"Check the dead and wounded in the timber," Ben told him. "Any alive might be persuaded to tell us something."

"Bet on that," Chuck said grimly.

"Rest of us get the light lines formed up. We're running out of time."

It took four minutes to get the DZ lit up. In the timber the sounds of an occasional gunshot could still be heard as Chuck's people found turncoats and the traitors put up a fight ... very brief fights, in most cases, for Chuck's people were pissed off to the max and not interested in any sort of niceties.

"Planes!" someone yelled, and Ben turned toward the east just as the lights of the first big transport could be faintly seen coming in low over the hills and mountains.

"Lights on!" Ben yelled.

Two long lines of light flashed on, marking the wide DZ in the valley.

The lead transport flashed its flight lights, signaling they had the DZ in visual.

Thousands of feet above the transports fighters circled, in case of trouble, but there was no more trouble in the huge park that night.

Dozens of parachutes suddenly blossomed in the night sky as the supplies were dropped. Chuck's people raced to retrieve the supplies. There was very little wind that night, and the supply drop went off without a hitch. Several tons of much needed supplies floated soundlessly into the valley, and then the night grew quiet as the huge transports made their turn and headed back toward the east.

"Let's see what we've got," Ben called.

They had rockets and launchers, M-60 machine guns and M-16's. Machine pistols with sound suppressors. Cases and cases of various types of grenades. Thousands of rounds of ammo. Boots and BDUs, socks and underwear. Berets and helmets and body armor. Medical supplies for every need and emergency. Cases of field rations. Water filtration systems and purification tabs. Portable stoves and heat tabs.

There were supplies strung out from one end of the valley to the other.

"Good God Almighty!" Chuck exclaimed. "When you call for a supply drop you don't kid around, do you, General?"

Ben chuckled. "I didn't call for a lot of this. But my people want me to be prepared for any eventuality."

"Well, we damn sure are now!"

"For a fact," Lara said.

"Let's get this stuff cached and take a head count," Ben suggested.

"I can tell you we've got four dead and several wounded,"

Chuck told him. "How many turncoats we had is still up for grabs. But I will find out. Bet on that."

There was no more time for conversation as men and women started coming in and picking up the supplies and loading them in small trailers hooked to three-wheelers and four-wheelers. They would divvy up the supplies come daylight, and discuss the fates of the turncoats and how to deal with them.

"I know how to deal with them," Lara said, considerable heat in her words.

Several other members of the militia groups in the park standing nearby nodded their heads in agreement, a couple of them adding some very earthy descriptive phrases along with the nods.

There was no way the turncoats were going to live very long after this night, not unless they moved out of North America.

Sad, Ben thought. The conditions in the USA had come to this: neighbor pitted against neighbor, father against son, brother against brother. Ten times worse than during the first civil war, a hundred and fifty years back.

The supplies were cached and the men and women of Ben's new command in the northeast got a few hours sleep. At dawn they were up and taking stock of what they had and how many men and women had turned on them.

"I'm getting reports in," Chuck said. "Ed was the ringleader. Nolan was in on it, too. There were fifteen others. Three of them are dead, four wounded, and we have them. One of them isn't going to make it . . . if he hasn't died already."

"Why did they do it?" Belle asked. "My God, I've known Ed for years."

"Money and power was Nolan's reason. Money and college for his kid was Ed's reason."

"I thought under Osterman's government anybody who wanted to could go to college." Ben said.

"That was the claim," Lara replied. "And still is. But it didn't work out that way—as was predicted by a lot of us when it was first brought up. There just isn't enough money, or teachers or schools."

"Anyone with half a brain should be able to see that not everyone is college material," Ben said.

"Osterman wants a nation of intellectuals," Chuck said. "I *guess* that's what she wants," he added with a shrug of his shoulders. "Hell, everything is so screwed up I don't think anyone knows anymore."

"She wants power," Ben told the group. "And her way in all matters. There is nothing wrong with being a dreamer. I had a dream, too. The trick is not letting that dream turn into a nightmare."

"Weland just died," a man called from the area where the turncoat wounded were being cared for. "He never regained consciousness."

"John Weland," Lou said. "I always thought he was with us a hundred and ten percent."

"It's times like these that could make a person get real discouraged," Chuck said. He stood up from his squat and shook himself like a big dog. "But I'm not going to let that happen. The group is solid again, way I see it. So let's get on with the job at hand and try to get this mess straightened out. The sooner we do, the sooner we can all start living some sort of normal life."

Those gathered around looked at Ben.

"My turn?" he asked with a smile.

"Your turn, General," Chuck said.

"That's easy."

"Easy, Ben?" Lara asked.

"What's next, that is."

The others waited.

Ben lit a cigarette and took a sip of coffee. "What's the nearest town?"

"In the park?" Belle asked.

"Might as well be."

"Saranac Lake," Belle answered.

"The police force there?"

"Solid Fed trained and solid Osterman supporters," Lara answered. "Ben, every police force in the USA is that way now. Any officer who thought differently is long gone—weeded out, forced out. The police have absolute power now. And you know what's said about absolute power."

"It corrupts."

"Right, and it sure as hell has done just that with these sorry bastards and bitches who now wear the badges in the United States."

"What about Saranac Lake?" Dave asked.

Ben grinned. "We take control of it ... tomorrow night."

Ben had not shaved in about a week, and his beard was naturally heavy. He was well on the way to having a full beard—a sculptured one. A few hours before the assault on the park town was to take place, he carefully trimmed and then shaved his upper cheeks and neck: the beard was coming along nicely. He didn't think it would fool anyone up close, but it might cause them to hesitate, and that would be all the time that Ben needed to get in the first punch, or shot, as the case might be.

He had asked and had been pleasantly surprised to find that Chuck's people had a comprehensive list of people with conservative leanings and those who were solid left wing. Militias and survivalist groups had begun compiling those lists several years back, and the lists were long.

"But those with conservative leanings have been disarmed, and are watched," Ben was advised.

"Well, they're about to be rearmed," Ben replied. "And they'll be taking over the policing of the communities we free from Osterman's rule. Once we're successful in half a dozen of these raids, other groups around the USA will start following suit. We're going to reclaim the USA, folks. One community at a time."

President Claire Osterman sat in the Oval Office in the new White House and silently cursed. The war with the SUSA was not going well. Not going well at all.

Her Federals had one minor victory to their credit, in Tennessee. They had captured Ben Raines. After that, Raines's Rebels had toughened up and started kicking ass all along the border.

Now Ben Raines had escaped from custody and was somewhere in the huge Adirondacks Park with a bunch of ragtag, idiotic, militia types.

"Shit!" Madam President Osterman muttered.

Her intel people had informed her about the supply drop in the park the past night—a massive drop of equipment. Her small, ill-equipped and poorly trained Air Force had scrambled a squadron of fighters to mix it up with the Rebels. Not a single Federal plane had returned. The goddamn Rebels had shot down every one of her fighters.

"Bastards!" she muttered.

She had to hire more mercenaries to fight the Rebels. She had no choice in the matter. One of her advisors had proposed bringing back the draft, and Claire had been horrified at just the thought. Good God! Decent people don't grub about in the military. That was something one *hired* done. If they got killed, well, society hadn't lost much of anything. Her own father had evaded the draft during that debacle in Vietnam years back, skipping off to Canada with a group of others from the university. She remembered how proud of that he had been. He had often told her that only people of very dubious intelligence served in the military; certainly not people of quality.

In order to hire more soldiers Claire would have to raise taxes. Just had to be done. Couldn't help it. People had to sacrifice in order to maintain a perfect society where everyone was equal. The citizens would understand. She was sure of that. Defeating Ben Raines and returning the SUSA to the Union would be worth it.

Of course, once all that was accomplished taxes would probably have to be raised just a teeny weeny bit more, for the reindoctrination of those misguided people who lived in the SUSA would be costly. It was certainly something that had to be done. Couldn't have a bunch of people running around believing that the average citizens had a right to own guns. Heavens, no!

Unthinkable.

Allowing a moment of silence in public school could certainly not be allowed, either. Absolutely not! Those foolish people who mumbled prayers to some mythical being would soon be contaminating the minds of truly intelligent people who *knew* the Bible was nothing but a good yarn, pure fiction.

And who knew what that damned Ben Raines was up to in the wilderness? For sure the goddamned troublemaker was plotting something against the government . . . that much was a given. But what? And why did he want all those supplies that were parachuted into the park? What kind of supplies were they, and what was he going to do with them?

Madam President Osterman leaned back in her massive leather chair, a frown on her face. As much as she hated Ben Raines, she could not allow herself to underestimate the man. She had done that several times in the past, and had soon regretted it. The bastard was smart, she had to admit that—albeit very, very reluctantly.

The problem with that damned park was that it was huge! When her State Police or Federal troops did go in after those miserable militia types, they never came back out. The park was booby-trapped, and very dangerous.

Claire pushed back her chair and stood up. She paused for a minute, looking out the window. What a lovely day. Then the face of Ben Raines entered her mind and spoiled everything. God, she hated that arrogant bastard.

She sure wished she knew what he was going to do next. She frowned again. Whatever it was, it would be destructive, that was for certain. Bastard enjoyed blowing things up.

Claire sat back down. She had developed a raging headache just thinking about him.

"Ben Raines, you rotten, right-wing son of a bitch!" she blurted.

he must she had done that scared him. In the darkness
then you repeat it to the General and make the list to
achieve them and leave you vulnerable.

The problem with that damned push was that it was
easy, when her hand radiated such heat, there he got in
there. It was her hair and the fingers that were laid
about the forehead he developed and so dangerous.

She pushed of him, but she leaned toward up. She pushed
for a moment, looked up into the window. What a lovely
man the General was happy enough at her smile and pulled
something. "No," she leaned in a soft faint beaded.

She smiled and her head went on before stepping to do that
the bones; again. Whatever from. Would the danger the
door was her either. Bruno sighed and blinking his the
closest on before down one and down speech a rising lower
arose out. Blinking about him.

"Bones, you come right into, yeah," and in it sure
rolled in.

Book Two

1935 will go down in history! For the first time
a civilized nation has full gun registration! Our
streets will be safer, our police more efficient,
and the world will follow our lead in the future!
—Adolf Hitler

Book Two

Chapter Sixteen

When a majority of a nation's population elects to support a socialist/communist regime, those opposed to such a form of government (the minority) have few options left them. They can revolt against the ruling government, but if the entire civilian population has been disarmed, their weapons confiscated (taken by force under threat of death or imprisonment) by government agents, their options become rather slim. Under such a form of government, block wardens, or watchers, suddenly rise to the fore. Neighbors, men and women and young people who were once friends, become suspicious and very wary of each other, for who knows who is reporting what to the town's central committee?

Once the entire civilian population is disarmed (except for certain selected individuals fanatically loyal to the democrat/socialist/communist regime) the normally law-abiding citizens are much easier to control with less manpower (excuse me, all you feminists: *person* power).

Those types who choose to wear or carry badges under such a restrictive and oppressive form of government also tend to get a bit cocky—very much impressed with their own self-importance.

Ben Raines and his new northeast command of militia and survivalists took all the steam out of the local federal police force just after sundown.

The dispatcher and the one person working the desk looked up and found themselves staring at a dozen heavily armed men and women, all wearing camo BDUs.

"Don't do anything stupid," Ben warned the pair. "And you'll live. Screw up and you're going to get seriously dead in a hurry. Understand?"

They both nodded their complete understanding of the situation and the ramifications involved. They were only too happy to comply.

Several of Chuck's people quickly disarmed the pair of Federal police and then emptied the gun racks and the small arsenal of the police station.

"Call your patrols back here," Ben ordered the dispatcher. "If I sense a code word being used to warn them, I'll kill you where you sit, understand?"

"Yes, sir," the dispatcher said. "I sure do."

"Do it."

Ten minutes later, the night shift of the town's police force were locked in their own jail. Twenty minutes after that, the other members of the town's federal police force had been rousted out of bed and were locked down.

"By God, I'll see you all hang for this!" the police chief blustered.

It was an empty threat coming from a man standing in his drawers.

"My, my, he sure has skinny legs and knobby knees, doesn't he?" Belle said.

"You dirty, rotten, filthy militia whore!" the police chief yelled.

"Got a mouth on him, too," Val observed.

"To hell with you, bitch!" the chief hollered. "I'll see all of you hang, you . . . you . . . traitors!"

Ben stepped closer to the barred door of the cell and the chief squinted and paled. "Ben Raines," he whispered. "You damned fascist!"

"You certainly are in a mood for name calling this evening, aren't you, Chief?" Ben questioned. Ben lifted the muzzle of his CAR and poked the chief in the belly with it. "Not too smart for a man in your predicament, I would say."

"I'm not afraid to die!" the chief yelled.

"You're a damn liar," Ben told him. "Everyone is afraid to die, whether they'll admit it or not."

"I'm not!" the chief hollered.

"OK," Ben said. He turned to Belle and Val. "You two take this bastard out back of the jail and shoot him."

"What?" the chief said. He began backing up in the cell. "Now you just wait just a damn minute here!"

Ben stuck the big key in the lock.

"Whoa!" the chief said. "I don't want to die. I changed my mind. What the hell do you people want here in my town?"

"Your town," Ben told him. "That's all we want."

The chief blinked a couple of times. "My town? Well . . . you can't have it! That's absurd!"

Ben turned as other members of his group herded in the mayor and half a dozen others of the town's leading citizens . . . including several females. None of those being prodded along by gun barrels looked very happy about the situation.

"The gang's all here," Dave announced cheerfully. "The town's leading socialists."

Ben pointed to a row of cells and smiled. "Take your choice of rooms."

"Now see here!" the mayor protested. "What's going on here? Who are you people?"

"Ben Raines," the police chief said. He pointed a finger at Ben. "Him."

"Oh, my God!" the mayor breathed as he and the others were being herded into two of the jails' four-bunk cells. "The Rebels have invaded us."

"Bread and water for thirty days," Lara said. "For all of them."

"Bread and water!" one of the female council members screamed. "Nobody can live on that. That's inhuman."

"Ah, hell, lady," Belle said, taking in the lady's rather rounded shape. "You can stand to lose a few pounds. It'll be good for you."

"How dare you!" the woman squalled. "Just who do you think you are?"

"Well . . . I suppose freedom fighters is a good way to describe us," Belle said.

"Freedom!" the council member hollered. "A bunch of damned terrorists is what you are."

Ben laughed. "One man's terrorist is another's freedom fighter, lady."

"You're nothing but a damned, right-wing, fascist Republican!" she hissed at Ben.

"That's not quite true," Ben replied. "Actually, I was an independent for years before the Great War, lady. Hell, I actually voted for several Democrats."

The woman sneered at him and said nothing.

Ben motioned his people out of the cell block area and closed the door. He turned to Chuck. "You've gathered together some people who support our movement?"

"We've got a dozen or so at a lodge on the outskirts of town. No one else in town knows what's going on. Everyone else is home watching TV or reading or getting ready for bed.''

"Good deal. All right. Let's go see these people."

The meeting was short, with Ben telling those present to wait for his signal before arming themselves with the weapons taken from the police and other 'selected citizens' who were supporters of the Osterman regime.

The weapons had been hidden outside of town; well hidden, but easily accessible.

"How long do we wait, and what are the odds of us failing?'' Ben was asked.

"The wait won't be long. The odds of failing are high. If we do fail, and there is a good chance we will, you'll probably all be killed during the attempt, or tried and convicted as terrorists and shot or hanged."

"Under this liberal regime that doesn't believe in the death penalty?" a woman asked, a slight but very sarcastic smile on her lips .

"Don't ask me to explain Osterman's philosophy," Ben replied, shaking his head. "The best I can come up with is it's a massive fuck-up with one hand not having the vaguest idea what the other is doing."

"That's not a bad explanation," a man said. "It's as good as any I've heard."

"What do you want us to do while the police and the other town officials are in jail, General?"

"Nothing, until others can join us in this minor rebellion," Ben explained.

"That's already happening in towns in and around the park," Chuck said. He lifted a small walkie-talkie and smiled. "I just heard from several people. The other groups didn't want to wait. The revolt is on!"

Everyone present smiled. Ben said nothing for a moment. He looked at each of the men and women for several seconds, wondering if many of them really knew what they were getting into. *Well,* he thought, *they're damn sure about to find out.*

"I guess it's fish or cut bait time, ladies and gentlemen," Ben said. "If you're in now, there's no turning back."

"Point of no return, General?" an older man said with a smile.

"That's it."

"Suits me," a woman said. "I'd rather die than go on living under a socialist regime. This isn't just *our country,* we all live and work here. We're not trying to run the lives of those who politically disagree with us, but we don't want them to run our lives, either." She shook her head. "I'm not saying this right. But everyone here knows what I mean."

Lara touched the woman's hand. "Yes, we do, Pattie. All of us do."

"Get the weapons we just cached," Ben said. "And be ready to use them . . . and I mean use them to kill without hesitation. And bear this in mind—there will be no turning back for any of you who take part in this revolt. Once you're committed, it's going to be all the way. Think about that. Give that a lot of thought. Take a few minutes to talk it over among yourselves. I'm going to walk over there by myself and smoke a cigarette while you talk. You're putting your lives and the future of your families' lives on the line."

"We know that, General," a man said. "We've talked it all out at dozens of quiet little meetings over the past couple of years. What you see here is the, well, hard-core, if you will. And this is not all of our little resistance group. There will be about fifty or so more people joining us as the night wears on—from eighteen years of age to men and women in their seventies. There will be about a hundred of us to begin with. Others will, of course, join in if they see we're going to win. You know those types."

"Oh, yes," Ben said. "I know the type very well."

Those types who complain about this, that, or the other thing, but refuse to do anything positive about it, Ben thought. *They would never join any organization or group who would actually consider taking up arms against the government . . . as a final act, after all else has failed. Oh no! Why . . . that would be unthinkable. Oh, no, is their thinking. Better to live under a near dictatorship than to actually fight and run the risk of getting wounded or killed.*

However, if a group of people were to actually fight the government and it appeared that group was going to win, well, now, that's different. Those constantly complaining, do-little-or-nothing types would be only too happy to join in the final stages of any campaign. After the shooting and all the personal risk-taking is over, of course.

Oh, yes, Ben knew those types quite well.

"It's going to be a sleepless night, folks," Ben said. "And it could very well turn out to be a bloody one. So give that latter note some thought for a couple of minutes while I walk over there and grab a smoke."

Ben walked over to a parked car, leaned against it, and had a cigarette while the group of men and women on the corner talked in low tones.

He wanted them to talk it all out—get it settled—because when all the resistance people were gathered Ben had final words to drop on them, and that was going to separate the sheep from the goats.

An hour later, Ben looked over the group, now numbering just under one hundred men and women. They had gathered in a local church. Those guarding the jail and manning the checkpoints on the roads leading into town were from Chuck's group, all of them wanted men and women with rewards on their heads. Ben didn't have to talk to them. They would stand.

Ben stood up in front of the group, but not behind the pulpit. Talking about killing from the pulpit seemed a bit hypocritical to Ben. "In about an hour, folks, we're going to start rounding up hard-line socialists. We're probably going to have to kick some ass while doing it. That means shooting. And when there is shooting, someone is going to get killed. People you know. People you have perhaps known all your life. A person who was once—before politics got in the way—your best friend. They might be your brother or sister, mother or father, son or daughter, aunt or uncle, niece or nephew, cousin. But when they point a gun at you, or come at you with a club or a knife . . ." Ben shrugged. "What happens next is up to you. But I warn you of this, and it is a warning, if you cause the death of a fellow Rebel—and from this moment on that's what you are, Rebels—because of your hesitation or outright refusal to act in a swift and decisive manner . . . I'll personally see that you are put in front of a firing squad and executed."

No one in the audience so much as blinked. Ben knew then he was dealing with men and women who were ready to lay down their lives for a cause, a belief.

"I've just received word that many of the towns within the boundaries of the park are now under Rebel control . . . at least for the moment. As soon as the park is firmly secure, we'll start moving out and keep moving until the entire upper section of New York State is free of this damn socialistic rule. The next step is to seize an airport, so we can be resupplied when the time comes. I've got a site in mind. That'll be my job. Your job is to wrest control from the current powers-that-be and bring at least this part of the nation back under Constitutional rule. We can do it. I know we can. I've done it. It's a hell of a lot easier than it sounds."

Ben paused for a moment, looking over the men and

women gathered in the church. "Any questions before we start kicking ass and taking names?"

One woman stood up. "General?"

"Yes, ma'am?"

"Let's cut the talk about it and do it!"

Ben laughed. "All right, ma'am. Let's do it!"

Chapter Seventeen

The resistance fighters began moving in all directions inside the park.

"We've got to move fast tonight," Ben had told the men and women just before they moved out. "We've got to hit hard and seize control of as many towns as possible before the state or federal government can react and send in help."

"And we won't be able to hold all the towns we take, will we, General?" Ben was asked.

"Probably not. We'll lose a few. But other groups around the nation have already begun to form up and strike. More will follow with each success we have."

"And if they don't?" a man asked Ben.

"We'll be in trouble and we'll have to pull back, regroup, and make new plans."

"Federal police!" a sentry outside the church yelled. "Coming in by helicopters. A lot of them."

"Go, people!" Ben said. "Get out of here. You know

what to do. Drive without lights until you're clear. Don't get taken alive. Shoot your way in and out of blockades. Do it, folks. Go, go.''

"Here they come, Ben!" Lara yelled from a side door. "It's the FPPS."

"Those goddamn Black Shirts!" Belle said. "Don't let those Federal bastards take you alive."

The Federal Secret Police, who usually came in by black helicopter and wore black jumpsuits when staging a raid, had become known as the Black Shirts.

The sounds of at least a dozen or more helicopters roaring in and over the town became louder.

"Attack!" Ben yelled, grabbing his CAR and heading for the door. "Take the offensive, people. Open fire now, damnit! Open fire on the bastards!"

Gunfire split the night, the sounds of the gunfire muffled down to nearly inaudible by the roaring of the helicopters.

The door gunners in the choppers opened fire with what sounded like M-60 machine guns, and one long burst tore into the side windows of the church and splintered the floor where Ben had been standing just seconds before.

"Shoot out those fucking searchlights on the choppers!" Ben yelled.

He lifted his CAR and gave the nearest chopper half a mag, the 5.56 rounds blowing out the high beam searchlight on the front of the helicopter.

"Shoot for the open side doors," Ben yelled to Lara. "Pass that word. Kill those gunners first. The cockpit on these new jobs is heavily armored."

Dozens of CARs—the chopped down version of the M-16—in the hands of resistance fighters on the ground opened up and began yammering. Several M-60 side guns on the choppers abruptly fell silent and one gunner toppled half in, half out of the door, held there by his harness.

Chuck ran to Ben's side. "Hell of a good move outfitting

everybody from the supply drop, General. I think we can more than hold our hold now."

"We'd damn well better do more than that," Ben yelled over the noise of battle.

"I hear you," Chuck said.

Then there was no more time for conversation as a dozen of the choppers landed and began spilling out Black Shirts. Ben jerked a grenade from his battle harness and held it up so those around him could see. They nodded and grabbed grenades.

Ben pulled the pin and held the spoon down until those around him had time to do the same. "Now!" he yelled, and chucked the grenade.

One of the grenades—no one would ever be sure who threw it—landed inside a helicopter door just as the chopper was settling down in an empty lot alongside the church. It blew, and so did the chopper. The chopper must have been carrying a lot of explosives, or its fuel tanks had just been topped off. When it blew, it colored the evening skies, shattered nearby windows, and dotted the landscape with hot metal and various body parts. The concussion caught a second chopper and flipped it, landing the chopper upside down. The second chopper didn't explode, but it sure ruined the evening of those Black Shirts who were inside—the resistance fighters on the ground further complicated their evening by opening fire on those who tried to escape the wrecked chopper.

The Black Shirts had not anticipated so great a number of resistance fighters, nor had they suspected the men and women would be so well-armed. They had landed smack in the middle of a firestorm.

And the firestorm was gathering strength as the fires of hate were fanned—the hatred of those opposed to living under any type of socialistic government had been intense, and had grown hotter as time passed and more and more personal liberties were taken away from citizens.

The resistance fighters were taking out their discontent on the Black Shirts.

Half a dozen of the pilots wisely aborted attempts to land in the middle of the maelstrom and roared off into the night skies. Those Black Shirts who were just unassing the choppers and had not found cover were cut to pieces by the resistance fighters.

One more chopper was damaged by several grenades and was forced to set down hard. Ben and those grouped with him opened fire on the chopper with everything they had. Several rounds finally punched—or somehow made their way—through the impact-loosened windshield and hit the pilot. In his panic, or final death throes, the pilot managed to really screw up matters for those on board. The chopper surged upward violently for fifty or so yards, slowly turned onto its side, and came crashing down to the ground.

Scratch one chopper and all the Black Shirts on board.

"Let's get out of here, Ben!" Lara urged.

"No!" Ben's reply was sharp. "We finish it. We don't leave until it's over. Pass the word."

"OK, Ben. You're the boss."

The town's residents wisely stayed inside while the shooting was going on. They knew the area's resistance groups had gathered, and were aware that the town's police were locked in their own jail, but there was very little that any of them could do about the situation. Most of the residents were members of the socialist/democrat party, and didn't believe in any private ownership of firearms.

They were, one might conclude, victims of, and prisoners in, a situation of their own doing.

Those residents of the town who were moderately conservative in their thinking but for whatever reason did not wish to take part in the revolt sat in their homes and wondered what this night would bring.

It was bringing death to any Black Shirt who refused to lay down his weapons and pack it in.

"Got some here who want to surrender, General!" a member of Chuck's group called as the gunfire was winding down.

"All right," Ben returned. "Stick them in the jail and get someone to see to any wounded."

"Ben Raines!" The shout came from behind a small building a few seconds later. "We know that's you out there. Listen, we've had it. We give up!"

"Suits me," Ben shouted. "Come on out with your hands in the air. Don't do anything stupid."

"We won't. I promise. Don't shoot."

The fight was over. The Black Shirts were confined to a two block area of the town in the park and they began wisely giving up, calling out to the resistance fighters.

"Get the town's doctors and nurses out here," Ben told Chuck. "Let's see to the wounded."

"That's a hell of a lot more than they would do for us," Chuck told him.

"You serious?"

"You bet I am. I've seen it."

"So let's show them we're better people."

"If you say so, General."

"I say so. Lara? While we're doing that, you find out how the other groups are doing, how many towns have been taken by our people."

"Will do."

Ben walked over to the group of Black Shirts and looked at them under the glow of a streetlamp, slowly and one at a time. It made them very nervous. They were scared, and none of them were making any effort to hide their fear. They had all studied extensive dossiers on Ben Raines and the Rebel philosophy, and knew that once a person or group had been declared an enemy of the state one's life expectancy could be very short. There was no middle road with Tri-Staters. You were their friend and you stayed the hell out of their business, or you were their enemy.

"You men and women have a choice now," Ben finally said after several minutes of walking up and down the line of Black Shirts. "You can quit your jobs and stop being an enemy of the SUSA, or I will turn your names over to my people and we will send teams in to hunt you down and kill you. No matter how this war goes—win, lose, or draw— if you continue to work against us you're dead. Think about it."

The Black Shirts stared at him in silence. The resistance fighters stared at him in silence. Both sides wondered if Ben really meant it.

"A decade ago," Ben continued, "the federal government tried to smash us out of existence. They failed, and most of those who took an active part against us were killed by members of what were called Zero Squads. They were called Zero Squads because the odds of their returning from their assignments were just about zero. Those who fought against us died. The killing went on for months. Think about it."

"Then what our government says is true—you people are nothing but thugs and murderers," a woman Black Shirt said. "That isn't war."

Ben smiled at her. "War is a matter of winning or losing, lady. It isn't nice. But I have to laugh at your suggestion of us being thugs and murderers. That's ridiculous! What do you people think you are, angels in black? You damn government agents kick in doors in the middle of the night and shoot citizens for merely attempting to exercise their constitutional rights. And you have the unmitigated gall to call us thugs and murderers? That's laughable and absurd!''

"We're obeying the direct orders of the Congress of the United States," a male Black Shirt said. "They make the laws, we enforce them."

"Just obeying orders, huh?" Ben asked. "Sure, you are. That's the same things Nazi war criminals said at the trials right after the Second World War. You people should read some history. It's being repeated here."

"Are you comparing us to Hitler's SS people and the Gestapo?" a Black Shirt asked.

"Hell, yes, I am! What's the difference? The government you work for has been trying for several decades to rid the United States of men and women who believe in the true interpretation of that document called the Constitution of the United States." Ben held up a hand. "I'm not going to stand here in the middle of the night and argue with you. You've all been brainwashed by the left-wing, your minds warped by the babblings of Osterman and her supporters. When we pull out of here, you're all free to go— after we take your ID's. Just remember what I told you. This is your only chance. You continue to fight us, you're dead." He looked over at Chuck. "Take their ID's and escort them out of here, please."

Ben walked down the block, very much aware of the citizens of the town peeking out through the curtains at him.

"Son of a bitch!" a citizen yelled, throwing open the front door of his house.

Ben hit the ground behind a tree.

The citizen opened fire, the shotgun blast tearing bark off the tree.

Ben crawled up on his knees just as the man fired again. This time the pellets blew a side window out of a car parked by the curb.

"You goddamn, right-wing bastard!" the local shouted.

Ben gave him a burst from his CAR and the man screamed and fell halfway back into his house, the shotgun falling onto the porch, his legs bloody from the slugs.

A half-dozen freedom fighters ran up to Ben, another half dozen onto the porch, a couple of them kneeling down beside the fallen man.

"Are you all right, General?" a woman called from the porch.

"I'm fine," Ben said, getting to his boots. "How is the citizen?"

"He caught lead in both legs. But he'll live to vote for Osterman . . . again."

"You're damn right, I will!" The wounded man moaned the words. "Claire Osterman is the greatest president this nation has ever had."

"He must have fallen on his head," Ben muttered. "The man is delirious."

Those freedom fighters standing around Ben laughed.

"Tom Dickson," a man said. "I've known him for years. And for years he's been an asshole."

"A little higher, and I would have given him a new one," Ben replied.

That brought another laugh from those standing around Ben.

"Secure the town," Ben ordered. "Disarm all Osterman supporters, and arm all those who support freedom—but warn them they might die for supporting freedom."

"Most are ready to do just that," Chuck said. "So the second civil war has begun, right, General?"

"It's really begun, Chuck."

Chapter Eighteen

By noon of the next day dozens of small towns all over the USA had been seized by various groups of men and women who were weary of being dictated to by the federal government. The federalized police, the mayors, and the town councils had been locked up. For a while, at least, the yoke of federal oppression had been cracked. Osterman sent in hundreds of federal agents, and by dark on the second day of the revolt about half the communities had been retaken by federal agents. A lot of blood had been spilled, on both sides of the political issue. In those communities that had been retaken by Osterman's goons, retribution against the freedom fighters was swift and terrible, but in most areas it did not have the effect Osterman had hoped for. Instead of crushing the spirit of those who desired to be free of federal control over their lives, it served only to strengthen their resolve.

Small groups of men and women who heretofore had been standing on the sidelines suddenly elected to step forward and be heard, to arm themselves with whatever they could find and take an active part in the growing and increasingly violent revolt.

Madam President Claire Osterman suddenly found she had a lot more than Ben Raines to deal with: she had a building revolution in every state that made up the USA. She and her socialistic allies were now facing a very nasty guerrilla war.

"A guerrilla war cannot be contained in a nation this size," some of the cooler thinking of Osterman's advisors warned her. "Just a few determined individuals can wreak havoc."

"Nonsense!" said those advisors who knew as much about warfare as they did the mating habits of the troglodyte. "We just catch the leaders of the revolt and execute them . . . publicly. That will take the steam right out of the movement and it will die. That's all there is to it."

The room erupted into a shouting match between the advisors . . . none of whom really knew what the hell they were talking about.

Those military leaders who were in attendance remained stoically silent. They knew the present administration hated the military (*loathed* was the word once used by the president). Not a single civilian present had ever served in any branch of the military. Guns frightened them.

Someone called for coffee and sandwiches to be sent in. It was going to be a very long afternoon.

Ben read the latest reports from around the nation and smiled. "It looks pretty damned good," he said, laying the reports to one side. "Better than I anticipated." He took a sip of coffee and lit a smoke. "We've got the Feds in a box, in a way. If they pull any units off the border with the SUSA, my people will pour across and do an end-around and really give Osterman's people a good butt kicking. Osterman just doesn't have enough Federal agents to handle all the hot spots in the USA. Lara, how is it looking as far as the individual units getting together?"

"Really good," she replied, smiling and holding up a thick folder of communiqués received over the past twenty-four hours. "The groups in ten states so far have come together under a loose bond of cooperation. But what they need is some real professional leadership."

"Someone to kick their asses and make them see they can't go it alone," Chuck said.

"I could arrange for people to go in," Ben said. "But if they do, they're going in as commanders, not advisors. That has to be understood up front."

"Many of the groups won't go for that," Lara told him. "That's been the problem for years. They all want to be independent."

"If they insist on staying independent, each with their own uncompromising ideas of how a government should be run, then they'll lose this fight. Hell, no one in the SUSA agrees with our philosophy one hundred percent. But it's the most workable form all of us could come up with and still have a government. Some are opposed to a national driver's license, others to a national health plan, others to this, that, or the other thing. But the pros still far outweigh the cons."

"I'll talk to as many groups as I can," Lara said. "See what they think."

"Do that. But advise them the Constitution is the document we base our government upon. I don't give a damn if it's five hundred years old, or was written day before yesterday. The original document and the philosophies of the signers and framers stand."

"Ben, many of the people up here just don't agree with

your ideas about using force to defend personal property,"
Lara reminded him.

"It's the oldest personal right in history," Ben said.
"Probably been in existence since humankind crawled out
of the caves or climbed down out of the trees. That fresh-
killed dinosaur tail belongs to me and my mate, and if you
try to take it I'm going to take this club and bash your
head in. Lara, no one has the right to take anything from
anybody—if they don't want them to—without due process
of law. Many of the problems society faced before the Great
War and the following collapse were created because we
got away from the basics. Many in power began making
excuses for those who broke the law. That will not happen
in the SUSA."

"All of us here agree with it, General," Dave said. "We're
with you a hundred percent."

"Fine. Now let's go take us an airport."

"Now?" Chuck asked, astonishment in his tone.

"Why not?" Ben asked. "It's as good a time as any."

The airport in Plattsburg lay just a few miles outside the
park boundaries. It had been repaired and updated and
reequipped, and the new runway was long enough to handle Rebel aircraft.

"Perfect," Ben said, studying the layout through binoculars. He lowered the long lenses and looked at Chuck and
Lara. "We'll take it tonight."

"Just like that?" Chuck questioned.

"Sure. All it takes is a little nerve and a few people."

"And how do we hold it?" Lara asked.

"The same way. It'll just be for a few hours. I've got a
unit of Rebels standing by to join us. As soon as we launch
our attack, planes already in the air and over the Atlantic
will turn west and be on the ground within two hours."

"And those militia people over in Vermont you spoke with this afternoon?"

"They'll be seizing some territory of their own. Relax, folks. It'll go smooth as silk and honey."

"That's easy for you to say, General. You've done this a thousand times," Chuck said. "Or more. An op this big is something new for us."

"It'll be good practice for you," Ben told them. "With any kind of luck we can pull it off without shedding a drop of anybody's blood."

Chuck looked very dubious. "Osterman has beefed up security around every airport in the nation, General. That's the very first thing she did when the war started."

Ben shrugged his shoulders. "No big deal. If the security people have any sense at all, they won't put up a fight. I hope they don't. If they fight, they'll die. It's just that simple."

"Simple for you, General," Marty said.

"No," Ben said. "That's the way you win battles, Marty. Fighting a war with complicated 'rules of engagement' is not the Rebel way. We go in to win. Period. That's why we've been so successful over the years. Anything less is a stupid way to fight a war."

"When do we go in?" Belle asked.

"At full dark. The planes are airborne now. Tankers are up ready to refuel. Right now, let's grab a bite to eat and get a bit of rest."

Ben and seven other people, including Lara, walked into the main terminal building at full dark. They had confronted and disarmed three security people outside without any trouble. As soon as the airline employees behind the counter spotted Ben and his team they stepped back and put their hands in the air. They were not armed, and wanted no trouble.

One young uniformed security guard had other ideas, though. He had visions of being a hero, and grabbed for his pistol. Those ideas got his legs knocked out from under him by a burst from Lara's CAR.

"The rest of you stand easy," Ben said. "Do that, and nobody else will get hurt."

"You're Ben Raines," a civilian blurted.

"That's right, mister."

"My God!" a woman said. "He's going to kill us all!"

Ben laughed at that. "Oh, I don't think so, lady. Not unless you pull a pistol out of your purse and point it at me."

"I don't own a gun," the woman said haughtily.

"Good for you," Ben told her. "That makes our job all that much easier."

"Control tower is ours," Lara said, after listening to her headset for a few seconds.

"Any trouble?" Ben asked.

"None."

The two other security guards in the main terminal stood quietly with their hands in the air while Ben's people took their weapons. They had no intention of becoming dead heroes. The young guard who had his pins knocked out from under him lay on the tile floor and moaned in pain.

"I thought I heard a shot a moment ago," Ben said.

"One security guard got stupid," Belle told him. "All it got him was dead."

"Pity," Ben said.

"Yeah," Dan replied. "I'm deeply touched."

"You people are savages!" a man yelled. "Nothing but filthy savages."

"Another Osterman supporter," Lara remarked.

"You damn right, I am!" the civilian yelled. "She's the

greatest president this country has ever had. And she'll have you traitors hanged."

Ben yawned. "I thought you socialist/democrats didn't believe in the death penalty."

"We do for people like you."

"Karl would be so proud," Ben told him.

"Huh?" the man said. "Karl who?"

"Marx. He would be thrilled with your form of government, I'm sure."

"I'm no damn communist!"

"No? Well, you're sure doing a great imitation of one. Fooled me."

"Airport is secure," Lara said before the civilian could respond. "For the moment," she added. "The local Federal police will be here shortly."

"They sure will," a woman said. "And then we'll see how tough you fascists are."

"Yeah," a security guard said. "They'll take care of you damned militia trash."

"Right," Nora said. "I'm sure they will." She laughed in the guard's face.

Ben had placed a squad of his people on the road leading into the airport. They were waiting, backed up by two M-60 machine guns.

"Ernie all set?" Ben asked.

"He's ready," Lara said.

Ernie was a former air controller who had been fired because of his openly stated views against Osterman and her socialist form of government.

Lara held up a hand. "Planes lining up for landing. Ernie says there are several dozen of them."

"Probably more than that," Ben muttered. "Cecil and Ike have overreacted . . . again."

"They're just worried about you, Ben," Lara replied.

"They should know by now I can take care of myself."

"And you like to lone wolf it, don't you?"

Ben smiled. "I rather enjoy it, yes." He looked over at the wounded security guard. A freedom fighter who had been an EMT before views of Osterman and her policies got him into trouble was looking after the man's wounds.

"Fifteen minutes to touchdown, Ben," Lara said.

"Let's get these civilians some coffee and settled down," Ben suggested. "It's going to be interesting when that commercial flight starts calling in for landing instructions."

"We can divert it."

"Is it prop or jet?"

"Prop."

"Oh, hell, let it land. We'll let these people get on their way."

Lara looked at him for a moment and then shook her head and laughed aloud.

"What's so funny?"

"You! You're the calmest man I have ever met. Nothing seems to shake you up."

Ben smiled at her. For the past few days sexual tension had been building between them. Ben had done his best to ignore the feeling—for he had learned the hard way that getting involved in the field was not a smart move—but the feelings just kept building between them.

"This guy's gonna be OK," the EMT called. "But he's going to need some surgery to get a couple of slugs out of him."

"Call an ambulance for him," Ben said. "Hell, the whole damn town will know we're here in a few minutes. No point in delaying medical treatment for him."

"Right, General."

Five minutes later the huge cargo planes began landing and taxiing off the main runway. The cargo masters went to work, quickly unloading personnel and equipment, and that was a job that was going to take most of the night.

"Good God!" Nora said, gazing in awe out of the terminal window. "I've never seen so many planes in all my life, and Ernie says there are dozens of planes circling or holding some distance out."

"We'll have more than a toehold up here when this night is over," Ben said, after listening to Lara's headset for a moment and then acknowledging the message. "Ike sent in several battalions of troops and armor and artillery to back them up."

"Several *battalions!*" Chuck breathed the words.

"Yes. Come on. Let's get out onto the tarmac and greet the troops." Ben smiled genuinely. "And I'll let you meet my son."

"That would be an honor, General," Chuck said.

On the tarmac, Ben waved at a young man standing off to himself watching the proceedings. Buddy Raines walked over and shook his father's hand. "Good to see you're doing well, Father. And I like the beard. Looks good on you."

"I'm about to shave it off, boy. Damn thing itches. Buddy, I want to introduce you around."

After the introductions, Ben asked, "All these people from your brigade, son?"

"Yes, sir. Three thousand of them."

"Ike order you in?"

"Yes, sir. You know he did."

Buddy Raines's 508 Brigade was made up in part of his old Special Operations Battalion. The Spec Ops were the bad boys and girls of the Rebels—Special Forces, Rangers, SEALs, Force Recon, Air Commandos, and French Foreign Legion all rolled into one. They were the most highly trained and lethal of all Rebels.

"How's my team?"

Buddy grinned. "Standing right over there," he said, pointing.

Ben's eyes followed the point, and he smiled. Jersey, Corrie, Beth, Cooper, and Anna were standing off to one side of the crowded tarmac. "Well, I'll be damned," Ben said. "I should have guessed you wouldn't be able to leave them behind." He waved them over and introduced them.

"The team we have all heard so much about," Chuck said.

"Nothing good, I hope," Jersey replied without changing expression. Only her dark eyes twinkled with humor. "I wouldn't want to tarnish our reputation."

Chuck smiled at the diminutive Rebel. His eyes shifted over to Corrie, then Beth, then Anna. All lovely, and each of them as dangerous as a den of rattlesnakes. He looked at Cooper; same coldness in the eyes. A very skilled and deadly group of young men and women, Chuck concluded.

Chuck cut his eyes to Buddy Raines. My God, the man was solid! He had heard that Ben's son was powerfully built. Now he knew it for a fact.

Chuck looked at Lara. She was watching the Rebels unass the planes. The men and women under Colonel Buddy Raines were all, as the saying went, "Lean, Mean Fighting Machines."

"I think the battle up here is about to take a turn for the better," Lara said, her voice just audible over the roar of planes landing and taxiing in.

Buddy had sized up the situation between Lara and his dad very quickly. Of course, the younger Raines knew his father well. "Yes, ma'am," he said. "I suspect it will. And I suspect it will do so very quickly."

Chuck's people stood and watched as tanks and trucks rumbled out of the massive transports. "Incredible," Belle said. "Just incredible."

"How about us finding something to eat?" Cooper said. "I'm hungry."

"You're always hungry," Jersey responded. "I swear to god you have a gut full of tapeworms."

"He's a growing boy," Beth said.

Over the sounds of huge transports landing and taking off, the sound of machine guns could just be heard. Buddy arched one eyebrow and asked, "Trouble?"

"I think the Federal police have arrived," his father replied. "And probably wish they had stayed home," he added.

Chapter Nineteen

The town's Federal police lost eight officers in the first four vehicles to arrive at the airport before they realized they had driven into a situation that five thousand officers would have been unable to contain. But by then it was far too late to turn back. The freedom fighters had closed off all avenues of escape, and for the lead vehicles it was a slaughter. Only a few shots had been fired by the town's federally trained, Osterman-supporting officers. The Federal police then did the only prudent thing: they surrendered.

Chuck's people brought the survivors of the night ambush to Ben. The federal officers stood in awe, looking at the heavily armed Rebels unassing the big transport planes.

"What's it going to be, people?" Ben asked the scared group of federal officers.

"What do you mean, General Raines?" asked one of the older officers.

"We're sure not going to keep you around, feeding and caring for you. Hell, we don't want you. You're not going to be facing unarmed citizens any longer. Come daylight, anyone who wants a gun can damn sure have one. And the first weapons to be given away will be yours, and from the police armory. So you'd better make up your minds which side you're on."

"How about us not taking sides, and just enforcing the law?" a man suggested.

"That's no good. You're federalized, and you swore an oath to support Osterman and her policies. How could I trust you to keep your word on that?"

"You just don't really understand how drastically crime has gone down since privately owned guns were banned," a woman officer said.

"I'll match our crime stats in the SUSA against yours anytime, lady," Ben responded. "And nearly everyone in the SUSA is armed. How about it?"

She glared with open hate at Ben, and did not respond.

"Scratch that one for sure," Ben muttered.

"You bet," Jersey said in a louder tone. "Shall I just shoot her now and put her out of her misery?"

"Now you wait just a minute!" the older Federal cop said. "Everyone is entitled to an opinion."

"Not when your opinions start interfering with my constitutionally guaranteed rights," Jersey said.

"Damn little militia whore!" the mouthy female Federal cop muttered.

Jersey heard her, and her eyes narrowed.

Ben stepped out of the way as Jersey handed her CAR to Cooper and stepped forward.

"This is going to be interesting," Ben whispered to Lara. "Watch."

"Haul your ass out here, bitch!" Jersey said.

"Are you going to permit this?" Lara questioned.

"Sure. Why not? You can bet no one is going to interfere. Not if they have any sense. Jersey is pretty and shapely, but tough as a boot."

Lara looked at him strangely and said nothing, just shook her head in disbelief.

"I won't lower myself to your level," the Federal cop said very haughtily.

"Well, la-di-da!" Jersey said, putting one fist on a shapely hip and mincing about a few steps. "The bitch has a big mouth and no guts to back it up."

Several of the freedom fighters laughed nervously, not understanding why General Raines was allowing this to continue. Buddy Raines stood back from the main knot of people, a slight smile on his lips.

"Come on, bitch!" Jersey waggled her fingers at the Federal cop. "You call me a whore, I'm gonna kick your prissy Federal ass for you."

The female Federal shook her head. Jersey laughed at her.

"Now stop this!" the older Federal cop said. "We're your prisoners, General. I believe there are rules that captors must abide by."

Jersey stopped right then and shrugged her shoulders. "Well, it was worth a shot. OK, lady. You don't get your ass kicked tonight."

Ben stepped forward. "Lock them down somewhere until we can decide what to do with them." He turned to Chuck. "What are your people finding in town?"

"Confusion among the Osterman supporters. Great joy among the conservatives."

"The Federal police?"

"They're being rounded up as we speak. Some resistance on their part. Only a few casualties. None of our people have been hurt."

"Weapons being distributed among those willing to fight for their freedom?"

"Yes, sir. Several hundred have already lined up to be armed. We're expecting several hundred more as the word spreads. About fifty of the first group have volunteered to act as police for the community."

"Good enough. And good work. Compliment your people for me, Chuck. A job well done."

"Thank you, General."

Walking away, back to the rear of the main terminal, Buddy fell in step with his father. "I have a question," the younger Raines said.

"Ask."

"What the hell kind of government did this Osterman person set up? It makes no sense to me. It isn't pure socialism, isn't pure communism. I don't know what it is."

Ben laughed. "I don't either, son. It's a combination of liberalism, socialism, and . . . something else that doesn't have a name."

"Ostermanism?"

Ben chuckled. "That's as good as any, I suppose. But I do know it's Big Brother all the way."

"What is so damned attractive about it? Obviously, something is. Millions of people openly embrace it."

"Cradle to grave care, Buddy. No one has to take personal responsibility for anything they do. Any act that is considered illegal or immoral by conservative-thinking people is not the fault of the individual committing the act. It's society's fault. Used to be a comedian years ago who humorously summed up that kind of thinking when he said, 'The devil made me do it.' "

"Really." Buddy's reply was very, very dry.

"That comedian didn't realize how prophetic his words would turn out to be."

"Ridiculous!" Buddy said contemptuously. "Society alone

can't make anybody do anything. I thought the people living outside the SUSA were through with that sort of nonsense."

"I thought they were on their way to being through with it. I guess we were wrong."

"So what comes next, Pop?"

"We start retaking this section of the USA, boy. We rearm the people and set up militia groups—or whatever they choose to call themselves—as we go."

"And when we pull out?"

"We'll hope—and pray, if you're the praying type—that the people we arm will stand firm and back up their beliefs with bullets."

"They didn't before."

"I think that maybe this time they will. The odds are better, at least."

"They will never adopt the laws of the SUSA, Pops."

"I don't expect them to. No candy-assed, left-wing liberal could live under our laws. Our laws are too simple for them. Too much responsibility is placed on the individual in our society, son. That goes against the liberal belief of no one taking the blame when they fuck up."

Buddy laughed in the night. "You have such a delicate way with words, Pops."

"I do, don't I? Gets the point across, though."

"It certainly does that."

Madam President Claire Osterman was clearly in mild shock after her military advisors had briefed her and then exited the new Oval Office . . . quickly.

In four days time—since the arrival of Rebels from the SUSA at the Plattsburg airport—Ben Raines and his ragtag militia and survivalist trash had managed to seize control of almost everything north of Interstate 90, with the exception of Syracuse, Schenectady, and Utica. And they were knocking on the doors of those freshly rebuilt cities.

"That rotten, right-wing, no-good Republican son of a bitch!" Claire yelled. Leaping out of her chair, she jumped up and down, occasionally pausing to pound on her desktop.

Her staff, standing outside in the corridor, could hear her cussing, and Claire was a pretty good cusser.

Claire calmed herself and sat down in her chair. She took several deep breaths and looked at the reports on her desk, left there by the advisors. They told a grim story.

Groups all over the nation were rising up and seizing control of the smaller towns.

"Goddamn militia trash!" Claire muttered. "Whacko gun kooks."

She read on. The Federal Police were overwhelmed, unable to cope with the worsening situation.

Claire closed the folder. She could not force herself to read any more.

One thing she knew for certain: It was all Ben Raines's fault.

Chapter Twenty

"I don't want any innocent people hurt or killed," Ben warned the freedom fighters. "And I sure as hell don't want any children hurt or killed. Is that clear?"

"Perfectly," Chuck said. "We're in agreement with that one hundred percent."

"How in the hell can a grown man or woman who works for and supports Osterman's policies be innocent?" a woman from another group asked. "That doesn't make any sense to me."

"Me neither," a man agreed. Others sitting around the office nodded in agreement. The man went on. "They're not for us, so they must be against us, right?"

"But they're not taking up arms against us," Lara told him. "That's the difference, Pete."

"Hell, they don't have any weapons to take up against us," Pete responded with a smile.

That got a laugh from the others in the meeting room.

"But if they did have access to weapons, they'd damn

sure use them against us," a woman argued. "You can bet your butt on that. So as far as I'm concerned they're the enemy."

About half of those in the room nodded their heads in agreement.

"That may well be," Ben said. "I'm sure many of them would take up arms against us, and probably will if given a chance. But for now they're just unarmed civilians, and I will not tolerate any of them getting hurt. That's the way it's going to be, people. Any one of you who takes their group and goes off on their own against my orders will be kicked out of this organization and receive no help from the SUSA, and I will publicly disavow that group. You will be nothing but terrorists, and I will order you shot on sight. Now, damnit, is that clear?"

It was. Perfectly.

"All right," Ben said. "You all know the objective. Let's move out and get into place."

Everyone in the various groups had been polygraphed or PSE'd. Four people had broken under the pressure and admitted they were working for the Feds. They had been executed. It was harsh punishment, but it was a harsh time in the land. Those men and women under Ben's command were not working to turn the USA into a second SUSA. They were simply working for the restoration of a few rights guaranteed them by the Constitution of the United States.

And, to a person, they were prepared to die fighting for the return of those rights.

"All right," Ben said. "Let's do it."

The brand new, just completed and staffed and equipped federal building was deserted from eight o'clock in the evening until six in the morning. Buddy's own people had made sure of that.

Ben checked his watch: seven forty-five. The cleaning crew should be leaving any time now. His own people were ready to move into place. First the water would be cut off to cripple the sprinkler system. Then his people would move in, a couple at a time, on the outside, planting explosives around the building. Then, at the last moment, vehicles would be moved into place, blocking all streets, preventing fire engines from getting to the building. Just as the explosives blew, mortar crews would begin lobbing in HE rounds. The building might not be totally destroyed, but it would suffer extensive damage, and millions of records would be lost.

"There go the first of the cleaning crew," Jersey whispered to Ben.

Ben lifted his night binoculars and watched the men and women exit the building. "Two more crews to go," he said.

"Everyone is sitting on ready," Corrie told him. "Mortar crews waiting for the word."

"Won't be long now."

The minutes ticked by until finally all the cleaning crews had left the building and the doors were locked for the night.

"Get the explosives in place," Ben said. "And set the timers."

That would present no problem, for the streets were nearly deserted due to the rationing of gasoline. "Cut off the water," he ordered.

The same scene was being played out all over the USA, in a dozen states.

A few minutes later Corrie said, "Water is off, Boss."

"Seal this area."

The vehicles were moved into place.

"Streets are sealed," Corrie reported.

"Everybody clear?"

"Clear."

"Mortar crews ready?"

"Ready."

Ben looked at his watch and counted down the seconds. The explosives went off with a tremendous crack. Glass from the building windows flew in all directions. The first six rockets from the mortars landed, and that only added to the noise and confusion.

"Pour it on!" Ben said.

"Federal Police on the way," Corrie told him after hearing from a spotter located blocks away.

"I'm sorry to hear that," Ben replied. "It'll be their last run."

Two dozen 81mm and 60mm mortar rounds had smashed into the building, and more were on the way when the first Federal Police car came screaming into view. The siren stopped abruptly as a rocket from a shoulder-held launcher turned the patrol car into so much burning, smoking junk. There would be no survivors from the rocket attack.

The Federal Building was now on fire, flames beginning to dance around and smoke pouring out of the shattered windows.

Ben took a final look and said, "Let's get out of here. That building is ruined."

Corrie gave the orders and Rebels and freedom fighters began backing away. Buddy's spec op people would fight a rear guard action until everyone was clear.

"FPPS people coming," Corrie said.

"Black Shirts?" Ben asked.

"Yes. A lot of them."

"We stand and fight," Ben replied without hesitation. "Pass the orders. Let's give Osterman and her American gestapo a hard lesson."

A few seconds later, local freedom fighters stationed on

rooftops began dropping grenades down onto the cars and trucks carrying the Black Shirts. Others opened up with automatic weapons fire. Still others waited with rocket launchers to finish off any who might break clear of the gauntlet.

It was the beginning of a very bloody night in the city.

The hammering of gunfire and the crash of grenades and rockets reverberated throughout the section of the city, and Rebels and freedom fighters fought it out with the Federal Police and the Black Shirts. Until now, Osterman's people had met only slight resistance from small disorganized groups, which for the most part were not well-armed and were sorely lacking in leadership. But this was very different: this was hard-core guerrilla warfare in America.

Ben and his team rounded a corner in an alley and came face-to-face with a group of Black Shirts. The Rebels instantly hit the ground and opened fire. The Black Shirts, not nearly so well-trained or experienced in combat, hesitated. That hesitation cost them their lives.

Ben opened up with his CAR, and his first burst knocked several of Osterman's Black Shirts spinning and down to the concrete of the littered alley, kicking and groaning and bleeding.

Cooper lobbed a grenade that took out several more of the Federal Black Shirts and Lara, Jersey, Corrie, Anna, and Beth finished the very brief firefight in the alley.

"Get their radios," Ben ordered. "Let's listen in."

The Rebels learned very little. There was not much on the Federal frequency except the excited and frequently frantic yelling of Black Shirts as they confronted teams of Rebels and freedom fighters.

"Where the hell are the local cops?" a Black Shirt yelled.

"I think they're staying out of this," came the reply. "At least many of them are."

"The yellow sons of bitches!"

Lara looked at Ben in the darkness and smiled knowingly.

"The police are wising up," Ben said. "I had hoped they would."

"If it will just spread nationwide," Beth said.

"Some will stay out of it," Ben replied. "Others won't. Time and blood will tell the story. Let's go. Our work here is finished for this night."

The night the freedom fighters took the offensive, fifteen new federal buildings were destroyed in the USA. Not one civilian was injured or killed. Millions of records were destroyed, and the night's activities dealt a crushing blow to the morale of Osterman's people.

Claire Osterman had felt her socialist/democrat party, her FPPS, and the federalized police had any situation that might develop under control. She could not have been more wrong. She had forgotten that many Americans have a habit of shoving back when pushed. A certain type of American will take only so much pushing before they start talking violence and forming resistance groups.

Millions of those types of Americans had given up on the USA and moved to the SUSA. There were still hundreds of thousands living in the USA who felt the Osterman administration had strayed too far away from the Constitution, and they wanted a return of many of their lost rights.

About ten percent of those still living in the USA were willing—or rather, had the courage—to shed blood to see the return of those rights. Those were the men and women who made up the freedom fighters. The other ninety percent were good talkers and complainers, but short on guts. As one Cajun had told Ben, "Those folks have alligator mouths and hummingbird asses."

Along the thousands of miles of battlefront, the Rebels

were holding firm. The Federals had advanced in a few places, only to be thrown back within hours. The Rebels did not want any land of the USA. They only wanted to be left alone and to live their lives in peace.

"But if this crap continues for any length of time," Ben told Buddy over coffee, "I will order an offensive launched against the USA. I won't put up with this much longer."

"President Jefferys feels the same way, Father. He told me so personally."

"I know that Cec is getting itchy about this matter. But I want to give the USA enough rope to hang themselves."

"That isn't very original, Father."

Ben smiled at his son. "I'll try to do better next time."

"Thank you. What's next for us?"

"Wait and see what Osterman does. I have a hunch she'll pull some units off the line down south and send them up here to try to stop us."

"They're certainly spinning their wheels down there," Buddy said with a grin. "They gain two miles, we throw them back three miles."

Ben nodded his head in agreement. "If she does send troops up here after us, they'll be mercenaries. The USA's troops are badly split about fighting us."

"Some units are, yes," the son gently corrected the father. "But many others have had years of brainwashing, and are totally opposed to our way of life."

"And all that was happening right under our noses," Ben mused softly. "I guessed as much all along—oh, hell, what am I saying, I knew it for a fact—but never gave it a whole lot of thought." Ben sighed. "That is, until it all reared up and smacked me in the face."

"And here we are."

"Better here than in Africa," Ben said.

"I heartily concur."

"Ike on the horn, Boss," Corrie said, sticking her head into the room.

Ben walked into the makeshift communications room and sat down behind the equipment, taking the mic. "Go, Ike."

"Ben, congrats on the operation the other night."

"Thanks, Ike. Everything went off without a hitch, as planned. What's up where you are?"

"Tired and pretty well demoralized Federals in several places, Ben. We've got militia and other resistance groups fighting the Feds in Oklahoma, Missouri, Kentucky, and West Virginia, and they're really giving the Feds fits."

"I heard about that. Groups are rising up all over the USA, Ike. But that isn't why you bumped me. Come on, ole' buddy, what's on your mind?"

"We've just received pretty good intel that Madam President Osterman has people all over the world busy recruiting mercenaries, Ben. Thousands of them."

"What does Mike say about it?"

"It was his people who reported it."

"Then it's firm, Ike." Ben paused for a few heartbeats. "Well, the news doesn't come as any surprise. She really doesn't have any other choice. Her options are severely limited. Our problems are going to come if she can get some sort of air force put together."

"She's not having much luck there. Eyes in the Sky tells us that China is involved in their own civil war, and it's a bad one. There are millions dead, and it's just getting started."

"You're building up to something, Ike. Come on, what's really on your mind?"

"I'm thinking it may be time for us to go on the offensive."

"I've been mulling over that very thing," Ben said. "It's

almost, but not quite, time for that. It all depends on what Osterman does next."

"And if she does fuck up?"

"Depends on the severity of her action. If she hires these mercenaries she's after—and I'm sure she will if she can find them—then we'll go on a rampage. We'll head straight up into the heartland of the country. Search and destroy, scorch and burn."

Ike whistled softly. "You have been giving it some thought, haven't you, Ben?"

"If she gets dirty, we'll get dirtier. She just doesn't know how mean I can be."

Ike laughed. "But I do, ole' buddy. Are you thinking hit teams?"

"That is something I've been giving a great deal of thought. But it isn't time yet for that."

"I agree." Ike paused again.

"I thought as much. Pick at least ten teams and start training them, though. If it comes to assassination, we'll go after the movers and shakers in Osterman's administration."

"Will do, Ben."

"Eagle out."

Ben hooked the mic and stood up. Buddy had been listening, a grim expression on his face. "You think it will come to that, Father?"

Ben nodded his head. "Yes, I do. I'd be willing to sit down with Claire Osterman and try to hammer out some form of compromise, but it would be meaningless. She wouldn't keep her word, wouldn't be satisfied. The left-wing liberals never do, and never are. I know. I've been watching them operate ever since I was a young man. Years back, the conservatives worked out a compromise concerning gun control, but the liberals wouldn't let it alone. They always wanted more and more and more.

Everything has to be all their way. They just kept pushing until . . . well, you know what happened. You're a student of history."

"Yes, I know what happened. And because of that knowledge I would be very dubious of any agreement with such a person as Osterman, or with anyone who is a supporter of hers. They are simply not trustworthy."

"The bastards are power hungry, too," Ben added. "Among other things."

"I think I'll leave before you really get wound up," Buddy told him.

"Good. Go away. I have work to do."

Chuckling, Buddy left the room.

Ben smiled and sat down behind a desk. He opened a map and began studying it. He would like to push further south in New York State, but knew that would be very risky. The population increased dramatically the further south one went. However, he also knew he might not have any choice in the matter. He could not keep his people static.

One of the problems Ben faced with the local groups was that they all had a lot of axes to grind. Retribution against those people in their communities who openly and solidly supported Osterman and her socialistic policies could very easily get out of hand.

Ben couldn't blame the local resistance groups one bit for feeling vindictive toward those men and women who happily and willingly wiped their asses with the Constitution and then shoved it in the faces of those who dared to disagree with that action.

Ben sighed and leaned back in the chair. He closed his eyes for a moment.

A moment was all he was allowed. Corrie walked into the room. "Boss, the FPPS just arrested half a dozen members of a local militia group. Osterman just made the announcement the trial was going to be a short one."

"And then?"

"The six will be hanged for treason."

"No, they won't," Ben stood up and reached for his CAR. "Get Chuck and Lara. We've got some planning to do."

Chapter Twenty-one

The six freedom fighters were being held in a downtown jail in New Syracuse, in a very heavily guarded facility. A team from Buddy's spec op group checked out the prison and reported back.

"It can be done, Father," Buddy told his dad, "but not easily."

"You don't think it's a setup?"

"I don't believe so. The place is literally crawling with Black Shirts."

"We don't have time to try to get a blueprint of the place. It's so new that if anyone tried that would be a dead giveaway that something was up."

"It's going to be loud and risky, Father," Buddy warned.

"Can't be helped. Osterman's supporters have to be shown that we will do exactly what we say we'll do. These people are under the command of the army of the SUSA. They're Rebels. And we take care of our own." Ben stood up and slammed a fist onto the desktop. "So let's do it, Buddy."

"My people are ready to go. Do we take any of the local groups?"

"Only the most experienced among them. This is not going to be any place for amateurs."

"When do we leave?"

"As soon as possible. We can be there in a few hours. Pick the fastest route to the city and send teams of your people ahead to neutralize any roadblocks."

"I have to point out anything like that will tell the Feds we're on the way."

"Can't be helped. Let's do it, boy."

Standing back a few yards from the father and son, Jersey smiled and said: "Kick ass time!"

Buddy's people did not finesse the taking out of the Fed roadblocks. They blew them wide open with rockets and rolled on through without giving the dead and wounded a second glance. Ben and his group were right behind the lead team of Scouts, pushing the Scouts hard.

The dozens of teams of Rebels and resistance fighters rolled through small towns on their way to New Syracuse. They met no trouble from the local police.

One local chief radioed to the FPPS HQ in New Syracuse: There is no way in hell I'm going to sacrifice any of my people to the Rebels. These people are out in force and out for blood, and by God it isn't going to be mine or my mens'.

I am ordering you to throw up roadblocks and halt this Rebel advance, was the answer.

I have four words for you, the police chief radioed back to the Black Shirt. Fuck you. I quit!

That sentiment seemed to be shared by all the local police.

The FPPS pulled as many guards as they could from around the jail and threw up roadblocks on the highways leading into New Syracuse from the north. They did not have the force or the will to match the fury of the Rebels. The Rebels and the freedom fighters tore through the roadblocks and slammed their way toward the jail.

The citizens watched from their homes as hundreds of Rebels and resistance fighters poured into their newly rebuilt city.

The men and women who made up the FPPS were bullies, but they were not fools. Those who were guarding the jail carefully laid their weapons on the ground and stood quietly with their hands in the air as the jail was completely surrounded by Rebels and resistance fighters. Many of them muttered somewhat brief but very sincere prayers.

Not a single shot was fired as the Rebels took control of New Syracuse.

Ben walked through the crowd of surrendered FPPS people until he was face-to-face with an older man who had been pointed out as the commander of the detachment.

"Your name?" Ben asked.

"Jim Barnes."

"Well, Jim, you and your people got smart this night. We'll see if the smarts continue. For now, get those six freedom fighters out here."

"Freedom fighters!" the commander of the FPPS blurted. "You call these terrorists freedom fighters? Are you serious, General Raines?"

"Yes, Commander. I am very serious. Get those men and women out here. And they'd better be walking and without injury."

"If they were hurt, General," Barnes said, "they were injured while being arrested, not while in custody."

"We'll have to see about that, won't we?"

"You don't believe me?"

"You work for Osterman, Jim. Do I have to say more?"

"I work for the United States of America. I enforce the laws of this government."

"I don't intend to stand in the middle of the street debating the dubious merits of socialism with you. Get those prisoners out here—right now!"

Jim waved his hand, and four men and two women were brought out of the jail. The crowd of local civilians that had gathered around the jail began cheering. Commander Jim Barnes flushed in anger at the jubilation.

"My, my," Ben said. "You're not as well thought of around here as you might have suspected, Jim. Doesn't that make you wonder about your everlasting allegiance toward Madam President-For-Life Osterman?"

The commander of the local FPPS glared hate at Ben. He opened his mouth to speak, then thought better of it and shut his trap.

"Destroy all the records," Ben said, turning to Buddy. "Then collect all the weapons, ammo, and other gear."

"And then?" Buddy questioned with a knowing half-smile on his lips.

"Blow the damn building!"

Commander Barnes paled at that. He muttered something under his breath.

"Something on your mind, Jim?" Ben asked, once more turning to Commander Barnes.

"That facility cost several million dollars to construct, General Raines. Taxpayer money. Aren't you going a bit far by destroying it?"

"Osterman went a bit far. We're just correcting her actions, you might say."

"At the risk of being shot by your terrorists, let me say that I will enjoy watching you hang."

"You're at the end of a long list of eager prospective spectators. But don't worry about being shot. That won't happen unless you try to escape."

The Rebels and militia and other resistance members were busy loading up guns and other equipment from the jail. Commander Barnes watched them work for a moment, then returned his gaze to Ben. "A lot of blood will be spilled because of this night, General Raines."

"I hope it will all be the blood of those loyal to Osterman."

"Some of it will be, I'm sure."

Boxes containing computer discs were carried out of the building and tossed onto a growing pile by the side of the jail. Gasoline was poured on the pile. When the fumes had dissipated, the mound of records was set on fire. Flames immediately began leaping into the night sky.

"Do you have a hobby, Jim?" Ben asked.

"What? A hobby? Why . . . yes, I do."

"And that is?"

"Computers. I'm something of a nut about computers."

"That might be a good vocation for you, don't you think?"

"Are you trying to tell me something?"

"As a matter of fact, yes I am. It just might be a good time for you to retire and start a new career."

Barnes shook his head. "I like my present job, General. I enjoy bringing traitors to justice."

"That's too bad. I really thought I detected a spark of decency in you."

That remark got to Barnes. "I'm as decent as any man! Who in the hell are you to judge me?"

"You work for Osterman. You can't be very decent and do that."

The FPPS man flushed and clenched his hands into fists. Then he slowly relaxed, and a very thin smile creased his lips. "That's good, General. Very good. But it won't work. You can't provoke me enough into taking a swing at you. As much as I might want to," he added.

"I wasn't trying to provoke you, Commander. Not into starting a fight, that is."

"You could have fooled me. What the hell were you trying to do?"

"Make you see that what you're doing is wrong. It's wrong to oppress people."

"I don't believe I'm oppressing anyone. I'm just following orders, that's all."

Ben's smile was tinged with sadness. "Just following orders," he repeated softly. "Are you a student of history?"

"I enjoying studying history, yes. Why? What has that to do with now?"

"Everything. But I guess you don't see it. Probably never will. And I'm sorry about that."

"I don't know what in the hell you're talking about."

Corrie motioned to Ben, and he walked over to her. She whispered to him, then backed off. Ben shook his head and cursed under his breath. "Get done with it here, people!" he shouted. "Shake it up!"

Lara walked up to him. "What's happening, Ben?"

"Osterman has hired her mercenary army. They're on their way. Our intel just confirmed it."

"And that means?"

"We've got a hell of a fight facing us, Lara. We've got a few weeks before they can all get here and get lined out. Then the shit really hits the fan."

"How many men could she have hired? And where did she find them?"

"A full division, I was just informed. And they won't be green troops. Where did she find them? All over the world. The USA is pretty closer to normal as far as government, industry, jobs, so forth. Seventy-five percent of the world is still in a state of chaos. Men and women will grab at a chance to make some money fighting."

Buddy walked up. "I just heard, Father. Ike bumped me."

"He sound worried?"

"Not in the least."

"He wouldn't be. I don't think that damned ex-SEAL ever worried very much about anything in his life. All right, let's get it wrapped up here and clear out. The building cleaned out?"

"Down to the walls and the floor."

"Blow it and let's get the hell out of here. We've got a lot of planning to do, and not a whole lot of time in which to get it done."

Chapter Twenty-two

After chatting with Ben for a few minutes, Cecil ordered every citizen of the SUSA to go on high alert. High school classes were canceled so the older kids could help on the farms, bringing in the crops. Factories again were running twenty-four hours a day, seven days a week. Citizens drew emergency rations. The SUSA got ready for possible invasion.

Ben left a team of Rebels in upstate New York and flew back to Base Camp One with his team and Buddy. Within an hour after landing, he was in a meeting with President Cecil Jefferys.

"The brigade commanders will be coming in later today," Cecil told him. "We'll schedule a council of war for tomorrow afternoon. I thought you and I had best hit the high points today."

"As soon as we know for sure where the staging area is for those mercenaries, we hit them with air strikes and missiles," Ben said. "I've alerted the missile crews, and they're on high alert. Our fighter pilots are chafing at the bit to go. I'm tired of screwing around with Claire Osterman. If she wants to get down and dirty, that's fine with me. I'll show her dirty like she's never seen before."

Cecil looked at his long-time friend. Ben's face was grim, and his eyes hard and mean. Cecil could remember only a few times in their long association when Ben had appeared like this. He nodded in agreement with Ben's words. "I knew that someday it might come to this," the President of the SUSA said. "But I kept hoping it wouldn't."

"Osterman and her goddamned socialist/democrats just won't let us live in peace," Ben replied. "God knows we have tried to get along."

"I will certainly agree with that," Cecil said. "I don't know what else we could have done."

"What's the mood of the people, Cec?"

"Ready for a fight. If Osterman's mercenaries and her Federal Army invade SUSA territory, they'll meet resistance such as they have never before known."

"Has Osterman begun evasive movements?"

"Oh, yes. We don't know where she is. She has stopped all public appearances, and is in hiding somewhere. We believe she is underground—literally."

"She has got to show her ugly face sometime. We'll nail her when she does."

"Then we'll have Harlan Millard to deal with, and he's just as bad as Claire Osterman."

"Or worse," Ben added. "I know it. But the people of the USA have to realize that the SUSA is here to stay. We're not going anywhere. They have to elect leaders who will try to get along with us. If they don't, we're going to be at each other's throats forever."

Cecil slowly shook his head. "Won't happen, Ben. Not

in our lifetime. Maybe never. If we somehow manage to get Claire Osterman out of the picture, Millard will step in. Shove him out of the way, some other liberal/democrat/socialist will step up, and here we go again. Up in the USA it's worse than it was just before the collapse and the Great War. Since you've been gone I've been reading the newspapers and monitoring the television from the USA. It's sickening. I've never read and heard such propaganda in my life. They've changed history to the point where it's unrecognizable. It bears little resemblance to the history you and I learned. I received a shipment of textbooks from the USA last week. Talk about political correctness taken to the max ..." Cecil shook his head. "We're fighting more than guns and bombs, Ben. We're combatting an entire generation of people who have been brainwashed into believing the government can solve all problems. Not only *can,* but *should* solve them. We're fighting a philosophy that is embedded in the brains of millions of people."

Ben listened, letting Cecil vent his spleen. Ben knew all that Cec was saying, but he also knew that being president of a large nation, just like being the commanding general of a huge army, is sometimes a lonely job.

Cecil wound down and looked at Ben for a moment, then smiled. "I'm preaching to the choir, Ben. Sorry about that, ole' buddy."

Ben returned the smile and waved off Cecil's apology. "We'll talk more when Ike and the others get here. What are you and yours doing for dinner this evening?"

Cecil grimaced. "Having a formal dinner with a representative from Great Britain." His face brightened. "Say ... I didn't know, of course, that you would be here. How would you like to attend?"

Ben quickly rose from his chair. He smiled and shook

his head. "Sorry, Cec. I'm, ah, meeting with my brigade
people this evening. But I sure wish I could be there."

"You're a liar, Ben," Cecil said with a laugh. "And not
a very good one, either. All right, all right. Get out of here.
I have work to do."

Ben left before Cecil could change his mind and insist
he attend that stuffy damned dinner. Cecil was good at
those formal affairs. Ben hated them.

Ben's team was waiting in the hall, and together they
walked out of the unpretentious building that served as
the capitol of the Southern United States of America. Nothing was very ostentatious about the SUSA. Here, practicality
took the place of pretentiousness. The philosophy of the
SUSA worked for those who chose to live there, and it
worked without fanfare or pomp.

The mood of the nation was much like the manner of
dress—casual for the most part. Ben Raines was, unargu-
ably, the most powerful man in the SUSA—Cecil Jefferys
would be the first to agree that Ben's voice was heard above
all others—but Ben seldom wore anything other than
BDUs or jeans when he was home, sometimes khakis.

Ben paused in front of the capitol office building and
studied the scenes all around him. People were going to
and from work, to and from shopping. No weapons were
visible, but Ben knew for a fact that plenty were close by,
ready to be grabbed in case the warnings went up.

"They're ready, Boss," Jersey said, watching Ben's eyes.
"And they'll fight to the last man or woman for the SUSA."

"It might come to that," Ben told her. "For when we
punch a hole up through the midwest, Osterman's people,
some of them at least, will come pouring into the SUSA."

"If they do, they'll damn sure wish they had stayed
home," Corrie said.

"And kept their noses out of another country's business," Cooper added.

"Occasionally, you do make some sense, Coop," Jersey said. "Usually when you agree with one of us."

Ben smiled as they walked along the wide sidewalk. That was something that was required for any new street or development anywhere in the SUSA: sidewalks. (For those not familiar with the term, a sidewalk is a strip of concrete that runs along both sides of a street. It's for people to walk on, and kids to ride bikes on, even occasionally knock adults down—accidentally. During the latter part of the last century, for whatever reason, many developers seemed to forget all about sidewalks. Ben was determined that was not going to happen in the SUSA.)

Ben and team came to a small park not far from the capitol building. Ben paused and then walked into the park and sat down on a bench. A woman was sitting on the bench across the rock walkway between the benches, watching her young son at play. She looked up at Ben, then quickly took another longer look. She paled as she recognized the founder of the SUSA and the commanding general of its army. She quickly rose as if to leave, motioning for her son to come to her.

"I don't bite, ma'am," Ben said with a smile.

She cut her eyes at Ben, flushed, then smiled. Then she laughed and sat back down on the bench. "It's not often we see the father of our country in the flesh, General Raines."

"Father of our country?" Ben said. "Well, that's a very interesting title to hang on me." Ben knew that was how many referred to him. He didn't like it, but there was really nothing he could do about it.

"What happens next with this Osterman woman, General Raines? If you don't mind me asking."

"I don't mind at all. I said to my commanders that the next move was up to her. She's made it. I haven't made up my mind yet how to respond." Not quite the truth, but Ben wasn't about to show his hand to anyone just yet.

"Kill her," the young mother said bluntly. "Kill her and all her top people."

Ben stared at the young woman for a moment. "Just like that, ma'am?" he asked softly. Others in the park, recognizing Ben, began to gather around, under the cold and very watchful eyes of Ben's team. Ben's ever-present security detail was scattered throughout the small park.

"Just like that, General. She and her socialist/democrats started this crap, not us. We never interfered in the way they ran their government. Nobody in the SUSA gives a damn what the USA does . . . as long as they keep their noses out of our business."

"It isn't time for assassinations," a man spoke up. "There may come a time for them, but that time has not yet arrived."

"Oh, the hell it isn't!" another man countered. "It's past time. Those are our sons and daughters and brothers and sisters on the line fighting. If killing Osterman and her supporters will end this war and let us get back to some sort of a normal life, I say do it."

Ben sat on the park bench and listened. In this small crowd, it was running about 99% in favor of killing Osterman.

It didn't surprise Ben at all.

The crowd began to pick up in number, in opinions, and in volume. Ben's security detail got a little nervous, and about half of them moved closer and worked their way into the crowd, surrounding Ben and his personal team.

"General," a man said, "if that Osterman bitch sends troops to cross over our border in force . . . I say you use everything that's in our arsenal."

"Wipe 'em out!" a woman shouted. "We all know we

have nuclear and germ and chemical weapons. By God, use them."

"Not nuclear weapons, Denise," a man said.

"I agree," a woman spoke. "No nukes. Even with our so-called clean nuclear weapons the results are just too terrible."

The SUSA had the highly advanced neutron bombs that would kill humans but not destroy buildings. Many of the same scientists who worked on the project in the USA before the collapse and the Great War were now working for Ben's SUSA.

"I'm not really sure why the USA hates us so," a young man remarked.

"Because we have a very small but highly efficient form of government," an older man answered, "while the USA went right back to a huge, complex form of government. We have a few hundred laws that we enforce to the letter, while the USA has thousands of laws that are constantly being bent and twisted and reshaped and redefined. In other words, young man, the Tri-States philosophy of government works smoothly while Osterman's socialist/democrats have screwed their government up something awful."

"But that isn't all of it, is it?" the young man questioned.

"No, you're very correct, that isn't all of it. The Tri-States philosophy of government won't work for everybody. We never maintained that it would. But it works for those of us who have at least a modicum of common sense and respect for the rights of others. It works for those of us who realize that as individuals we alone must take responsibility for our own actions and deeds. We don't blame society for our successes or failures."

Ben smiled. He recognized the speaker now—a professor at a local university. Ben had met him several times when forced into attending some function. There were no liberals in the SUSA's university system . . . damn few *anywhere* in the SUSA.

The professor summed it up. "Our system works, young man, and those living outside our borders just can't handle that."

"And we'll fight to keep our way of life," said a man who looked to be in his seventies, considerable emotion in his voice. Then he smiled proudly. "I was with the first bunch out in the northwest. One of the last of the original Tri-Staters." He tapped his leg with his cane. "Lost my left leg during the assault by Federals." His smile faded. "And lost my wife during the last fight here, when we were over-run with punks. But I damn sure killed my share of those rotten bastards, and I'll do it again if the Feds get this far in. Bet on it."

The crowd broke up shortly after that until it was just Ben and the college professor left sitting on benches. Ben smiled at the man. "Afternoon, professor."

The professor returned the smile. "General Raines. Good to see you again. How goes the war?"

"So far, so good. I suppose you've heard about Madam President Osterman's hiring of mercenaries . . . it seems to have spread like wildfire."

"I heard. It sickened me, but didn't surprise me. And I doubt it surprised you."

"No. Not at all."

"We will win this conflict, won't we?"

"Oh, yes, we'll win. I don't know how much of the USA will be left intact, but we'll win. Have no illusions about that."

"Do you think the SUSA will ever be allowed to exist in peace?"

"Someday, yes. But not in our lifetime." Ben rose from the bench and held out his hand. The professor took it.

"Good luck to you, General Raines."

"Same to you."

Ben and his team walked on. The professor sat alone on the park bench and watched him walk away. "Someday," he whispered. "Someday."

Chapter Twenty-three

The final opinion among the brigade commanders was in, and their answers came as no surprise to Ben: Invade the USA. Hit the USA hard and fast, and take the war to their doorstep. Let them have a taste of it.

Mike Richards had just sent a terse message from Europe: Mercenaries on their way. ETA, ten days.

"We can't get enough people up north in time to prevent their landing," Ben said. "The Feds have begun shifting some troops around in anticipation of our trying that. So we won't even attempt it. Besides, I'm not at all certain the mercs are coming in by ship, or if they are, if that's where they're docking. That information was just too easy to come by. It's my opinion they'll be landing at various ports on both coasts, as well as coming in by plane. I've delayed air strikes until we learn for sure where the staging area will be."

Ben smiled with a savage curving of his lips and took a sip of water. "When they do land, they're going to find their host country cut up into several pieces." Ben eye-balled each brigade commander for a few seconds. "We go on the attack, people. Day after tomorrow at 0600 hours. Move hard and fast. If it's in the way, knock it down or burn it. 501st, 503rd, 505th, 507nd, and 509th brigades will advance into USA territory. The others will spread out and hold. You all know the drill. No point in wasting time going over covered ground. Get back to your units. Good luck, people."

Ben shook hands and chatted briefly with each commander, a few moments longer with his kids—Tina, commander of 509 Brigade, and Buddy, commander of 508 Brigade.

"Get your bottom lip stuck back in, boy," Ben told his son with a smile. "Stop pouting about not going in with us. Your people are going to be busy holding what you've got."

"I am not pouting, Father!"

"Sure looks like it to me," Tina said, giving her brother a rude elbow in the ribs.

Buddy sighed with great patience.

"I just got this, Boss," Corrie said, walking up holding a message pad. "General Walter Berman has just been named commanding general of all troops east of the Mississippi River. No word on who is commanding west of the river."

"Berman is a mercenary," Ben mused. "That's a slap in the face to the USA forces."

"They may have all stood down," Buddy suggested.

"Maybe," his father agreed, "but as soon as we enter USA space they'll be right back in it. They'll have no choice in the matter."

"There's more," Corrie said. "Berman has promised Osterman that he will personally hunt you down and bring you in, dead or alive."

"Very ambitious of him," Ben said. "I can't really say I wish him luck."

"I thought Osterman wanted you alive so she could publicly hang you, Father," Buddy said.

"That order has been rescinded," Corrie told them. "And . . . ah, there is more, too." She looked at the other team members as they quietly gathered around.

"Let's have it, Corrie," Ben pressed. "Come on, how bad could be it?"

"It isn't good, Boss," Corrie replied.

"Well?" Ben stared at her.

"It happened just about an hour ago. The Feds were tipped off about the location of some militia members in upstate New York. There was a raid on the edge of the park. A lot of militia members who are aligned with us were captured and then lined up and shot."

Ben felt a coldness wash over him. "Go on, Corrie."

"None of the Rebels we left up there were taken. They were at another area of the park."

"Lara?" Ben asked.

"She's dead, Boss. That entire group was captured and shot—Chuck, Belle, Nora, the kid, Jimmy . . . everybody. There were no survivors."

"I see," Ben's words were softly spoken. "Well . . . instant justice, huh?"

"Yes. Osterman style. New orders from the White House, just issued a few hours ago. Rebel sympathizers are to be arrested and sent to reindoctrination camps for extensive reeducation. Active Rebel supporters are to be shot on sight."

"That sure as hell opens up a brand new can of worms," Ben said softly. "Doesn't it?" Without waiting for any reply, he continued. "Madam President is pulling out all the stops."

"Sure gettin' down and dirty, Boss," Cooper said.

The other team members nodded in agreement, Jersey saying, "Extensive reeducation? That's just a fancy term for communism."

"Hardline socialism, for sure," Beth said. "Not that there is a great deal of difference between the two."

"I'm sorry about Lara Walden, Father," Buddy said. "I liked that lady."

"Yes. Well . . . so did I, son. So did I."

Ben looked at his kids. "You two have your orders. Let's get cracking."

Ben walked off to stand alone for a few moments. *Things that might have been,* he thought. I have a full memory trunk of such things. Goes back more years than I care to think about. Getting real dusty now.

Ben and Lara had made love several times in the quiet hours alone and spent a few hours talking about personal things: what they would like to do in the future . . . if the future held anything at all for either of them.

Ben sighed softly as he stood alone, away from his team. Time to close and lock another door; another door at the end of a very long and twisty hallway. *Been too many of them,* Ben thought. *Too damn many doors that I have had to close and bar and walk away from in my life.*

How many more?

Of course, he had no idea about that. Despite what many believed, Ben was as human as anyone else. He could not foretell the future.

He would miss Lara. They had talked about her coming back to the SUSA with him. She had decided against it at that time, said her place was with her people in upstate New York.

"Shit!" Ben muttered, looking off into the distance.

Behind him, his team waited.

Ben looked back. Buddy and Tina were gone. Time for

him to get gone, too. Bury another memory. Close another door. Throw away the key.

Ben wondered where Lara was buried. And if the Feds who shot the group even took the time to bury them.

Probably not, he concluded.

Ben walked back to his team. "Let's go to work, gang. We've got a war to win."

Chapter Twenty-four

Ben and his team landed in Central Tennessee and were on the road north an hour later.

"It's almost a repeat, Boss," Corrie said after listening to a short radio transmission.

"What is?" Ben asked.

"The Feds tried to slam through at several places in Texas. The Texas Home Guard stopped them cold and then proceeded to kick the shit out of them. Ran their asses all the way back where they came from."

Ben smiled. "There are almost two brigades of Texas Militia and Home Guard. Those people are fighting for their homes and families. And for God and their country . . . which in this case is the SUSA. I don't worry about the Texas border."

Corrie held up a hand and Ben waited.

"Patrols from our 501 Brigade have crossed over into the USA at several locations. Meeting no resistance."

"Tell them to halt their advance. Wait until we get to the border and I look things over."

"Ten four, Boss."

Several hours later, Ben stood on the Kentucky/Tennessee border viewing the scene through binoculars. It all looked very tranquil. He lowered the long lenses and said, "Let's go across, gang, see what we've got. Order everyone across. Up and down the line."

No resistance. No Federal troops to be found. The first town they came to was deserted, utterly devoid of human life. A few cats and dogs were spotted, but that was it.

"Corrie?" Ben asked, questions in the single word.

"Nothing, Boss. Intel thinks the residents were evaced during the night. But they don't know where they went, or were taken, as the case might be."

"How far in does this go?"

"Eyes in the Sky thinks about fifty miles all up and down the border."

"Recon?"

"Pilots reporting nothing, Boss. First concentration of Federals about sixty miles straight north."

"And there are no civilians?"

"Not a one spotted yet."

"Order all units to halt their advance until we can determine what the hell is going on."

"Ten four, Boss."

"Scouts out."

An hour later, Scouts were reporting back from all locations that very few civilians were to be found. Those that remained in the contested sectors were for the most part very elderly . . . and very stubborn.

"Let's go talk to some of these people who remained behind," Ben said.

* * *

"I remember you from five or six years ago," one elderly man said to Ben as he sat on his front porch. "You and your people came through here and chased off a bunch of punks who was tormenting me and my wife. I never did get to thank you proper for that. So, thank you, General Raines."

"You're quite welcome, sir," Ben told him. "Now will you answer a few questions for me?"

"Sure. All you have to do is ask."

"Are you alone here?"

"My wife's buried in the backyard. She died . . . oh, three years back."

"No children to take care of you?"

"We had five kids, General. Three boys and two girls. The oldest boy disappeared during the Great War. Don't know what happened to him. Never saw or heard from him again. The girls married and left home. Moved up north somewhere. Other two boys went bad on us. Stealing and night rambling. They're still alive, I think, but I'm not sure where they are. Don't much give a damn, neither. Rotten little bastards."

Ben carefully hid a smile. The old man was not shy about his feelings. "Why didn't you leave with your neighbors, sir?"

"Didn't want to go, that's why. I've lived right here all my life. I was born not five miles from this very spot. I intend to die right here."

"I'm surprised the government didn't force you to leave with the others."

"Nobody forces me to do a goddamn thing, sonny boy!"

Anna had to turn her head to hide her smile at the term 'sonny boy.'

"I figured you Rebels would be along. I been listening to the real radio."

"The real radio?"

"Yeah. Rebel radio. You folks tell the truth with your newscasts. Used to be the Democrats told the truth. Republicans was a pack of liars. Then the Democrats started lyin', and the damn Republicans was the ones told the truth. Then there come the time when neither one would know the truth if it bit 'em on the ass. 'Bout that time the whole world went belly up and crazy. You folks down in the SUSA is sorta single-minded 'bout some things, but you damn sure beat the shit out of President Osterfuck and her commie government."

Ben smiled. "That's . . . ah, a very interesting way of describing your president."

"There ain't no way that damn bitch is *my* president, sonny boy. Altman was all right. I think that was his name. He tried to do right. Osterfart and her commie buddies killed him. You can bet on that."

"And replaced the supreme court."

"Yep. They damn sure did that, too. Fucked everything up royally is what they done."

"Mister, why don't you let us move you into the SUSA and get you out of harm's way?"

"You gonna move my old woman, too? And my brother and sister? My parents is buried on that ridge over yonder. You gonna move them, too? I don't think so. Hell, General, I'm over ninety years old. I've lived through bad times before. If I don't make it through this fight . . . well, so what? I seen the Second World War come and go, then the Korean war, then Vietnam, then the collapse and the Great War. I've lived through a shitpot full of bad times. Tell you the truth, I'm just plain tired. Maybe it's time for me to exit this fucked up world. No . . . I think I'll just sit right here and watch what happens."

"How many folks do you think resisted the order to leave, old friend?"

"Hundreds, General. Town folks, they all tucked their tails 'tween their legs and done what they was told to do. But folks like me, in the hills and hollers, we stayed. Can't nothin' run us out, 'ceptin' death."

"Can we leave you anything? Medicines, food, anything at all?"

"I'd like to have some tobacco, if you have any to spare."

"All you need," Ben replied, motioning for Cooper to get the old man some smoking tobacco.

"Anything else?"

"Can't think of anything else I need, General. But thanks for offerin.' "

"Take care of yourself, friend."

"You do the same, General."

Back on the road, Ben told Corrie, "Tell the Scouts to start prowling the back roads. Let's see how many people ignored the evac order."

Most of the towns were deserted, the people evaced north, but in the country—the 'hills and hollers,' as the old man had put it—many people had stayed.

"No resistance anywhere in our sector so far," Corrie said. "A lot of fighting being reported all along the Texas border, however."

Ben and his people pushed on north for a few more miles that day before Ben called a halt.

"Do you want to destroy the towns, General?" Ben was asked by his field commanders.

"No," Ben replied without hesitation. "Not unless the people left in the towns open fire on us."

Two days later, the Rebels had advanced about fifty miles north in all sectors. With the exception of Texas border, very few shots had been fired from either side. The Federals kept backing up, pulling the Rebels deeper into USA territory.

"That's it," Ben ordered at noon of the third day. "I don't know for sure what the hell is going on, but whatever it is, it's about to come to a halt."

"There are no Federal troops moving in behind us," Ben's intel reported. "Those citizens who refused to be evaced are just that—citizens."

"Can they tell you anything?" Ben asked.

"Not much. Most of them are senior citizens who stayed because they didn't want to leave. They are not armed, and many of them are friendly toward us. At least they're not hostile toward us," the intelligence officer added, amending that slightly.

"What did they tell you?"

"The residents were evaced out over a period of two days. It was a hurry up operation. One suitcase per person only."

"Where were they taken?"

"No one we spoke with has any idea. The only thing they know for sure is that many of the residents weren't very happy about leaving."

"It's screwy," Jersey said, after the intelligence officers had left. "We've never hurt civilians. Not unless they were shooting at us. It's as if Osterman *wants* us to occupy this territory."

Ben looked at Jersey for a long moment, looked at her so long it was making her nervous.

"What, Boss? Have I got a piece of spaghetti hung up in a tooth, or something?"

Ben laughed and shook his head. "No! I just had a thought, Little Bit. I may have figured out—at least in part—what Sugar Babe is up to. Thank you."

"Thank me for what?"

"For giving me the idea."

"What idea?"

Ben was heading for the como truck. He had a lot of talking to do with Cecil. He wanted to see what Cecil thought about the germ of an idea that Jersey had just hung in his head. If it survived several mental washings, there was a good chance it just might possibly backfire on Madam President Claire Osterman and make her look more like the arrogant fool Ben knew she really was.

Ben was smiling as he walked toward the communications truck. "Gotcha, Sugar Babe!"

The newly elected Secretary-General of the United Nations, Jean-Francois Chapelle, did not mince words with President Osterman. "It won't work, Madam President. General Raines saw through your plan."

"Whatever in the world are you talking about, Mister Secretary-General?"

"Your scheme to make Raines's Rebels and the SUSA the aggressors in this civil war. A war which the USA started, I might add."

Claire elected to remain silent.

"General Raines in now in the process of pulling his troops out of USA territory. He has assured me that if the USA will refrain from attacking the SUSA, all hostilities will cease immediately."

Madam President Claire Osterman remained silent.

"You are now free to allow those thousands of residents who live along the border with the SUSA to return to their homes and businesses. Your ruse didn't work."

"I really don't know what you're talking about, Monsieur Chappelle. I do appreciate your concern, however misguided."

"Of course, Madam President. Good day."

Claire Osterman leaned back in her chair and began

226   *William W. Johnstone*

cussing. Softly at first, then louder and louder, until she
was shouting a stream of obscenities.

All of it directed at Ben Raines.

Naturally.

Chapter Twenty-five

"Madam President is livid," Cecil told Ben. "Her plan to have the United Nations condemn the SUSA for aggression was a total bust."

"Now what?"

"We hold where we are and wait for Osterman to make her move. She will. She hates me that much."

"When the mercenary army arrives?"

"Yes. Intel reports they will be landing on both coasts at various ports. Also coming in by plane. General Berman will be the overall commander of all armed forces."

"That man doesn't like you very much, Ben."

"I know."

"He sure knows you from somewhere. Perhaps by reputation only?"

"Has to be, Cec."

The two old friends chatted for a few minutes longer before Cecil had to ring off and get ready to attend some fancy function. Once again Ben thought how fortunate he was not to have to put on a tux and stand around making small talk with a bunch of stuffed shirts. Cecil enjoyed it. Ben hated those functions, and usually ended up sticking his boot in his mouth, for he was no statesman. He was not known for having a lot of tact, and usually told of a situation or problem exactly as it was. He was not politically correct. He told the truth, and the truth is often not PC. He was a soldier, pure and simple, and loved the field with all its hardships.

He walked outside of the old long-deserted home on the Tennessee/Kentucky border he was using for a CP, and stood for a moment in the late afternoon sun. His team was lounging nearby in the shade of a huge old tree. Corrie was taking a break from her normal duties as Ben's personal communications officer.

The Federals were fifty miles away to the north, and the residents along the border were slowly returning to their homes, unsure of what they would find. No home or business had been bothered by the Rebels. Everything was exactly as the people had left it.

A runner from the como truck approached Ben. "Message from General McGowan, sir." She handed Ben a piece of paper.

Ben thanked the young woman, unfolded the paper, and read: BORING AS HELL HERE, BEN. I THINK I'LL TAKE A NAP.

Ben chuckled and tucked the paper in a pocket. "Tell Ike to forget the nap and go on a diet instead," he told the young woman.

She looked startled. "Sir?"

Ben laughed and patted the runner on the shoulder. "No reply."

"Yes, sir."

Ike's weight had been a standing joke between Ben and Ike for years. Ike was tubby, and that was that. He was strong as a full-grown grizzly bear, and when he got angry his temper was about the same. Ike liked to eat . . . a lot.

There had not been a shot fired in several days. The Federals were waiting for the mercenaries to show up. After that, Ben didn't know what was going to happen. The Secretary-General of the UN had asked Claire Osterman to cease hostilities. Ben had learned that Osterman had told the Secretary-General—in so many words—to go to hell.

She had added that she was the President of the USA, and she would deal with the breakaway nation of the SUSA in any damn way she saw fit, so butt out!

Good ole' Claire Osterman, Ben thought. *Diplomat to the core.*

Ben went back into the house, poured a mug of coffee, then returned to the front yard and sat down in a camp chair and rolled a cigarette. As he sipped and smoked he noticed a flurry of activity around the como truck. Then Corrie got up and jogged over to the truck, fitting her headset on as she ran.

Ben watched and waited, thinking, *Something's up.*

Corrie left the como truck and ran over to Ben.

"What?" Ben asked, snubbing out the cigarette butt under the heel of a boot.

"Guerrilla raids deep in the SUSA, Boss. All over the place. Several dozen enemy teams involved. At least that many."

"How much damage?"

"Extensive in some areas. Power plants, water treatment facilities, office buildings. A number of citizens killed, scores wounded. No one has a firm figure yet."

Ben looked down into his coffee mug. It was empty. Anna took it from his hand. "I'll get you a refill, Pops."

Ben nodded his head in thanks. He was so angry he was afraid to try speaking for fear his voice would betray his very dark inner feelings—revengeful, killing emotions. Osterman had sent spec op teams in to kill civilians deep in SUSA territory. Madam Socialist President didn't realize it yet, but she had just cracked open the lid of Pandora's Box.

Corrie held up a hand as her headset crackled. After a moment, she said, "Danjou, Rebet, and Pat O'Shea have been wounded. All the other brigade commanders escaped injury. There was a series of hit and run attacks on brigade HQ's. Mercenary special forces came up from the rear."

"How hard hit are the three?"

"Serious, but not life-threatening. All three have been flown back to Base Camp One for treatment."

"Tell the XO's to take over immediately, and to await orders."

"Right."

"How many troops did we lose during the attacks?"

"Minimal, Boss. Getting numbers now."

"Get those orders out, Corrie. Then get me a link with Cecil. I'll be in the house."

"Will do, Boss."

Five minutes later, Ben was talking with the President of the SUSA.

"We've got about a thousand civilians killed, Ben, and the number is expected to go a lot higher. Hundreds and hundreds injured, many of them not expected to live."

"Women and kids, Cec?"

"Most of them were civilian workers. Women with kids in the various company's day care centers."

"Goddamn Claire Osterman!"

"My sentiments exactly. Plans?"

"I've been so angry I haven't taken the time to formulate any plans. But you can bet I will."

"I have no doubts of that."

"I'll be in touch."

"Ben? Don't do anything stupid. Give any action some thought. Will you do that for me?"

"Yes."

"I'm going to try to talk with President Osterman."

"Give her a message from me, Cec—Tell her to kiss my ass!"

"Ben—"

"Talk to you later." Ben signed off. He sat at the field desk for a few moments, his thoughts dark and bloody.

Corrie walked into the room. "Boss, most of the federal spec op teams are still at large. Security thinks we've got some Federal sympathizers back home helping them."

"Probably."

"They're reviewing records now, but that's going to take some time. They said a number of suspected Federal sympathizers seemed to have disappeared."

"I'll just bet they have. If they find them, try them and then shoot them."

Corrie looked at Ben. He was dead serious. "I imagine they will do just that, Boss."

"I certainly hope so," he said, tight-lipped.

Corrie left the room. When Ben got like this, anything was likely to happen . . . and probably would. Ben Raines was pissed to the max.

Ben poured another mug of coffee and picked up a field telephone. Then he paused, shook his head, and slowly replaced the receiver. He didn't know where Claire Osterman was. Besides, she wouldn't speak to him even if he could make connection with her location.

He leaned back in his chair, thinking: *I really don't have a great deal to say to her. It's all profane, and what the hell good would that do, other than to make me feel better temporarily? It wouldn't do a thing to alleviate the suffering of those civilians down in the SUSA.*

But then, what would?

"Nothing," he muttered, answering his own question.

The field phone jangled, and Ben picked it up. "General Walter Berman on the line, Boss," Corrie said. "You want to talk to him?"

"Sure. Why not? I imagine the son of a bitch wants to gloat about killing civilians. Put him on. I have a few things I want to say to him."

"General Raines." Berman's voice boomed in Ben's head. "Has some of that cockiness left you now that you realize your precious SUSA is very, very vulnerable?"

"Go on, Berman," Ben said evenly. Ben was determined to keep a firm lid on his anger . . . for a while, at least.

"I hear your traitorous civilian population really took some hard hits."

"So I understand."

"Too bad I can't work up any sympathy for the kids who got killed. But nits grow into lice, you know."

"You should be an expert on lice."

General Berman laughed. "You can't make me angry. Not today. I'm in too good a mood to let that happen."

"Too bad. I was rather hoping you'd choke on all the hate that's in you."

"I do hate you, Raines. That is a fact. And I certainly despise any person who is stupid enough to follow your dubious philosophy."

"It isn't my philosophy, it's the will of the people. I just happened to be there in time to see a dream become reality, that's all."

Berman cussed Ben, but the profanity was without rancor. "And I'll be there to see it fall apart down around your ankles, you fascist bastard."

"Fascist?" Ben laughed. "What have you been doing, hanging around Sugar Babe Osterman? Probably. You're both cut from the same cloth."

"She's a fine person, Raines. She really has the good of the USA in her heart."

Ben leaned back and laughed at that. When he could speak, he said, "God, you are a fool. Expound some more for me, I need a good laugh."

"You cocky asshole!"

Ben again laughed, sensing he was getting to the man and wanting to keep it up. The general had a short fuse. Ben would keep that in mind. "You're a nothing soldier, Berman. You make war on civilians—women and helpless children, babies—"

"You son of a bitch!"

"You don't know what it takes to be soldier. You don't have what it takes to be a soldier—"

"Goddamn you, Raines! By God, I'll show you, you sorry son of a bitch!"

"No, you won't. You're a coward."

"Coward! Me?"

"Yeah, you. Who else am I talking to?"

"I'll kill you!" Berman shouted. He was on the very edge of losing it.

"Baby killer, that's you. Hell, you're not a man. You don't have the courage to fight men."

"I'll fight you any damn time, any damn place. Just say the word!"

"Naw, Berman. Hell, you wouldn't show up."

"Try me, you asshole!"

"I'd be wasting my time on a yellow prick like you. Why bother?"

Berman began cussing, and Ben smiled.

"If you did show up, you'd bring an army with you. You're that afraid of me."

"Afraid of you?"

"That's right. Hell, when you do have me prisoner, you can't hold me. You're nothing but an incompetent fool.

Just like the people you have following you, you arrogant, pompous prick.''

Berman's reply was nonstop cussing.

"Oh, shut up!" Ben shouted. "It's always been my theory that people who have to constantly punctuate their conversation with vulgarities are very low in intelligence. You just proved it beyond any reasonable doubt, you halfwit."

"You sorry bastard!"

"There you go again."

More cussing.

"Where in the hell did Sugar Babe Osterman find a fool like you?"

"I'll kill you, Raines! Goddamn you, I'll skin you alive, you piece of shit!"

"She must have looked in every nuthouse worldwide to find you—"

"It'll take you days to die, you bastard! I promise you that, you—"

"Oh, be quiet, Berman. Your ranting and raving is giving me a headache. Can't you say anything that makes any sense, you Girl Scout."

"Girl Scout!" The words came through the receiver in a roar.

"Well . . . perhaps not. That would be a terrible insult to a fine organization. Not yours, dickhead, the Girl Scouts."

"I know who you're referring to, Raines."

" 'To whom I am referring,' you ignorant asshole. My God, did you even get out of grade school, you halfwit?"

Berman launched into a new round of wild cussing and dire threats.

Ben smiled. Maybe he could get Berman so worked up he'd have a heart attack. He shook his head. No, he thought, he wouldn't want that. He wanted to kill the mercenary himself, personally, up close. Ben wanted to look into the man's eyes and smile at him seconds before the bastard expired and went tumbling straight into the fires of hell.

"I'm going to enjoy killing you, Berman. I'm going to love every moment of it."

"You've got that all wrong, Raines. You're the dead man. You're walking around dead and don't even realize it, you stupid, middle-aged, over-the-hill fool."

"I'm middle-aged, for sure, but I've got a few good years left before I'm over the hill."

"You might have a few weeks left you, at most. But don't count on that."

"I'm getting very weary of this conversation. Do you have anything else on your mind? No, let me rephrase that—you have nothing on your mind, you're incapable of thinking. So with that, I shall say good-bye."

Berman was still screaming obscenities when Ben, smiling, hung up.

Chapter Twenty-six

The security forces of the SUSA stayed busy for the next week, rounding up known Federal sympathizers for questioning. It didn't take long for one to break and start telling all. After that, things got nasty in the SUSA . . . real quick.

Unlike in the USA, trials didn't last long in the SUSA, and punishment came hard and fast. Confessions were read and sentences were passed and carried out within thirty days. Treason carried the harshest penalty: death by hanging or firing squad. Very few of the Federal Spec Op teams were taken alive.

Along the border with the USA, the Rebels watched and waited for the action to start. On both coasts the ships carrying the mercenaries docked, and the mercenaries were transported to a staging area.

Ben Raines and his Rebels waited.

Those brigade commanders who were wounded in the

sneak attacks were still in the hospital, but mending well and rapidly. They would be back to duty in a few weeks.

"Internal Security sure wrapped up the situation down home in a hurry," Anna told her father one warm afternoon.

"They aren't people you want on your butt, Kiddo," Ben replied.

"I'm glad we have them, though. I guess all nations have to have something like our I.S. people."

"Unfortunately, yes they do. Especially now, in the SUSA. But you never hear about our Internal Security until something like the sneak attacks occurs."

"Pop? What happens next? I mean, with us and the Federals?"

Cooper and Beth had wandered over and sat on the ground. Jersey and Corric spotted them and they came over and sat down, too.

"There's going to be a hell of a fight, Anna. According to Intel, about fifty percent of the USA's regular military is going to stay out of it. Those taking an active part will be young men and women, for the most part, young enough to have been brainwashed by parents and teachers from grade school through college, who have adopted Osterman's weird philosophy of government."

"I still haven't figured out just what Osterman's form of government is," Beth said. "I've studied it closely. And I just don't know."

"It doesn't have a name," Ben said. "But it's very close to socialism, with a dash of communism and something else that doesn't have a name tossed in for good measure."

Before anyone else could ask another question, a runner from the como truck approached Ben and handed him a slip of paper, then stepped back, waiting for a reply.

Ben read the brief message and nodded his head. "Tell

Ike message received," he said. "And to take appropriate action."

"Yes, sir."

After the runner left, Ben said, "Intel just reported that the mercenaries are advancing toward our lines. We'll be shooting at each other in a couple of days."

"Well, it had to happen," Cooper said. Then he sighed. "Peace was kinda nice while it lasted."

"Agreeing with you is getting to be a habit, Cooper," Jersey groused with a fake frown. "This has to stop."

Ben smiled and stood up. "You said yesterday you were getting bored, Cooper."

"I changed my mind, Boss."

"That's a woman's prerogative, Cooper," Jersey told him.

"Do we cross the line over into Federal territory, Boss?" Corrie asked.

Ben shook his head. "Not yet. The civilians have moved back home and are just getting settled back in."

"Something President Osterman sure as hell took into consideration," Jersey said.

"I'm sure of that," Ben replied. "Her raid on the SUSA brought it all home very clear to me—the elderly, the sick, civilian women and kids . . . they're off limits."

"No matter what, Boss?" Jersey asked.

"I hope so, Little Bit. I sure hope so."

Ben stood on the Rebel side of the border and waited for the artillery battle to begin. He watched through binoculars for the first physical sign of enemy troops, but so far he had seen nothing.

"Going to be a long war, isn't it?" Beth asked softly, standing by his side.

"From all indications, yes it is. Intel reports that Osterman has factories producing war materials operating around the clock, seven days a week.''

Anna unwrapped another piece of gum and stuck it into her mouth. "I thought Osterman and her followers were opposed to war."

"Oh, they are," Ben said with a grin, lowering his binoculars. "As long as everyone does everything—without question—Osterman and her wacky form of government dictates, Osterman and Millard will preach peace until they fall over."

"Spotter planes report they're taking the wraps off artillery," Corrie said.

"Let's get to the bunker," Ben suggested. "It's going to get hot and heavy here in a few minutes."

"Ah . . . Boss?" Jersey said.

"What?"

"President Jefferys has ordered your security people to move you back several miles from the front."

Ben stared at her for a long moment. "He did *what?*"

"Ordered you moved back several miles," a security officer said, walking up. "Are you ready, sir?"

"I sure as hell am not." Ben glared at the officer. "Who the hell are you?"

"Captain Fordham, sir. You promoted me in Africa."

"Oh. Yeah. I remember now. Well, let me tell you something, Captain, I am not moving back from the front. So go guard me from a hundred yards off." He turned to Jersey. "How long have you—all of you—known of this order?"

"Since this morning," Corrie spoke up. "The security council of the SUSA voted on it, and the vote was unanimous, Boss. Sorry. But that's the way it is."

Captain Fordham had not moved. He stood a couple of feet from Ben, one very large young man. Several more very large young men walked up to join him.

"This is mutiny!" Ben said.

"No, sir," Captain Fordham said. "It's orders to us from the President of the Southern United States of America. I'm just carrying them out, that's all. And your team was ordered not to say anything to you about it, General."

"I see. Well, here's what you do—tell Cec you carried them out, and let it go at that."

"Cec, sir?"

"Cecil Jefferys, son. The President of the SUSA. My old friend."

"Are you ready to move back several miles, sir?"

Ben sighed. He knew if the captain insisted, he would go. He certainly was not going to be carried away kicking and screaming like some sort of lunatic. That thought amused him, and he hid a smile. "If I said no?"

"I suppose we would have to radio the president for further orders, sir."

"And that wouldn't look good on your record, would it, Captain?"

"No, sir. Not at all."

"You have a place all picked out, I suppose?"

"Yes, sir. We do."

"For how long?"

"Beg pardon, sir?"

"How long have you had the place picked out?"

"Ah . . . about a week, sir."

"I see. Cec screwed me."

Captain Fordham didn't look at all comfortable with that statement. He offered no reply, but his expression was that of a man who needed to fart but couldn't.

"All right, Captain. I certainly believe in obeying orders. We'll head for the new location. Give me a few minutes to get my gear together."

"The wagon is packed, Boss," Cooper said, looking rather

sheepish. "We were ordered to get your gear together about an hour ago."

"Who ordered that?"

"Captain Fordham, Pops," Anna told her father. "He has written orders from President Jefferys."

Ben nodded his head. "OK. That settles that. Let's do it, then."

Before anyone could say anything else, a Rebel yelled, "Incoming!"

Ben and team and the security people hit the ground just as the first several rounds impacted with earth and exploded. Hot steel began whistling all around them as shrapnel filled the air. They all immediately began crawling toward the bunkers.

"I suppose we'll have to delay my moving to a different location," Ben yelled to Captain Fordham.

The captain made no reply. He did have a very disgusted look on his face.

Ben fell down the incline into the covered bunker, his team right behind him.

When the team was all inside Ben lit a lantern and said, "Where's Captain Fordham?"

"He went to the bunker just east of us," Cooper told him. "He made it."

Rebel artillery began answering the Federals onslaught, giving back two rounds for every one received.

Cooper looked around him.

"What are you looking for?" Jersey asked, noticing his wide-eyed gaze.

"Bats and other creepy stuff," Cooper replied. "I don't like these places. They remind me of caves, and I never have liked caves."

"There are no bats in here, Cooper," Jersey told him during a lull in artillery fire. "And the only thing that comes close to being creepy is you."

"You really know how to hurt a guy, don't you, Jersey?" Cooper asked, putting on his best 'I'm so offended' face. He couldn't quite pull it off.

The ground trembled with impacting artillery rounds, and conversation was impossible for a moment. When a few seconds of relative silence clung over the countryside, Ben said, "I'm not angry at any of you people for not telling me about Cecil's orders to move me back. He's been threatening to do it for months, and you people were under orders to keep your lip buttoned about it."

"We thought you'd be furious," Anna said.

"Not at you people," Ben replied.

"At President Jefferys?" Corrie asked.

"Not really. Cec is doing what he thinks is best for me and the SUSA, that's all."

The incoming artillery rounds had lessened, mostly due to the Rebel artillery crews deadly on-target accuracy in returning fire. The Rebels had the Federals out-gunned in all departments, and the Rebels were, at least up until the arrival of the mercenaries, much more experienced in combat.

Ben had some thoughts on that, too. He had said, "We'll just have to wait and see how experienced the mercenaries are. I've got a hunch the majority of them are not that experienced in combat. They've probably all tasted war to some degree, the world being in the shape it's in, but most signed on for the money, I'll bet."

The incoming artillery picked up again, and once more any conversation in or out of the bunker was impossible. Corrie was struggling to hear what was being sent. She had removed one small earplug and had slipped on headphones. She had both hands covering the phones for extra noise protection, and was still having a tough time hearing.

"Hell, yes, we're receiving incoming!" Corrie shouted. "By the fucking ton! Can't you hear it?"

Ben smiled at her in the dim light of the sputtering lantern, and she shook her head in disgust and lip formed the words, *Base Camp One.*

Ben nodded his head in understanding and mouthed the word, *Cecil?*

Corrie nodded, too, and waggled one hand from left to right.

Ben held up the middle finger of his right hand and pointed to it with the index finger of his left hand. He formed the words, *Give this to him!*

She laughed and shook her head.

"Nothing's funny!" Ben heard her shout.

Ben walked over to the three steps leading up and out of the bunker and stood for a moment. They were really getting creamed this early morning. Had to be a softening up for a troop advancement across what was left of the old no-man's-zone. The wide strip was still there, but most of the mines had been exploded by mortar and heavy artillery fire over the past weeks. The Federals had cut a wide path through the zone, and probably just as soon as the barrage lifted, they would be coming across in droves.

There was another unexpected lull in the barrage and Ben asked, "Is this crap happening all along our border?"

Corrie shook her head as she worked on the table in the dim light. "In only half a dozen spots, Boss. I'm mapping them out now."

Just as Corrie reached over to turn up the lantern, a round landed almost directly on top of the heavily fortified bunker. The roof caved in, burying Ben and his team under a mass of dirt and timbers.

Chapter Twenty-seven

Ben coughed and spat out a mouthful of dust and heaved a sack of dirt off of him. He kicked at a broken timber with his left boot until he could free his right boot. He could clearly hear Jersey cussing.

Then Cooper lent his voice, alternately cussing and coughing in the dust-filled air.

"Are you all right, Pops?" Anna asked.

"I'm fine, Baby. You hurt?"

"No. How about the others?"

"OK, here," Beth said, standing up and giving Corrie a hand up. All of them were covered with dust and dirt.

"Shit!" Corrie said. "That round must have landed damn near right on us."

"General!" a Rebel shouted. "Are you hurt?"

"No. I'm all right. The team is fine."

"Federals are pouring onto the strip, sir. In spots all up and down our sector."

The artillery barrage had stopped.

Ben climbed out of the bunker. His CAR was buried under a ton or more of debris. "Get me a weapon," he told a group of Rebels who had come running over. "Get weapons for all of us."

"Yes, sir."

"Where is Captain Fordham?"

"His leg is broken, General. Several of his people are hurt. They're being transported to a MASH unit as we speak."

Weapons and ammo belts and grenade pouches and rucksacks were brought to Ben and his team. Cooper was handed a SAW—Squad Automatic Weapon—and he busied himself checking it out. Ben and his team took a moment to brush as much of the dirt and dust from them as possible.

Ben did not have to issue any orders concerning the steadily advancing Federals. All his people, from platoon leaders to battalion commanders, knew exactly what to do, and they were busy doing it.

"Check on our transportation, Cooper," Ben told him. "See if it survived the barrage." Ben looked around him. The immediate area was pockmarked with smoking holes in the ground. "They gave us a good dose of artillery, and they were right on target. The mercs may be better than I thought."

"The fire was coming from a mixture of troops, sir," said a Rebel sergeant standing nearby. "A combination of mercenary and regular USA Army. They are about a thousand meters away at this moment, advancing steadily toward this position."

Ben looked at the man and smiled. "Thank you, Sergeant."

"You're quite welcome, sir. Now you had better move back a few miles."

Ben sighed. "You're part of Captain Fordham's bird dog group, right?"

"Yes, sir. That is one way of putting it."

"Just my luck."

"Shall we move out now, sir?"

"All right, Sergeant. All right. Come on, gang. Let's find Coop and get the hell out of here."

The big wagon had survived the artillery barrage intact, and a few minutes later Ben and his team were heading south, escorted by his security detail.

Ben was thoroughly disgusted.

"You knew it was coming, Pops," Anna told him. "Cecil's been threatening to do it for months."

"That doesn't mean I have to like it."

The team exchanged knowing glances. They all strongly suspected that Ben was already making plans to shake his security detail. He did not like people telling him where he could and could not go.

"How far south are we going, Coop?" Ben asked after a few miles and moments had passed by in silence.

"Ten or so miles, Boss." Cooper was somewhat evasive with his reply.

"Ten miles or so!" Ben exploded. "Goddamn, we'll be so far back we'll have to use carrier pigeons."

"Ten or so miles," Coop repeated. "Those are my orders, Boss. Straight from President Jefferys. Beth has the written directive in her rucksack."

Ben twisted in the seat and glared at Beth.

She met his gaze without flinching. "Yes, sir, I do have the orders. You are to direct the war operation from a safe and secured location. Those are President Jefferys' orders."

"Shit!" Ben said.

Anna put a hand over her mouth to hide her smile, but not before Ben caught it.

"You find this amusing, girl?" he demanded. "I'm sup-posed to run a war from Mars or some goddamn place?"

She could no longer hide her humor at the situation. She burst out laughing.

"Wonderful," Ben muttered, as his entire team, includ-ing Cooper, began giggling and laughing. Then the humor struck home and Ben smiled and slowly shook his head. "You guys had better understand I'm not going to put up with being muzzled for very long," Ben advised them.

"Where you go, we go," Jersey told him.

"Keep that in mind," Ben replied.

"I might as well tell you before we get to your new CP, Boss," Corrie said. "So it won't come as a shock to you."

"You mean there are more surprises in store for me?"

"I'm afraid so," Beth said.

"I've got a feeling I'm not going to like what you're about to tell me. Am I?"

"I doubt it, Boss," Corrie said.

"You see," Beth said, "I mean, what it is . . . well, Presi-dent Jefferys and the security-council feel that you're car-rying too much responsibility, that's what it is."

"Uh huh," Ben said. "Go on."

"And they—the security-council, that is—all agreed that you needed some help."

"Did they now?"

Jersey picked it up. "That's right. They didn't ask us how we felt about it, by the way."

"They didn't?"

"No, sir," Cooper said quickly. "They sure didn't."

"That's the truth, Pops," Anna said. "No one asked us. Not a thing."

"I believe you. Well . . . Oh, now wait a damned minute. I think I'm beginning to see where all this is leading. And I'd better be wrong in my thinking, or all hell is going to bust loose around here."

248 *William W. Johnstone*

The team exchanged nervous glances.

"Maybe," Corrie said, "we'd better pull over, Coop. I'll radio the security detail."

"Good idea," Cooper said. "I want some running room."

Ben glared at him. "That bad, huh?"

"I . . . ah . . . don't much think you're going to like the rest of the news, Boss. As a matter of fact, I'd bet on that."

"We'll pull over just up ahead, Coop," Corrie told him. "Security has picked out a spot."

"Right."

"It's up to my security detail where and when I stop from now on?" Ben questioned.

"That's . . . ah . . . just part of it, Boss," Jersey said.

"I can hardly wait to hear the rest," Ben said.

"I wouldn't bet on that," Anna muttered, too low for her father to hear.

The short column pulled over a few minutes later, and Ben and his team unassed the wagon.

Under the shade of a grove of trees, Beth said, "You've been assigned a staff, Boss."

Ben stared at her in silence.

"Fourteen people, I think," Corrie said.

Ben cut his eyes to her and remained silent.

"They're going to take some of the workload off you," Anna told him.

"I have been assigned a staff," Ben said softly.

"That's right, Boss," Cooper said.

"Fourteen people."

"That's right," Jersey said. "At least that many."

"Interesting." Ben's word was calmly spoken.

The team looked at one another. Ben sure was taking the news well.

"But I have a staff . . . sort of," Ben said. "They've been doing a good job."

"They're spread out all over the country, and they don't travel with us," Corrie pointed out.

"And this bunch will travel with us?" Ben asked.

"Ah . . . yes, Pops," Anna hesitantly replied. "That's the word I get. We get."

"And every time I turn around I'm going to be running into one of them."

"Well," Cooper said. "Ah . . . it probably won't be that bad, Boss."

Ben withered him into silence with a hard look.

"A fucking staff!" Ben said, getting up from his squatting position. "Fourteen goddamn people getting in my way—"

"Maybe it was sixteen," Anna said. "I forget exactly."

"Wonderful," her father said. "It just keeps getting better and better."

"They'll be here in a couple of days," Beth told him.

"Isn't that nice?" Ben replied.

None of his team chose to respond.

"We'd better be moving, sir," a lieutenant from the security detail said, walking up. "We just received word that a lot of Federals have infiltrated this area."

"When the hell did they come in, and where?" Ben asked, standing up.

"Intel thinks they've been here for several months, at least. Maybe longer. Where did they come in, sir? That's anybody's guess."

"All right," Ben said. "Let's haul ass."

Ben turned, and a small round appeared in the lieutenant's forehead. He was dead before he hit the ground. Had Ben not turned when he did the bullet would have taken him in the head, and he would have been cooling on the ground.

Ben and the team dropped to the ground, and the security detail fanned out.

"Sound suppressor on that sniper rifle," Jersey said. "I never heard a sound."

"He might be two thousand yards away," Ben replied. He looked around him, carefully studying the terrain. "But I don't think so. I think he's on that high ground to the northeast. That's the only place where he could get a clear shot to here."

Corrie was on the horn immediately, passing that information along. "Gunships will be here in a few minutes," she told Ben.

"Everybody stay down," Ben ordered. "No heroics. Corrie, tell security to do the same. Let the birds handle this."

In only a very few minutes, a dozen gunships came roaring in and proceeded to tear up the landscape with rockets and 30mm ammo from its chain guns. Each gunship was armed with up to seventy-six 2.75 inch rockets, armed for this mission with high explosives.

Most of the infiltrators never had a chance, for just behind the highly advanced Apache battle helicopters came half a dozen ultra modern Hueys, each armed with three 7.62 M60 machine guns—one on each side and one mounted under, the belly mount operated from the cockpit—25mm cannon, and 40mm grenade launchers. The heavily armed Hueys were flying hunter/killers, and on this day they performed magnificently.

"We've got prisoners," security radioed back to Corrie, and she informed Ben.

"Bring them in," Ben told her. "I want some information from these people, and I want to look at them eyeball to eyeball. And get somebody to make some coffee. We're going to be here for a while."

There were eight survivors of the sky attack, one of them so badly injured the medics took one look at him and shook their heads. They gave him a shot to ease his pain and let him die in peace . . . if dying can ever be described as peaceful.

"Thank you for that, at least, General Raines," said one of the prisoners.

"We treat our prisoners as humanely as field conditions permit," Ben said, turning to look at the man.

"That's not what we were told."

"Then you got some bad information. What is your name?"

"Dick."

"Last name?"

"That is my last name. Dick."

"And your rank is major?"

"Yes."

"First name?"

"Major."

"No," Ben said, shaking his head. "I know your rank. What is your first name?"

"Major."

"Your rank is major, and your first name is Major?"

"Yes."

"Major Major Dick?"

"That is correct."

"This is ridiculous! I am in no mood for games, Dick. Don't start with me."

"I am not playing any games, General. "My name is Major Dick. My first name is Major, my rank is major."

"Incredible."

The prisoner opened his mouth to speak, and Ben waved him silent.

"No . . . forget it. I'll just call you Major. That should cover it all."

Ben talked to the major for a few minutes. Major Major Dick gave Ben his serial number, and that was it. That was about all Ben expected to get out of the man. The man might have an unusual name, but to outward appearances, at least, he was tough and capable.

Major Dick and his men were taken back to the front lines for transport to a POW facility. The enemy dead were buried where they fell. The young lieutenant was body-bagged. He would be buried in a cemetery the Rebels had started weeks back, just after the first offensive by the Federal troops.

Ben drank his coffee, and then the short column started out again. They rode in silence for a few miles, Ben finally saying, "Cooper, I thought you said my new CP was only ten or so miles south of the lines?"

"Well," Cooper replied. "It's really not far, Boss. But it is more than a few miles."

"How far?"

"Oh, maybe thirty or forty miles, Boss," Beth said.

Ben twisted in the seat. Stared at her. "Thirty or forty miles?"

"Right, Pops," Anna said. "Just a few miles north of the center of the state."

"Wonderful," Ben muttered. "I certainly should be safe there."

Ben's mind was already working on how best to ignore this order from Cecil and the SUSA's security council without making it seem he was thumbing his nose at President Jefferys. That was something he wanted to avoid.

There was no way anybody was going to keep Ben Raines out of action . . . at least not for very long.

He'd think of something.

Soon.

Chapter Twenty-eight

Ben began settling into his new CP, waiting for his staff
to arrive. As soon as they did, he would start making plans
on how to get rid of them and get himself back to the
front lines.

The offense by the Federals had fizzled out and turned
into a near slaughter for the mercs and Federal troops
who were chosen to spearhead the attack. Most of them
did not make it across the wide no-man's-strip before they
were cut down. After the offensive failed, the Federals
withdrew and were, according to the best guesses of intel,
planning their next offensive.

Ben's new CP was located in what used to be a minimall
on the outskirts of a town that was abandoned just after
the collapse of government and the Great War. His CP
was in the largest space in the minimall, and partitioned
off by office dividers. Ben had the entire rear of what used
to be a huge retail store.

A number of reporters from the USA had abruptly

requested permission to report on the war, and much to everyone's surprise Ben had no objections to that. He granted them permission immediately.

"I think he's sick," Cooper had said. "Everybody knows he hates liberal reporters."

"I think he's got something up his sleeve," Beth said. "This isn't like him at all."

"I think he just wants some comic relief," Jersey countered. "We all know how the Boss likes to put the needle to liberal reporters."

"I think Jersey's got it," Corrie said.

"You're all correct to some degree. Especially Beth. Pop is planning some, but he's bored, too," Anna told the group. "He's been here a day and a half, and already he's edgy and restless." She glanced at her watch and sighed. "I'm not looking forward to any of this. The new staff will be here in about an hour. And the reporters will be here later on this afternoon."

Cooper nodded his head in agreement. "Should be a real interesting day."

"That's damn sure one way of putting it," Jersey said.

A Rebel from the security detail had walked up in time to hear the last few comments. "The arrival of the staff has been delayed a couple of hours," he informed the group. "Bad weather down south."

"Oh, goody," Beth said. "We get to meet the reporters first. I can hardly wait."

"I'm just all aquiver with anticipation," Anna said.

"I'm thrilled," Corrie said.

Jersey belched. "A bunch of candy-assed, whiny, crybabies. Shit!"

"Isn't she quite the lady?" Cooper said to the Rebel from security. "You should see what she does for an encore."

"Spare me that," the Rebel replied, and walked away.

"Here comes the Boss," Beth said.

Ben walked up and stood with his team for a moment. "I just got word the reporters will be here in a few minutes. One of the members of the security-council asked if I was going to greet them wearing my dress uniform."

His team laughed at that. Anna said, "And you told the security-council member?"

"I didn't have a dress uniform. She said they would have to see about getting me one. I told her not to bother, I wouldn't wear the damn thing if they got it."

"How come the security-council is suddenly sticking its nose into our business?" Jersey asked.

"Oh, they're not trying to run the war," Ben told his team. "They know better than to even attempt that. But their concern for me is genuine. I'm grateful, but I really wish they would just butt the hell out."

"Choppers coming in," Anna observed.

"That'll be the reporters," Ben said.

"How come you gave this Osterman-loving bunch the OK to come in and snoop around, Pop?" Anna asked.

"I needed a good laugh, Kid. And I imagine this group will provide me with plenty of laughs. Especially Ms. Cynthia Ross-Harris."

"One of those," Jersey muttered. She looked at Ben. "You've mentioned her a time or two."

"I knew her back before the Great War. I didn't know her well, but I knew her. She was a raging liberal back then, thought the government had the answer for everything. She still does," Ben concluded.

"Choppers are on the pads," Beth said. "Are we supposed to go over and greet these assholes? You know they're going to do a number on us."

Ben laughed. "Beth, your language has taken a turn for the worse of late. You used to be such a quiet and demure young lady. What happened?"

"She's been hanging around Jersey too long," Cooper said. "The original Apache guttermouth."

Jersey reached down and picked up a wrist-sized stick from the ground, about two and a half feet long. Cooper got ready to run. Jersey gravely handed her CAR to Beth. "Hold this, please. I have to swat a bug."

Cooper took off.

Jersey was right behind him, about three steps to the rear, cussing and swinging the stick, but Cooper's legs were longer and he was a better runner. He raced ahead of Jersey, all the time slinging verbal taunts over one shoulder.

"I'll break your goddamned head!" Jersey yelled. "You halfwit!"

Cooper laughed and flipped her the bird as they headed for the center of the parking lot of the old minimall.

Ms. Cynthia Ross-Harris and a group of reporters were just exiting the choppers and were preparing to walk across the parking lot toward Ben's CP when Cooper and Jersey came running and cussing past. The Rebels were used to the antics of the pair, and paid them little attention. Ms. Ross-Harris and the others were somewhat taken aback.

"You sorry turd!" Jersey hollered, waving the club. "Call *me* a guttermouth, you prick!"

"My word!" a reporter from an eastern newspaper blurted as the two ran past him. "Are we under attack?"

"That son of a bitch is!" Jersey yelled, pointing toward Cooper. "I'm gonna put some knots on his head."

"No discipline whatsoever in this army," said Ms. Ross-Harris. "I don't understand why so many people hold them in such high esteem."

"Disgraceful behavior," another reporter said. "You certainly would never see anything like that in our army."

"Absolutely not!" said another reporter. "We have professionals in our armed forces."

Jersey and Cooper had circled the growing knot of

reporters a couple of times, and now both were taking a short rest in the parking lot before the chase resumed.

"I wonder which one is Ms. Prissy-Ass?" Jersey panted.

"Probably the one who looks like an advertisement for one of those old adventure mail-order catalogs we used to see all the time when we were prowling around deserted buildings," Cooper replied, wiping the sweat from his face.

"Yeah. She must have twenty pockets in that jacket. Wonder what she carries in them."

"Nothing."

"Well, why the hell does she wear the jacket, then?"

"It's fashionable, you hick redskin. Don't you know anything about being in style?"

"Hick redskin?" Jersey yelled. "Why, you white trash, possum-eating, swamp-crawler—" She picked up her club.

Cooper stuck his tongue out at her and took off, Jersey right behind him.

"At least I didn't grow up eating Gila monsters and rattlesnakes!" Coop yelled over his shoulder.

"I'm going to make you look like a Gila monster, you goober mouth!"

"Goober mouth?" Coop yelled.

"General Raines," Ms. Cynthia Ross-Harris said, walking up to Ben as he stood at the edge of the awning covered walkway of the minimall. The others in her group were still watching Cooper and Jersey race around the parking lot. "Your troops putting on that little show for us?"

"Nope. Those two have been at each other for years. I suspect they'll get married one day. Did you ever find a man, Cynthia?"

"I haven't been looking, General Raines."

"Too bad. A stiff dick would work wonders for your disposition."

Cynthia leaned close to Ben and whispered, "Fuck you, Raines. You pig!"

Ben laughed, and that got the attention of the other reporters. They all walked up to where Ben and his team—minus Cooper and Jersey—were standing.

"Quite a group," Ben observed, looking over the twenty or so reporters. "It's a good thing the entire bunch didn't come down in one plane. All of you leaning left would have caused the plane to fall out of the sky."

"Very amusing, General," said a middle-aged man. "Ha Ha."

"Well, well," Ben said. "Mister Harry Bell. The socialist's best friend. What rag are you working for these days . . . since New York City no longer exists?"

"The city will rise again, General. A massive rebuilding is taking place. As if you didn't know."

"Like the Phoenix from the ashes, eh, Harry?"

"Something like that, General," the New York journalist replied coolly.

"That's good. I always did like to visit New York City." Ben smiled at the man.

Harry's returning smile was very thin.

Ben spoke to each of the reporters, and they were led off to their quarters. He would meet with them later.

Jersey had stopped chasing Cooper around the parking lot and they were resting, sitting on the sidewalk curb, talking. Both received some strange looks from the reporters . . . which they ignored.

"Security is getting edgy, Boss," Beth said to Ben. "They've received reports that a large number of infiltrators are in this area."

"Their objective?"

"You."

Ben paused in his rolling a cigarette. "They never give up, do they?"

"Doesn't seem like it."

"What does security have in mind?"

"They might want to move you again."

"Where?"

She shrugged her reply, then said, "They don't know. They're talking about it now."

"I've been expecting some attempt at an end-around by the Feds." Ben smiled—very knowingly, Beth thought. "Our lines are so long, and there are so many gaps a division could walk through."

"I saw you studying the maps, pinpointing the areas where the Feds concentrated on blowing the mines in the strip."

Among other things, Ben thought. "They did a good job of it, too. One area is just west of here, the other is just east."

"This bunch of reporters wanted to see some action. Looks like they might get more than they bargained for."

"I really need to get them out of here for their own safety, but if I tried that they'd think . . ." Ben paused and shrugged. "Hell, who cares what they think? They're going to blast me with words no matter what happens. They knew the danger coming in, or should have. If they get their asses shot, it's their fault."

Anna walked up. "Why is security so uptight?" she questioned. "What's going on?"

"Infiltrators, Kiddo."

Corrie walked up and said, "Infiltrators have been spotted, Boss. East, west, and south of us. A major offensive by the Feds is just getting underway north of us."

Ben was silent for a moment. The security detail at his CP was not nearly large enough to beat back any major attack launched against them. They were, as the old saying goes, between a rock and a hard place.

"You can bet some Federals will be under orders, if they break through our lines—and they will in some places— to drive south as hard as they can and box us in here,"

260 William W. Johnstone

Ben said. "It's what I would do if I knew the commander of all Feds was stationary in one spot, with only a company or so of troops. Son of a bitch!"

"This was not a good idea," Cooper remarked.

"Cooper," Jersey said. "You are belaboring the obvious. Shut up."

"Be quiet!" Corrie snapped. "Both of you. Squabble some other time." She held up a hand. "I'm getting a lot of transmissions."

Corrie was the unofficial leader of the team, and Jersey and Cooper shut up immediately. Beth and Anna exchanged glances and smiles.

"Fed troops advancing toward this area as we speak," Corrie said. "From all directions."

"Get those reporters back on the choppers and get them out of here," Ben ordered. "Do it, Anna. Move!" He turned to Cooper. "Get the wagon ready to roll, Coop. Move!" He looked at Jersey and Beth. "Draw supplies. You know what we need. Take off. How close are they, Corrie?"

"In another fifteen minutes you can ask them personally, Boss."

Ben smiled at her. "That close, huh?"

"You bet."

The sudden whine of the choppers' engines filled the afternoon air.

"Corrie, bump Base Camp and tell them to do something about those new staff members coming in. Divert them somewhere."

"Done, Boss. First thing."

"I should have guessed that. OK. What are we forgetting before we bug out of here?"

The reporters ran to the choppers and scrambled aboard.

"Short visit," Corrie shouted over the roar of the choppers, gesturing toward the reporters.

"Long enough for me," Ben replied.

A couple of minutes passed. The choppers lifted off and the reporters were out of harm's way. Rebels were hurriedly loading gear into the backs of trucks in preparation for bugging out.

"There's Coop," Corrie said.

"The team is with him," Ben said. "OK. Everyone is accounted for. Let's get the hell out of here."

A mortar round landed just in front of the big nine passenger wagon and blew out the front window. Water started pouring from a busted radiator. The team appeared to be unhurt.

"Get out of there!" Ben yelled. "Grab what you can and get clear."

The team scrambled out of the wagon, grabbing backpacks, rucksacks, and weapons, and ran over to Ben and Corrie.

Ben took a pack and rucksack. "Get in that deuce and a half over there," Ben told his team. "I'm right behind you in the next truck. I've got to get something from the office."

"I'll stay with you," Jersey said.

"You'll get your ass in that truck like I told you," Ben said. "Move, all of you!"

The team obeyed orders. None of them liked it, but they did what they were told.

Ben had parked a HumVee behind his office. He had plans for that vehicle. He waved at his team as the truck pulled away. "I'll catch up with you!" Ben yelled.

The team waved at him.

"The hell I will," he muttered. Ben had known about the infiltrators before anyone else connected with his CP. He had intercepted a message from communications . . . before Corrie had a chance to see it. It seems that General Walt Berman was feeling his oats, and had insisted upon leading the team of infiltrators now converging on Ben's CP. Ben had radioed intel about the message.

"Has this rumor been confirmed as fact?" Ben had asked. "Berman is really leading this group?"

"It's a fact, General. He is definitely leading one of the teams."

"The man is a fool!"

"Yes, sir. But he has sworn to kill you personally."

The infiltration teams had not materialized when intel had said they would, and Ben dismissed the report as pure rumor. Hours later, rumor became fact, and Ben had put on a good show of not knowing anything about it. It had been difficult to keep a straight face while doing it. He was pretty sure that Anna had picked up on the ruse but had not been able to really figure out what he was up to. By the time they did figure it out, it would be too late for any of them to do anything about it.

"I guess I'm a pretty good actor," he muttered, ducking behind the minimall, tossing his gear into the Hummer, and cranking it up. "I should be nominated for an Academy Award for my performance this afternoon."

He checked the vehicle for gas. Full tank and several full gas cans in reserve. There were cans of water and food and ammo.

He was set.

The area around the minimall became quiet as the last of Ben's security detail pulled out. He had aced his security, and his own team.

Ben smiled. "Working so far," he said. "The Raines luck is still working."

Ben checked a map. He knew that Berman was leading 'A' Team in from the north. B Team was coming in from the south. C Team from the west. D Team from the east.

"OK, General Berman," Ben muttered, slipping the HumVee into gear. "You wanted to meet me eyeball-to-eyeball, you son of a bitch. You're going to gct your chance.''

He turned on the radio and set it to scan the Federal frequencies. The Rebels had all of them. It wouldn't take Ben long to get a fix on Berman.

Then the two commanding generals would settle this thing. One way or the other.

Chapter Twenty-nine

Ben slowly drove the back roads, listening to the chatter as the scanner locked onto Federal frequencies. He listened for talk of landmarks that would help him find Berman's team. Finally, just as the sun was going down, Ben pulled in behind a falling down piece of a barn, tucked the Hummer under what remained of the roof of a lean-to, and had something to eat.

Nobody had to tell him that what he was doing was totally stupid. He knew that. He and Walt Berman had been talking back and forth for days, the insults getting more and more personal, until Ben finally remembered where he had met Berman . . . long before he'd been his prisoner at the nuthouse.

Berman had not been his name then. It had been years back, long before the collapse and the Great War. Ben had been doing contract work for the Company, and Berman's talents as a hired gun were for sale to any country, any cause, that had the money to hire him.

Berman had been an international terrorist.

Ben remembered that just before the collapse, he had learned that the Agency had put a contract out on the man who now called himself Berman.

Obviously Berman had survived, and made quite a name for himself as a soldier.

The man called Berman also hated Ben Raines, although Ben had no idea why. Ben finally gave up trying to figure it out. The why wasn't all that important, anyway. Ben intended to kill the bastard . . . one way or the other.

Call it male pride or whatever anyone wanted to call it—perhaps a sudden surge of testosterone. Whatever.

Ben ate his meager—but filling, if not a bit tasty—supper of cold rations, then made himself a cup of coffee using a tiny field stove and a heat tab. He rolled a cigarette and smoked and drank his coffee slowly, enjoying each sip. He listened for the sounds of combat, but could hear no shots or explosions.

He knew that the Rebels had shifted troops around and had thrown up a circle around this part of Tennessee . . . those had been the last orders Ben had given before bugging out. Berman and his infiltrators were trapped—he had outfoxed himself. All Ben had to do, really, was just stay hidden and let his troops finish off Berman and his men.

But Ben had no intention of doing that.

That would be too easy.

Ben had vivid memories of the aftermath of the terrorist attack deep in SUSA territory: dead and maimed civilians, mostly women and children and elderly.

And Ben had learned that Berman planned the entire operation.

"I'm going to kill you, Berman," Ben whispered. "Believe it, you bastard."

From listening to radio transmissions Ben learned that all the reporters had made it out safely, not that he really gave a damn whether any of the left-leaning bastards and bitches had or not. He was quite certain that if any of them had gotten hurt or killed he would have been blamed for it. He'd been doing battle with liberals—verbally at first, before the collapse and the Great War—for years . . . usually to no avail. There was no compromise in liberals. For socialist/democrat it was either all their way, or no deal.

Ben's team had all made it out safely. He had talked very briefly with Corrie just before pulling behind the old ramshackle barn, and assured her he was all right. He made it plain that he wanted to be left alone to tend to some personal business. He made it a direct order that there would be no rescue teams sent in after him unless he requested them. He had Corrie tape the order and play it back to him.

"Strange order, Boss," Corrie had told him. "Lots of people are not going to like this."

"I can't help that. This is something I have to do, and that's that."

"What is it you're going to do, Boss?"

"Personal, and for the time being, Corrie, private."

"OK, Boss. I have no problem with that. You take care."

"I will. I'll contact you when the job is over."

"I sure hope so, Boss."

"Eagle out."

Ben fixed himself another cup of coffee, and when it was brewed he rolled another cigarette and sat and readied himself to watch a very lovely sunset.

"Very peaceful place," he whispered. "Nice way to finish a day." He sipped his coffee and relaxed and enjoyed the view.

A few seconds later he heard the sounds of a vehicle on the old blacktop highway in front of the deserted farm. He couldn't tell, as yet, which direction the slow moving vehicle was coming from.

Ben took his CAR and rucksack from the seat of the Hummer and slipped inside the old barn, working his way carefully toward the front of the building.

"Federals," Ben muttered, catching sight of the military painted truck. "This will be a better way to finish a day, I believe."

Thoroughly trained professional soldiers do not think of enemy soldiers as male or female, or even as human beings. They are the enemy, and it is time to kill or be killed. Survival instinct takes precedence over all. Training and experience push everything else out of a professional warrior's mind. That same warrior might risk his or her life to save the life of a child or an elderly person caught up in a dangerous combat situation, or even a horse or dog, but he or she doesn't give a good goddamn about someone wearing the uniform of the enemy . . . not if that warrior in question wants to live.

The bed of the truck was covered with a tarp over a frame of some sort, so Ben had no idea how many men might be in the bed: One, or half a dozen or more, it really didn't make any difference. If they stopped to do a search of the old farm, he was going to kill them all. That was the way it was. That was the way it had to be. A soldier has no choice in the matter, no other option.

The truck drove slowly past the old, rundown house and barn. The driver gave the place only a cursory glance— too damn relaxed a look from him to suit Ben—and the other two soldiers in the cab didn't turn their heads. That was, to Ben's mind, a dead giveaway that they felt something was amiss and would be back to check it out.

He had not seen any one of the three in the cab use a radio. Of course, they might very well be radioing in their location now that the farm was behind them.

Ben waited. The minutes ticked past in silence. Then

he heard the sounds of the truck returning, coming up the road very slowly.

"Stupid," he muttered. "They should have returned on foot through the woods to the south."

The truck stopped and the driver cut the engine. Half a dozen uniformed and well-armed men got out of the tarp-covered bed, and three more unassed the cab of the truck.

"Nine to one," Ben whispered. "And I've got about forty-five minutes of good daylight left. Going to be interesting."

The nine men stood and talked for a few minutes, then began to fan out: three on each side, three facing the front of the decrepit old house.

Ben didn't see any need to wait for an invitation. "Might as well open the dance right now," he muttered.

He lifted his CAR and took out the three men walking up the ragged and overgrown front yard. He burned a full mag into the trio and then quickly ejected and stuck home a full thirty round magazine, shifting locations in the litter of what remained of the front room as he reloaded. There was some returning fire, but Ben was not hit.

"Lonnie?" one of the three men on the south side of the house called.

Lonnie, Ben guessed, was one of the trio who now lay dead or dying in the front yard. He did not reply.

"Eddie?" the same man called.

Nothing from Eddie.

"Vance?"

A moan from the front yard.

"How hard are you hit, Vance?" The voice came from the north side of the house.

"Belly," Vance called. "My guts are on fire, Peter. Help me."

"Can you see him, Carl?" Peter called.

"No. All I know is he's in the house."

"There's a HumVee parked in the back," another voice added.

"I need something for the pain!" Vance yelled. "Goddamnit, somebody help me."

"Shut up, Vance," Carl shouted. "We'll get to you. Just hang on."

"Hang onto what?" Vance groaned. "I got Lonnie's brains all over me. When he was hit he pulled the trigger and shot himself in the head. Blew his fuckin' head all to pieces and his brains all over me."

The gunfire Ben had heard.

"Is Eddie dead?" another voice on the north side called.

"Deader than hell," Vance moaned. "He took half a dozen rounds in the chest."

"Let's blow him out of there." Another voice called the suggestion.

"I want that Hummer," Carl yelled. "Hold up with the grenades for a while."

"Yeah," this voice came from the other side of the ramshackle house. "My ass is sore from ridin' in the back of that goddamned truck."

"Vance?" Carl called.

Vance did not respond.

"Vance?" Peter yelled.

No response.

"He's either passed out or dead," yet another man called. "Probably dead."

"How do you figure that, Miles?" Carl yelled. "You close to him? Can you see him?"

"I seen him get hit," Miles called. "He took half a dozen rounds in the belly. He got tore up pretty bad. Them rounds lifted him damn near off his feet and then doubled him over. He's dead."

Ben popped the pin on a Fire-Frag and chunked it out

a caved-in part of the north side of what remained of the house.

"Oh, shit!" he heard one of the mercs yell just a couple of seconds before the deadly grenade blew.

Ben bellied down on the rotted floor a second before the Fire-Frag blew and sent shrapnel all over the place.

Before the echo of the explosion had died away, Ben scrambled across the rotted floor to the other side of the house and chunked another grenade. Before it blew, he was running hard as the old floor would allow out of the rear of the house and diving behind a pile of rotting fire-wood.

The Fire-Frag blew, and Ben heard someone screaming in great pain. *Serves you right for picking the wrong side in this fracas,* he thought.

Ben lay behind the pile of old firewood catching his breath and acutely aware that he was not as young as he was behaving. The landing on his belly hurt, and Ben would not be ashamed to admit that to anybody.

"Carl!" someone screamed. "Oh, Jesus, his guts and balls and legs and other shit are all over the damn place."

"Whose guts?" Carl yelled.

"Davy. He's dead."

"I got one dead over here, too," Carl yelled. "Whoever that son of a bitch in the house is, he's taking us out and taking his own sweet time doing it."

"That fuckin' grenade landed right in front of Davy. He froze at the sight."

"Davy knew better than that."

"What the hell difference does that make now?"

There was no response from Carl.

Ben waited.

"All right!" Ben now could recognize Carl's voice. "Blow that goddamn house apart! Do it right now!"

Ben waited, peering out one side of the rotting pile of

firewood until the pins of the grenades were pulled and the grenades were tossed and in the air. Then he moved while the mercs were bellied down on the ground, out of the path of the shrapnel that was sure to fill the air.

Ben scampered as fast as he could, staying as low as possible, over to the south side of the house, about twenty-five meters away from the mercs, and bellied down just as the grenades blew. The rotting remains of the old farmhouse blew apart. The walls puffed out and then disintegrated, and the roof collapsed with almost a contented sigh. Dust filled the air for seconds. That was all the time Ben needed.

Ben raised himself to his knees and burned a magazine of 5.56 rounds into the mercs on the south side of the house. The Federal mercenaries were just getting up to their knees to take a look at the damage done to the house.

Ben knew they were mercenaries because of their shoulder patches. His intel people had advised him of those patches. Ben had smiled then. They were miniatures of the skull and crossbones of the old pirate flag, the Jolly Roger.

The mag of 5.56 rounds tore up flesh, cracked and splintered bone, and sent the mercs to whatever place their Maker had picked out for them.

"Good riddance," Ben muttered as he crawled over to the three shot up mercs.

One was dead, one was unconscious, and the third was not long for this world.

The conscious merc took one look at Ben and gave a bloody curving of the lips, more of a pain-filled grimace than a smile. "We sure picked a mean son of a bitch to try to kill on this beautiful day, didn't we, General?" the mercenary gasped. Both his hands were holding his perforated belly.

"You sure did," Ben whispered. "You know my name, boy. How is that?"

"Hell, General. Damn near everybody in the world knows who you are." He closed his eyes and groaned as waves of pain ripped through him.

"Miles!" Carl yelled from the north side of the house. "What the hell was that shooting?"

"Your name Miles?" Ben asked.

"No. That's him with half his head gone. I'm Peter. That's Wilhelm to your left."

"Answer him, Peter."

"Why?" the merc challenged. "You want to answer him, be my guest."

"Tough to the end, hey, Peter?"

"You'd better believe it, General."

Peter then smiled faintly, closed his eyes, and died without making another sound.

Ben took a quick look past the ruins of the old house. He didn't think he could toss a grenade that far with any accuracy, and he wasn't going to try. He cut his eyes for a couple of seconds. The old lean-to where he had parked the Hummer had survived the concussion from the explosion and was still intact.

Ben mentally counted the dead or badly wounded. *Seven*, he thought. *Nine mercs to begin with.* That left two, both of them on the other side of the jumble of wood that remained of the old house. One of them was Carl. Ben didn't think he had heard the other's name mentioned. Not that it made any difference—neither one of them were going to walk away from this fight . . . not if Ben had his way.

"Where is that son of a bitch?" he heard the voice ask.

"Hell, I don't know," Carl replied. "He damn sure wasn't in the house, was he? But I think Miles and Peter and Wilhelm have had it."

"He's out-guessing us at every step."

"So far," Carl replied. "This isn't over yet."

"He killed Miles and Peter and Wilhelm. It's damn near over. Just the two of us left."

"I can count, Frank."

"So can I. And I don't like the odds, Carl. Let's get the hell out of here."

"No way, Frank. We finish this right here and now."

"You finish it, Carl. I'm gone."

"Steady down, Frank. Get a grip on yourself."

"Fuck you, Carl!"

"Don't make me shoot you, Frank. I will, damn you."

"Then do it, Carl. I'm gone."

"Damn you, Frank. I will."

Ben couldn't hear all of the conversation, but he certainly got the gist of it. He heard another exchange of angry voices. Then he heard the single gunshot.

"Damn," he muttered. "I think Carl really shot him. So much for camaraderie."

"All right, you son of a bitch!" Carl yelled. "I guess it's just you and me now."

Ben said nothing. He looked up at the sky. Almost dark. The light was tricky now.

"You hear me, you bastard?"

Ben remained silent.

"You got a name?"

Ben pulled a grenade from his battle harness and slowly removed the pin, holding the spoon down.

"Answer me, damn you!"

Ben waited. "Your move, you dickhead," he whispered to the gathering darkness.

Carl burned half a mag in Ben's direction while he was shifting positions. Ben kept his head down, but heard it when Carl stumbled on some shattered boards as he made his run to the north side of the ruins of the old house.

"Good move, Carl," Ben muttered. "For me, that is. Gets you closer to me. Maybe close enough. We'll see."

Ben popped the spoon and tossed the grenade. It was an awkward throw, and landed a few yards short of the far edge of what was left of the house, but it served its purpose. The blast filled the dusky air with dust and splinters and rusty nails. The dust covered Carl's eyes with a grainy film, and the splinters and nails peppered his upper body and face.

Carl started screaming in pain and shouting, "I'm blind, you rotten bastard. You've blinded me, goddamn you to hell. You've blinded me!"

Ben charged out from behind cover and stopped and leveled his CAR when he saw Carl stumbling and staggering around by the side of the house.

Ben shot him.

The rounds from the CAR knocked the mercenary backward and set him down on his butt. With one hand on the ground, bracing himself, the merc used his other hand to wipe the sweat and dust from his face until he could see Ben.

"Goddamn you, now you've killed me!" Carl said.

"Seems that way, doesn't it, Carl?"

"You're no young kid, that's for sure. You've got some miles on you. That makes it better." Carl blinked several times. Then he tried a smile. "General Ben Raines. Well, I'll just be goddamned. That makes it even better. I'll die easier knowing one of the best took me out." The mercenary moaned and fell over on the ground. He gasped for breath for a few seconds, then seemed to settle down.

"I'll make no promises, but I'll try to bury you all in some fashion."

"Don't bother, General. I've left a thousand men I've killed on the ground to rot."

"As you wish."

"All my men dead?"

"Dead or dying."

"You're damn good, you are. You better be good, Ben Raines. You better be damn good. I heard about that deal you and Berman worked out."

"Did you now? What did you hear?"

"That you and him was gonna settle an old score *mano a mano*. Any truth to that?"

"Yes. But I don't know what the old score is."

"He does. But he never said."

"Makes no difference. I'm going to kill him."

"You might just do that. You're damn sure tricky enough."

Ben walked around the battle area. All the mercenaries were dead, and when he returned to stand over Carl, Carl had slipped into eternity.

Ben looked around, trying to spot a suitable place to put the bodies. Then he thought about burying them. There was a shovel in the Hummer.

Ben finally decided to leave the bodies where they had fallen.

"Hell with it," he said.

He wasn't in any mood to dig a big hole, anyway.

Chapter Thirty

Ben pulled the mercenary's vehicle behind the lean-to and removed some rations and ammo from the truck, stowing them in his Hummer. The mercs had all been carrying regulation M-16's with bloop tubes, and Ben took two of them and all their 40mm grenades, filling two rucksacks. Why they hadn't used the rifle grenades was something that Ben didn't understand.

Ben loaded up and pulled out, driving about five miles up the old blacktop before cutting down a gravel/dirt road. The road was nearly overgrown with weeds, and to Ben's eye did not look as though it had been used much in a long time.

He cut off into what had once been a pasture, and topped a low hill. His headlights picked up an old shotgun house butted up against a thick stand of timber.

"Home for the night," Ben said, and he pulled on down the hill and around to the rear of the old tenant house. "And none too soon, either," he added.

STANDOFF IN THE ASHES   277

As soon as he unassed from the Hummer, the weariness hit Ben hard. He'd been running on pure adrenaline for several hours, and fatigue had finally caught up with him. He sat down on the ground and put his back to the side of the Hummer, resting there for a few minutes.

He caught a few moments rest and then got out his portable stove and made a small pot of coffee. He ate some crackers and peanut butter from one of his accessory packs and then had a cup of coffee and a smoke. He slowly began to feel better, in spite of the numerous bruises on his body from throwing himself and landing on the hard ground several times. The gear on his battle harness was not meant for a human body to land on.

"You are no kid, Raines," he whispered to the night. Then he smiled. "But then, you're not over the hill yet."

Just don't put a hill in front of me and tell me I have to climb it right now, he thought with a grin. He chuckled at his own joke.

His grin faded as his thoughts shifted to Berman. He wondered if he would ever know why the man hated him so. Probably not. Not that it really made a serious difference one way or the other, but it did trouble Ben somewhat.

Ben placed his coffee mug on the ground and stretched long and hard. It hurt a bit, but he felt better afterward. Then he took off his boots and rubbed his feet, and that really felt good.

Ben wrapped a blanket around him against the slight chill of the Tennessee night, and then he finished the last of his freshly brewed coffee. He set the mug aside and decided he'd close his eyes for a moment.

He awakened hours later. He checked the luminous hands of his watch. Three-thirty in the morning. Before he moved around much, Ben remained where he was for several moments and listened. He could detect no sounds that weren't natural to the area and the night.

Then Ben crawled to his feet and stretched several times, working the stiffness out of his muscles and joints. Picking up his CAR, he slowly and silently prowled the area for several moments. Nothing set off his mental alarms.

Ben returned to his vehicle and brewed his first cup of coffee of the day. While his coffee was brewing he ate a packet of dried fruit and grimaced at the sour taste—not tart, just plain sour. He forced himself to finish the packet, then made a mental note to have his people back home do something about the fruit. To Ben's taste buds, the fruit was nothing short of awful.

He rolled a smoke and fixed his coffee and sat down on the ground sheet to enjoy his first waking moments of the day. He was still a bit sore, but knew the soreness was temporary and would vanish with the day's passing and a little physical activity.

He turned on one of the radios he'd taken from the mercenary's vehicle and let it scan, the volume set low. Nothing was happening that he could pick up. Then he switched radios and found a station broadcasting from deep in SUSA territory. The news was not good.

Federal agents were cracking down hard on anyone who belonged to or vocally supported militia or survivalist groups. Members of militias or survivalist groups were now officially classified as traitors to the USA and shot if they resisted capture, hanged when they were taken alive—after a trial, of course. Anyone who vocally supported militia or survivalist groups was promptly arrested and immediately sent off to reindoctrination camps. Those camps were springing up all over the United States.

"Nazi Germany all over again," Ben muttered. "I predicted it would come to this."

Ben listened to the other news from the SUSA radio station: there was worldwide condemnation of the USA's war against the SUSA. And those in the free world—such as it was—had told Madam President Osterman they would not assist her in any way in this fight.

"What a sorry state of affairs this is," the prime minister of a friendly country was quoted as saying. "After all the Rebels have done for this world, to now have to fight a civil war. It's disgusting."

Madam President Osterman had no response to those remarks, but Ben had to smile, thinking that she privately probably blew several gaskets over what the prime minister had to say.

"Serves the socialistic bitch right," Ben muttered.

Ben brewed and drank another small pot of coffee and waited for the sun to start poking its beams over the eastern horizon. He stowed all his equipment and topped off the gas tank. He checked his CAR and one of the Federal's regulation M-16's taken from the battle site, laying a rucksack of 40mm grenades on the seat next to his.

"Time to go," Ben said, just as the first touches of silver began to lighten the eastern sky.

He cranked up, dropped the HumVee into gear, and pulled out. He reached for the light switch and then paused and drew back his hand. Something, some inner warning, went off, urging him to cool it with the lights.

Ben stopped just before he reached the crest of the small hill and got out, carefully making his way to the top of the hill. In the distance, off to his left, he could just make out the lights of several vehicles as they came down from the north. He watched as the lead vehicle slowed, then he lost sight of it.

"Bet they cut off on this old dirt road," he muttered, then watched as headlights suddenly appeared, driving slowly down the dirt road.

Ben went back to the Hummer and got the regulation M-16 and a rucksack of grenades.

"I'm in a good spot for a battle," he muttered. "If

it comes to that, and it probably will. I've got the high ground."

Ben laid out his weapons and rucksack and bellied down on the crest. He waited and watched.

Ben smiled knowingly as he watched the lead vehicle slow down and then turn into the old pasture. The vehicles, a HumVee and two pickup trucks, stopped about halfway between the old dirt road and the hill where Ben lay waiting. "Here we go," Ben whispered, pulling his M-16 to him and slipping a 40mm grenade into the bloop tube.

Using his binoculars, Ben carefully inspected the scene before him while he got the range. Eight men were standing around talking, making no attempts at concealment or cover against possible enemy fire. Ben began to have some serious doubts again about the caliber of men chosen for this mercenary army. So far, Berman's troops hadn't shown him very much in the way of professionalism.

The distance was well within the range of the grenade launcher—about three hundred and fifty yards. The men below him were paid mercenaries, wearing the shoulder patch which silently spoke of that designation.

As the news reports had stated, fifty percent or more of the former regular U.S. military was staying out of this war. But Ben knew that could change in a heartbeat. He hoped it wouldn't. However, he knew that might well be just wishful thinking.

Ben again lifted his binoculars and studied the men below him. They seemed to be in some sort of argument which appeared to be getting rather heated, and Ben couldn't determine just who was in charge. Surely somebody was.

Then one of the men stepped away from the group and pointed up the hill. "That's the man in charge," Ben muttered. Ben wished he had his old Thunder Lizard, his M-14. If he had that weapon the group below him would very quickly be leaderless, for Ben was a very good shot, but three hundred yards was stretching it for the M-16 . . . at least, for Ben it was. Shooting downhill was tricky under the best of conditions.

"Come on, boys," Ben quietly urged the mercenaries below him. "Let's get this show started. I've got things to do and a man to see today. If I can find the son of a bitch, that is."

One of the mercs knelt down and inspected the ground. Ben watched him through the long lenses. The man stood up and pointed up the hill.

"Found my tire tracks, did you?" Ben whispered. "Well, congratulations, and good for you. Now let's get going and do something, you assholes."

The group of eight mercenary soldiers turned as one and looked up the hill. They could not see Ben, hidden in the tall grass and scrub brush. But from the way they suddenly started behaving, Ben figured they knew somebody was on the hill, or strongly suspected.

"No point in waiting for them to get cranked up and going," Ben said.

He gave them a rifle grenade. It fell short, but the explosion sure got the mercs moving. Two of them got turned around and started up the hill, running about seventy-five yards toward Ben. Ben burned a mag downhill and knocked both of them spinning.

"Two down, six to go," he said to the early morning breeze that fanned him.

Ben tried another 40mm grenade, and this one landed behind the line of vehicles. The third one was right on target, landing between the Hummer and a pickup truck, doing extensive damage to both vehicles.

Ben could not hear any cussing coming from the mercenaries—he was too far away—but he figured they were turning the air very profane. The two mercs he'd cut down were not moving. They were out of the game permanently. "You picked the wrong side, boys," Ben said.

Ben tried another 40mm grenade, and this one was all the way off the mark, off to one side. The fifth one landed just where he wanted it: right on the hood of the lone vehicle left. The hood went flying off, along with various pieces of the engine. The truck did not catch on fire, which suited Ben just fine. He didn't want someone from Berman's command coming to investigate a column of thick smoke spiraling into the air.

"All right, boys," Ben said. "Come and try to take me."

Ben could afford to say that, for he was sitting in the catbird seat: he had the high ground, good cover, and open meadow on both sides that ran for several hundred yards left and right in case the mercs attempted an end-around.

Ben's only drawback on the crest of the hill was the range. It was really stretching it for his M-16. Ben suddenly remembered that when he was a kid, an older friend of his had an old World War Two M-1 Garand. Ben got to fire it several times, and loved the old M-1. That round could reach out and touch someone hundreds of yards away.

"Progress," Ben muttered. "Sometimes it ain't all it's cracked up to be."

Ben really didn't have a thing against the M-16. It was a fine weapon 99% of the time. This was just one of those times when that one percent seemed huge.

The minutes ticked past. Now it had turned into a waiting game. The mercs were behind the ruined vehicles, and Ben had not seen a radio among the group. That meant the radios were in the vehicles.

"Well, the smoke be damned," Ben muttered. "I can't let those guys get to a radio and call for help."

Ben started lobbing 40mm grenades down the hill. On

the third try the gas tank on one of the trucks blew, the explosion tossing one merc about twenty feet off to one side, mangled and dead, and set two more ablaze like human torches.

Ben lay on the hill and watched the two mercs burn until they collapsed and were still. "And then there were three," he said. "Now what, boys?"

A few moments passed with no movement from either side. The vehicle fire died out and the smoke dissipated. Ben looked up at the sky. Clouds were beginning to move in, and Ben guessed rain was not far behind.

"Come on, boys," Ben muttered. "Let's get something going here."

The three remaining mercs had no fight left in them. Ben watched in amazement as the three men took off running as hard as they could, back toward the old dirt road. He did not fire at them; at that range it would have been nothing more than wasting lead.

Using his binoculars, Ben watched the three as they made the dirt road and turned toward the blacktop road. They were walking now, probably feeling secure. They occasionally turned and looked back toward the battle site, but they made no attempt to return.

He watched them until they were out of sight, then quickly loaded up the Hummer and headed out. When he reached the dirt road, Ben cut away from the blacktop, heading in the opposite direction, continuing down the old dirt/gravel road . . . more dirt than gravel.

Ben had no idea where the old road would take him. He just wanted to put as much distance as possible between himself and the battle site as quickly as he could.

The road took him past several old and long-deserted farmhouses; no signs of life. Ben drove for several miles before he came to an intersection, a crossroad that gave him three choices: left, right, or straight ahead.

Ben cut to his left, wondering where in the hell the road would take him. He checked the mileage on his odometer and then drove for five miles, the road taking more twists and turns than a hole full of snakes. He came to several crossroads and changed directions each time.

"Good God!" he blurted. "Where in the hell am I?"

He had his radios on, but so far had been unable to pick up anything. He had no idea what was going on. He did know one thing for certain: he was lost.

Chapter Thirty-one

Ben finally came to another crossroad—one of the roads was blacktop, although in pretty sad shape—and to what remained of an old combination general store and gas station. Ben turned onto the gravel driveway/parking lot—much of it now weed-grown—pulled in behind the old store, and tucked the Hummer in close to the rear of the building.

He glanced at his watch and was surprised to learn he'd only been wandering about for just slightly over an hour, though it felt to Ben he'd been driving all morning.

Ben got out of the Hummer, taking his CAR. He stood for a moment and just listened. He could hear nothing that did not fit in with nature. Birds were singing and squirrels had begun jumping about in the trees behind the store, chattering irritably at Ben's presence.

He stepped into the rear of the store—easily done because the back door was missing—and looked around. He was in what had once probably been a storeroom, barren now except for about a foot of litter that covered the floor.

Ben made his way into what was the main part of the store. He didn't expect to find anything, and he sure as hell wasn't disappointed. What the Rebels hadn't taken years back—if indeed the Rebels had passed through here and taken anything—others had taken in the years since then.

A lingering odor wrinkled Ben's nose. It was very unpleasant.

Ben looked around for a moment and then went back outside into the fresh air. Because the old store didn't smell too good, Ben suspected there was or had recently been something dead in there . . . like a human body.

Ben walked over to the blacktop and looked up and down, hoping to see a road sign. No such luck. He really hadn't expected to find a road marker. Then he got that familiar edgy feeling that many experienced combat veterans develop: someone, or some *thing* was watching him.

Ben cut his eyes and caught a glimpse of movement in the brush alongside the road. Black and white movement. He smiled as a furry face poked out of the brush. A dog. A rather large dog.

Ben knelt down and held out a hand. "Come here, fellow. Come on. You hungry?"

The animal came charging out of the brush with such speed it startled Ben.

"Damn!" he said, putting out one hand to steady himself.

Then the animal was all over him, rubbing up against him and licking his face.

Ben first thought it was a Husky, but he was wrong. He took a closer look. It was a Malamute, and a big one. Ben guessed the Mal to be about a hundred or so pounds. He checked the sex. Female—a damn big female. From the way she moved, Ben guessed her age at about four years, maybe three. Wearing a very ragged collar that was too tight, she was very friendly and had at one time, probably recently, been in the company of humans.

Ben loosened the collar, and the Mal licked his hand. Ben laughed and said, "Well, now what, girl?"

She licked his face.

"All right. Let's go find you something to eat. Not that you look undernourished. But you sure could use a bath. You smell sort of doggy."

Ben got to his boots and started walking toward the old store. The Mal followed right along. "Somebody has trained you pretty well, girl. Without a leash, most Malamutes I've been around would have been five miles down the road."

The dog just looked at him.

"Beautiful eyes," Ben said, smiling at her, and they were—a bright brown that seemed to shine with health.

Behind the old store, Ben opened several packs of MREs—stew and chicken and rice—dumped the mess onto a wrapper, and placed the food on the ground.

The Mal ate quickly, all of it, and then tried to eat the wrapper. Ben grabbed one end of the tough paper and he and Mal had a very short tug of war, which she won hands down.

"Incredibly strong animals," Ben said. "And very strong-willed, too." He watched as the Mal trotted off with the wrapper. She stopped a few yards away and licked the wrapper clean. While she was busying herself with that, Ben fixed a canteen cup of water and walked over to the dog.

She looked at Ben, then at the water, then she lapped it up. Ben fixed another cup and she drank that, then lay down by the Hummer. She didn't go to sleep. She never took her eyes off Ben.

Ben fixed himself some crackers with some sort of mystery meat and had that . . . he tried to get the dog to eat some of it, and even she turned up her nose at the crap. It sure as hell wasn't very tasty—and as a matter of fact it smelled like glue—but it filled him up while his coffee was brewing.

"I know you have a name," Ben said to the Mal. "But I don't have a clue what it is and you're not able to tell me. So if you stay with me, and I hope you do, I've got to name you something. I can't keep calling you Dog."

The Mal came over and lay down beside Ben. Ben put a hand on the dog's head and petted her. In a very few moments, they went to sleep together. He had found a friend.

"The problem is, Mal," Ben said to the dog as they rode down the old blacktop, "I'm looking to hunt someone to kill him. What am I going to do with you when Berman and I meet? I don't want you to get hurt."

The dog deep-voiced back at him in the odd way that Malamutes have of 'talking.'

"Right," Ben said. "Absolutely. That was going to be my next question."

The clouds and the storm that had been threatening had moved on east, and the day had turned out bright and warm. Suddenly, far up the road, on a straightaway stretch, Ben caught a glimpse of sunlight off a windshield or chrome. He quickly cut off the highway and into a pasture, then into a small stand of trees. He cut the engine and got out, taking the regulation M-16 and a rucksack of 40mm grenades.

He looked at the Mal. "You stay," he told her. "Stay right here!"

Surprisingly, the Mal jumped into the rear of the Hummer and lay down.

"Good girl. Good girl!"

Before Ben closed the door he lowered one side flap, so if the worst happened and he did not return the Mal could get out.

Ben walked to the edge of the timber and waited, binoculars in hand. Four vehicles came into sight, driving slowly. All the vehicles had a white star on the doors. Regular Federal troops. Ben hated to see that, and would not fire on regular American troops unless they fired on him.

The four vehicles, two Hummers and two pickup trucks, drove slowly past. Using his long lenses, Ben watched as the men looked all around them, missing nothing that was visible to them. They drove on past and Ben relaxed a bit.

Ben waited for several minutes before returning to his Hummer. The Mal was right where he'd left her. "Good girl," Ben told the her, petting her. "You've had some good training, and it stayed with you."

Ben cranked up and pulled out, heading in the opposite direction from the Federal troops. He turned on his radios and let them scan, hoping to pick up something that would lead him to Walt Berman. For the most part, both Federal and Rebel frequencies were silent.

Ben followed the blacktop to the top of a hill and pulled off, driving over a meadow and into a stand of brush and timber. He took a Federal walkie-talkie and keyed the mic.

"Hey, Berman," Ben said. "You washed up son of a bitch! Are you listening, you bastard?"

Nothing came back at him.

Ben tried again. "Anybody out there seen the self-appointed general asshole named Berman?"

Nothing.

"This Ben Raines, you traitorous mercenary pricks. Somebody talk to me."

Nothing.

"I know somebody is monitoring this," Ben said, after releasing the mic key. "Probably both Berman's people and my Rebels."

Ben waited for a moment and then tried again. "Anybody out there seen that yellow-bellied, two-bit tin soldier who calls himself Walt Berman? If you have, give him a message from me. Tell that piece of shit that Ben Raines is going to first whip his stupid ass, then I'm going to kill him."

"What are you trying to do, Ben?" Ike's voice popped out of the radio set on Rebel frequencies.

Ben ignored the question from his old friend and second in command of all Rebels.

"Talk to me, Ben," Ike persisted. "I know you can hear me. What the hell are you trying to prove?"

Ben smiled at the voice, but did not respond to the question. Mal stood up in the back and gave Ben a lick on the side of his face.

"Come on, Ben," Ike urged. "Talk to me."

Ben picked up the mic to the radio linked to Rebel frequencies. "It's personal, Ike. Now shut up and leave me alone, will you?"

"No way. Ben, you're the commanding general of the finest military force in the world. You can't—"

Ben reached over and turned the radio off. "Sorry, Ike. But this is something I have to do, ole' buddy." He didn't think he had stayed on long enough for Ike to have his location pinpointed. Ben picked up the small handheld unit and punched the TALK button.

"Well, have you assholes managed to locate that banana republic general of yours?"

"He'll be here in a few minutes, General Raines," the voice popped out of the tiny speaker.

"Good. I'll bump you in a few minutes. When Berman

gets there, tell the two-bit prick to stand by for my transmission."

"That's affirmative, General."

Ben waited for a few minutes, then tried again. This time Berman came on the horn.

"Raines, you bastard!"

"Hello to you, too, you pea-brained piece of crap."

Berman spent the next couple of minutes cussing Ben, and the mercenary commander was pretty good at it.

When he paused for breath Ben radioed, "If you could fight half as good as you cuss, you might someday be qualified to lead a platoon, Berman. Or maybe even a company. But that might be stretching credibility just a bit."

That set Berman off again. Ben waited until the man paused for breath. "I know that even a dimwit such as you will have equipment to pretty well pinpoint my location, Berman, so let's cut the crap and get down to it."

"What do you want, Raines?"

"To kill you, shithead."

"In your dreams."

"You man enough to meet me alone, Berman?"

"You goddamn right, I am. Just name the date and place."

"What's wrong with right now, dickhead? Or do you need more time to set up troops to help you? You damn sure aren't man enough to do the job yourself."

Berman started cussing again.

Ben calmly rolled himself a smoke, smiling at the angry profanity pouring out of the radio. He lit up just as Berman was running out of steam. Ben punched the TALK button.

"You're beginning to repeat yourself, Berman. And you're really starting to bore me. You have to be one of the most vain and certainly one of the dumbest sons of bitches I have ever had the misfortune to encounter."

"You son of a bitch!" Berman screamed the words so loudly they were distorted coming out of the speaker.

"Now, now, watch your blood pressure, old fellow."

"Old fellow?"

"That's what I said, Berman."

"We're the same goddamn age, you prick!"

"Now how would you know that, Berman?"

That question was followed by about thirty seconds of silence. Finally Berman said, "Figured it out, did you, Raines?"

"Some of it, yes."

"You were a contract operative for the Company, just like me, Raines. Well, almost like me. You always got the better assignments."

"They didn't fully trust you, Bateman. That's it. I knew it would come to me. Al Bateman."

"How about the rest of it?"

"You'll have to fill me in."

"Remember Joan, Raines?"

"Who?"

"Joan. Joan Tillson."

"You have me there, Berman—Bateman. I don't recall any Joan Tillson."

"You sorry son of a bitch!"

"Who the hell is Joan Tillson?"

"Damn you to hell, Raines! You're a liar. How about operation Lion's Den?"

"I wasn't on that op."

"You're a liar. You were in Capetown just before I got there. Dawson told me you were."

"Lars Dawson?"

"Yes."

"Lars Dawson is a liar. The man hated me. I sent in the report that kept him from being named Chief of Station."

"You're the liar, Raines. You let Joan down. Failed to

back her up. Got her killed. I loved that woman, and I hate you for that."

"You're wrong, Bateman. I never heard of Joan Tillson."

"Liar. Liar!"

"This is getting ridiculous. Your people have my location locked in?"

"Yes, they do."

"And you're going to tell me you're coming to meet me man to man, I suppose."

"You know I am. I'm going to kill you."

"You're a coward. You'll probably bring a company of troops to help you out. You're so damned afraid of me you're probably pissing on yourself as we speak."

The mercenary commander launched into another round of almost wild cursing. Ben smiled and waited until the man paused for breath.

"Come on, Berman—Bateman. Or are you going to continue stalling and showing how damn cowardly you really are by doing nothing but cursing?"

"I'm on my way, Raines."

"Alone, General Bullshit?"

"I'll be alone, you prick!"

"I'll believe that when I see it."

"One hour. You've got one hour to live!"

"Come on, dickhead. I'm so worried about it I think I'll take a nap."

Ben silenced Bateman's cussing by turning off the radio.

Chapter Thirty-two

Ben shifted locations about half a mile, to a large wooded area that seemed to run for a long ways, perhaps as many as four or five miles, taking in numerous hills and brushy country. Ben had no idea what else might be in that heavily forested area, but he had him an idea he was damn sure going to find out.

He had no idea what direction Berman would be coming in, but he suspected it would be from the rear, if there was a road behind that wooded area. Or he might be coming in by chopper. Ben would just have to wait and see.

He fixed Mal a large container of water and opened several packets of food for her, placing it all in the rear compartment of the Hummer. Then Ben geared up.

He put on his body armor and then slung a rucksack of Fire-Frag grenades and full mags for his CAR over one shoulder. He checked his sidearm and clip pouch on his web belt.

Mal sat in the back of the Hummer and watched it all with interest. She made no attempt to leave the rear compartment. Someone, Ben concluded, had spent a lot of time and patience training this big dog. They had done a wonderful job, plus the dog certainly had a lot of intelligence for it to stick. Malamutes were not, Ben knew, the easiest animals to train. They were strong-willed and very independent.

Ben ate some crackers and cheese and made a pot of coffee. While the coffee was brewing he filled his canteen with water, then sat down and rolled a smoke and drank his coffee and relaxed for a time.

He waited fifteen minutes then stood up and slipped the Federal walkie-talkie into a pocket. He petted Mal and said, "You stay, girl. I'll be back, and that's a promise. You stay here! Stay!"

Mal lay down and looked at him.

"Good girl. Good girl. Stay."

She licked his hand and Ben turned and walked off without looking back.

The Hummer was well concealed, and Ben didn't think any troops Berman brought with him—and he was sure Berman would do just that—would find the vehicle. Besides, Ben was going to be standing out in the open about a thousand or so yards from the Hummer, waiting for Berman to arrive.

He timed it just about right, and had Berman pegged as to how the mercenary commander would arrive. A few minutes after Ben got into place, he heard the heavy whacking of helicopter blades. He stepped further out into the clearing just as the chopper began a slow circling.

Ben pressed the talk button on the walkie-talkie. "Berman, is that you, asshole?"

"Coming in to kick your ass, Raines. Got your will all made out?"

Ben smiled and said, "How far does this stand of timber run?"

"Couple or three miles, and it's about a mile deep to the south. That the proving ground?"

"That's it."

"Suits me."

"Berman, I'm going to step back into the timber until you get your ass out of that chopper and the chopper is airborne and out of sight."

"Don't you trust me, Raines?"

"Hell, no!"

"I do have honor."

"I doubt it."

"You son of a bitch! I gave my word I would come alone, and by God, I'm alone."

"You've probably got two or three companies of your men coming in from all directions," Ben told him. That was not said solely to needle him. Ben firmly believed Berman was setting him up for the kill should he fail. Ben knew the mercenary had no intention of losing this fight.

"I do not!" Berman insisted just as the chopper was making its final approach before setting down in the clearing.

"We'll see. I'll be waiting just inside the timber. I'll step out when the chopper is clear."

"All right."

Ben stepped back into the timber and pulled on a pair of tight-fitting leather gloves. There was something he wanted to do before he and Berman started hunting each other with killing on their minds.

Moments later, the two middle-aged men met face-to-face for the first time in years. They stood staring at one another. Neither man offered to shake hands.

"You haven't changed that much," Berman said. "A few more lines in your face, more gray in your hair."

"Same with you—*Berman*. I'll stay with that name. I've gotten used to it."

"Suits me."

"That the name you want on your tombstone?"

"Fuck you, Raines. I'll be the one burying you, you conceited asshole!"

Ben popped him on the side of the jaw with a hard right fist that flattened the mercenary.

Ben waited, his CAR ready to bang. Berman shook his head to clear out the cobwebs and lay on the cool ground, staring hate at Ben.

"You got the balls to stand up and go a few rounds with me, Berman?"

"You goddamn right I do, you lousy bastard!" Berman pushed his weapon, an AK-47, away from him.

Ben propped his CAR against a tree and stepped back, shedding his battle harness, his rucksack, and web belt.

Berman stood up and took off his light backpack and battle harness. The two men faced each other.

"I should have killed you years back, Raines. After you left the Company and were writing your shitty articles and cowboy books."

"Why didn't you make a try?"

"I was out of the country." Berman took a swing at Ben and Ben moved his head to one side a few inches, the punch just missing him.

"That the best you've got, you dickhead?" Ben smiled as he taunted the man.

Berman answered that by shooting a jab at Ben that connected. Ben backed up and shook his head. The jab hurt; Berman had power. Ben fired back with a left that Berman wasn't expecting, and the punch caught the man on the side of the jaw that rocked his head. Ben followed that with a right that Berman succeeded in only partly blocking. The deflected blow caught him in the upper face, on the cheekbone. Berman grunted at that and backed up.

Ben pressed the man, and Berman caught Ben in the belly with a hard right that hurt. Ben countered with a hard straight right to Berman's chest, right over the heart. Berman gasped and backed up, his fists over his face, trying to catch his breath from the heart-hurting blow.

Ben hammered the man in the belly with lefts and rights, backing him up until he kicked out with a boot that caught Ben on the knee. Now it was Ben's turn to back up, favoring his painful knee.

Berman grinned. "That hurt, didn't it, you asshole?" He pressed in. Bad mistake.

Ben anticipated that, and put a little applied judo on the mercenary. Berman hit the ground on his back with such force it knocked the breath from him. Ben thought about kicking the man to death right then and there, then rejected the idea . . . for the time being, at least. He wanted to hammer on the mercenary commander for a few more minutes. The idea that he might get his own ass whipped did not enter Ben's mind.

Berman slowly got about halfway up and Ben uncorked an uppercut that caught the man smack on his snout. Blood and snot went flying and Berman hit the ground again, on his back.

Berman glared up at Ben and cussed as Ben backed up. "Why don't you finish it while you've got the chance?" he gasped, blood leaking from his busted beak. "I damn sure wouldn't give *you* any breaks."

"I know you wouldn't. And I should. But I want to hammer on you awhile longer."

Berman made a wild dive for Ben's legs and caught one, bringing Ben down to the ground. Ben kicked out, and his boot caught the mercenary on the shoulder and knocked him back.

Both men scrambled to their boots and stood facing each other for a few seconds. Blood was leaking from Berman's mouth and nose. Ben lifted his fists and Berman did the same. Then they went at each other again.

"This is for Joan!" Berman shouted, taking a wild swing at Ben.

Ben ducked the swing and smashed a fist into Berman's belly. "I keep telling you, you prick, I don't know any Joan." Ben shook his head in disgust. "You took this job just so you could kill me over a person I never met and never heard of? That makes you a fool."

Berman charged at Ben, both fists flailing the air. Ben sidestepped and hit him in the face with a right and then clubbed him on the back of the neck with a left.

Berman staggered and twisted around. Ben hit him again, with a left and a right to the face. Berman got wobbly in his knees and Ben pressed in, punching hard. He hit him half a dozen times before the man went down, his face bloody and swelling. This time, he did not even try to get up.

Ben backed up, studied the mercenary for a moment, and decided he was through for the time being. Ben peeled off his gloves. He slipped into his gear and picked up his CAR. Berman was still on his knees.

"I'll be waiting for you in the middle of this timber," Ben told him. "Then we'll see just how good a soldier you really are."

"Gonna kill you," Berman gasped.

"Wishful thinking, that's all. Just wishful thinking on your part."

Berman cussed him for a moment. Then he spat out blood and got to his boots. He swayed for a moment as he faced Ben. "I'll be along, Raines. And I'll kill you."

Ben shook his head and turned away. Then he heard a

metallic click and spun around. Berman had drawn his pistol and had jacked a round into the chamber.

"Don't do it, Berman!" Ben told him, lifting the muzzle of his CAR.

"Nobody whips me this way, Raines. Not and get away with it." He lifted the 9mm.

Ben shot him.

Berman jerked as the rounds tore into his chest. For a few seconds, he stayed upright, on his knees, a very puzzled look on his face.

"Maybe you didn't know Joan," Berman whispered as the pistol slipped from suddenly weak fingers.

"I didn't," Ben said. "I told you that."

"Raines? I got one more thing to tell you."

"What is it?"

"Fuck you!" Berman said, and then he fell over dead.

Chapter Thirty-three

"This way!" Ben heard the faint shout coming from the clearing. "That wasn't an AK."

Ben looked down at Berman's body. "I knew you'd bring troops with you, you lying bastard." Ben knelt down and picked up the dead mercenary's small backpack. He knew instantly and without looking what was in it: grenades and extra mags for Berman's AK-47. Ben took it and the Russian-made AK.

Ben quickly headed deeper into the woods until coming to a rise of ground. Too small to be called a hill, it was still the high ground. Ben quickly climbed up to the crest of the rise and was delighted to see a natural trench running across the top of the rise. On the back side was the remains of a fallen tree. Ben began putting together a sort of barricade, using broken limbs and stones placed in front of the natural trench, which was about two and a half feet deep.

On his left side, there was a sheer drop off of about thirty feet; Berman's mercs wouldn't be coming up that way. To his right, halfway down the small hill, was a partial clearing which offered scant cover, at best.

Ben got into place in the trench and behind his make-shift barricade and waited.

It wasn't long before he spotted the first of Berman's mercs making their way cautiously through the thick brush and timber. He had Berman's AK ready to bang. The round for the AK was a little less likely to be deflected by heavy brush.

"He's on that hill just up ahead," Ben heard a man call.

"What hill?" someone challenged. "Whole goddamn country is one hill after another."

"When he starts shootin' you'll know," another called. "You can bet on that."

"I need to call for someone to send a chopper for the general's body," a fourth man said. "They're not gonna believe he's really dead."

"Well, he's dead, all right. It was a damn fool thing for both of them to do."

"Not really. I understand it. General Berman hated General Raines. It was just something that had to be settled, that's all it was."

"Well, it's damn sure settled. Berman's dead. I guess you'd have to call that settled."

"Enough chatter," the first man said. "McVey, you and Chuckie and Mallory start up that hill."

"That's your ass, Barton," one of the three called. "Berman's dead."

"So?"

"Who's payin' us our money now? Somebody answer that one for me."

"I'd say he's damn sure got a point there, Barton. Who is paying us?"

"I don't know," Barton called. "But this is personal

now. Money or no money, I been with Berman a long time. We owe him this, way I see it.''

"Fuck that. I don't owe him nothin.' I fight for money, not friendship.''

Yet another voice was added. "Damn right, I ain't fightin' for the pleasure of it.''

"You got that right,'' another merc said.

"Get up that goddamn hill like I told you,'' Barton snapped. "I still give the orders here. Now, do it!''

Ben watched and waited for someone to make a move. Then one man attempted a run across a small clearing. Ben gave him a burst from the AK and the mercenary went down in a tumble, his legs mangled from the short burst of lead. He lay on the ground and screamed in pain.

Ben wondered how many men Berman had trucked in just behind his arrival. So far he had heard enough voices for maybe a squad, but Ben didn't think he would be that lucky. Surely as much as Berman had hated Ben and wanted to see him dead, he had brought more than that.

The mercs below him opened fire on his position and Ben was forced to hunker low in the trench, knowing that at least a couple of the mercs were on the move during the cover fire.

Ben smiled and took a couple of grenades from the rucksack and popped the pins, then tossed them down the hill, throwing the mini-bombs in a high arc.

"Grenades!'' someone yelled.

Both grenades exploded about ten feet off the ground and several of the mercs began yelling.

"I'm hit, I'm hit!'' one yelled.

"Shut up, damnit!'' the man that Ben could now recognize as Barton shouted.

"Oh, Jesus!'' another merc called, his voice slurry. "My neck . . . my face is . . .''

His words trailed off into a painful bubble.

"Where the hell are the others?" a merc called.

"Berman said they'd be here if he needed them."

"Well, we goddamn sure need them now!"

"Was he gonna call in?"

"I don't know."

"Who's got the radio?"

"Barton does."

"No, Barton doesn't," Barton called. "Franklin does."

"That was Franklin yellin' about his face and neck," Chuckie called.

"Can you get to him?"

"I can try."

Ben waited a few seconds and pulled the pins on two more grenades and chunked them over the side.

"Get down!" a merc yelled.

The warning came about two seconds too late. The grenades blew, and that was followed by several more explosions. When the debris stopped falling there was almost dead silence for half a minute.

"What the hell was that?" Barton called.

"One of the grenades landed right on Chuckie," someone called. "It set off the grenades he was carrying. Chuckie is all over the place in bits and pieces, and Wesley don't have a head. I'm outta here, Barton."

"Get your ass back here!"

"Fuck you. I'm gone."

"I'm with you, Dick," Mallory said. "I'm gone."

"You yellow bastards!" Barton yelled.

There was no reply. Mallory and Dick had cut out for safer grounds.

"Shit!" Ben heard Barton say. That was followed by someone beating a path through the brush.

Barton had followed Mallory and Dick.

Was there anyone left?

Ben didn't know.

What about the wounded mercs? Did those who had just pulled out leave them to die?

He didn't know about that, either. What Ben did know was that he couldn't spend a lot of time waiting around there. Some of Berman's mercenaries would certainly show up with blood in their eyes ... probably led by Barton when the man got his nerve back.

Ben crawled to the end of the shallow trench and chanced a look below him. He could see huge splashes of crimson splattered about in one spot and chunks of various body parts—remains of the merc after the grenades on his battle harness exploded. Ben shook his head at the sight; what a mess. The first merc he'd downed was lying in the clearing and not moving. He could see nothing of the other dead or wounded.

Ben cautiously made his way down the rear of the small hill and into the brush, circling wide and heading back to where he'd left Mal in the Hummer. He really had serious doubts about her still being there. He'd been gone a long time: a couple of hours.

When he reached the Hummer, she was gone.

"Well," Ben said. "I was asking a lot of her."

A bit sad at losing the dog, Ben put his gear in the vehicle and turned around as he was removing his battle harness. Mal was sitting a few yards away, looking at him, as if to say *Where the hell have you been?* Ben smiled and knelt down, holding out his hands. The dog came to him and Ben petted her for a moment.

"You ready to take a ride, girl?"

She gave him a lick on the side of the face.

A few minutes later, Ben was on the road, Mal sitting on the front seat, watching the passing scenery with doggy interest.

Ben turned on the radios and the talk was all over the frequencies. The Rebels had attacked the Federals from all sides and put them in a full rout, forcing them back across the border as fast as they could go. The Rebels had taken several hundred prisoners.

The Federal assault on Rebel territory was over, and Raines's Rebels were clearly the victors . . . again.

Ben drove for several miles, not sure where he was. Finally he pulled over to roll a cigarette and try to get his bearings. He had just lit up when suddenly the sky was filled with Rebel helicopters. Several of them landed in a clearing off to Ben's right. Ben put a hand on Mal to calm her down; she was getting very nervous about the hammering of the huge blades.

His team piled out of one chopper and ran toward him. Mal bared her teeth as they approached.

"It's all right, girl," Ben told her, petting her. "They're friends."

Jersey was the first one to reach the Hummer. "You all right, Boss?"

"I'm fine, Little Bit."

Mal looked at the young woman.

"Holy shit!" Jersey said. "Who is that?"

"I found a friend."

"You sure did," Anna said from the passenger side of the Hummer. "Is it all right to pet him?"

"Her," Ben corrected. "Malamutes are usually very people-oriented. But this one is very different from others I've been around. I'd let her approach you before doing anything."

An officer Ben did not know by name but had seen a few times walked up. Ben thought he was a major, but since many Rebel officers did not wear rank insignia, he wasn't sure about that. "General," he greeted Ben. "President Jefferys said that when we found you we were not to let you out of our sight again, and we were to escort you back to Base Camp One immediately."

"Did he now?"

"Yes, sir. He sure did, sir. Ah . . . is that your dog, General?"

"I think I belong to her," Ben replied. "But maybe it's a mutual thing."

"Whatever you say, sir. That is a very large animal, General."

Ben noticed the officer was eyeballing the Malamute warily. "She's no lightweight, for sure."

Mal was busy licking Anna's face while she petted her. Anna had no fear of dogs, and the Mal had sensed it.

"Shall we go, sir?" the officer asked.

"In a little while," Ben told him.

"Ah . . . sir," the major persisted. "President Jefferys said immediately, General."

Ben cut his eyes to the major, then slowly got out of the Hummer. He looked directly at the officer. "In a little while, Major."

The major knew better than to push it any further. One simply did not push a commanding general, and one sure as hell didn't push Ben Raines. "Yes, sir. Whatever you say, sir."

"Thank you." Ben turned to his team, all gathered around the Hummer. "Somebody get my gear out of this vehicle, please. Then we'll have a cup of coffee and I'll relax a bit."

"Right, Boss," Cooper said, moving around to the rear of the Hummer. "Sounds like a good idea to me, for sure."

"Who cares what you think, Coop?" Jersey told him, a twinkle in her eyes. "Get the gear. Why not make yourself useful for a change?"

Cooper looked up and silently mouthed the words, *Screw you!*

Jersey gave him the middle finger.

The major looked pained at the exchange.

A very senior sergeant that Ben had known for years walked up. "Howdy, General."

"Sergeant Major Jensen," Ben greeted the CSM.

"There are die-hard mercs and young hotdog Federals all around this area, General," the CSM advised Ben. "It isn't wise to stick around here."

"You are suggesting that we depart as soon as possible, Top?"

"Yes, sir. I would say quickly, General."

"Very well, Top. Let's do that."

There are ways to smooth troubled waters—especially when dealing with generals—and the CSM knew them all.

The major looked very pained at how easily the Command Sergeant Major worked Ben.

That was why sergeants ran the army.

Chapter Thirty-four

Cecil was furious, and making no attempt to hide his anger. "Of all the stupid, arrogant, unthinking, goddamned, stupid-assed stunts you have pulled in the past, this one damn sure takes the prize. Good God, Ben, you're the commanding general of our armed forces. You're a national treasure, a legend. What the hell were you thinking?"

"You're upset with me, aren't you, Cec?" Ben asked with a smile.

"Upset!" Cecil shouted. "Jesus Fucking Christ! You're goddamned right I'm upset."

"Don't hold back, Cec. Let your feelings out. Tell me how you really feel." Ben sipped his coffee and grinned at his longtime friend.

The President of the SUSA sat down behind his desk and put his face in his hands. "I give up," he muttered. "I just by God give up. You'll never change."

"Look on the bright side, Cec," Ben said cheerfully.

"What bright side?"

"Berman is dead. His mercenaries are, at least for the moment, leaderless. The civil war is at a standstill, giving us time to shift troops around and resupply all units—or a standoff, might be a better way of putting it. Rebel losses have been very light. Sure, there is a bright side."

Cecil grunted noncommittally.

The big Malamute was getting bathed and dipped and groomed at a local vet's office.

Madam President Claire Osterman had gone on the air in the USA to announce and condemn the brutal murder of General Walter Berman at the hands of Ben Raines.

And Ben was in the process of getting his ass chewed in the office of President Cecil Jefferys.

Cecil pointed a finger at Ben. "I'm going to surround you with security people, Ben. I'm going to make sure you never, ever get another chance to pull this type of stunt again. You understand me, ole' buddy?"

Ben smiled. He loved a challenge.

"I don't like that smile. Damnit, Ben! You've got to start accepting your part in the running of this nation. You've got to stop taking these wild chances."

"I'm a soldier, Cec. Not a statesman."

"So were a lot of other commanding generals throughout history, Ben, but they didn't behave as though they were twenty year olds trying to prove something."

Ben grunted.

"Let's don't butt heads on this issue, Ben. Let's don't have a showdown. That wouldn't be good for us or the nation. You agree with that?"

"Of course, I do. No showdowns, Cec."

"Good. That's settled, then."

"So have you been in contact with Sugar Babe?"

"I have spoken with some people in her inner circle several times over the past three days."

"And?"

"We all agree the fighting must stop."

"That's entirely up to them, Cec. I'm ready to end the fighting anytime a reasonable compromise can be worked out."

"We're trying to work something out."

"With a liberal socialist democrat? Good luck, Cec. Just keep one hand on your wallet if you meet with them, and for sure don't believe anything they agree to do."

Cecil stared at his friend for a long silent moment. "What is the alternative, Ben?"

"War, Cec. A war that eventually the SUSA will win."

"Yes, we'll win it, in time. But you said yourself it would create a wound that would never heal."

Ben smiled. "Or words to that effect."

Cec looked at Ben, a very serious expression on his face. He held up a hand. "No jokes, Ben. Not now. My people are working very hard with Osterman's office to bring this war to a close."

"Don't trust them, Cec. You can't trust socialist democrats to keep their word." Ben leaned forward and put his hands on the desk. "Somebody's been hoodooing you, Cec. Socialist democrats don't compromise. They'll tell you they will, and then turn right around and stick a knife, so to speak, in your back." Ben grimaced. "Sometimes stick a knife in your back literally. I wouldn't trust one of the sons of bitches out of my sight."

"Ben, don't you think I know all that? Hell, I don't trust them. But these talks are being closely monitored by the United Nations. And you know how they feel about us. There isn't a country on that monitoring committee that doesn't owe their very existence to us."

Ben shook his head. "You think a socialist democrat wouldn't tell a lie to the UN? Horseshit, Cec! They've got one thing on their minds, and that one thing is their own agenda. You watch those mealymouthed lying assholes,

Cec. They'd tell a lie to God because they wouldn't believe it was actually God confronting them. You be careful, Cec. Be very careful, and don't promise those bastards anything. They don't believe in God, Cec. They're far too intelligent to believe in God."

Again, Cecil stared at Ben for a long moment. "You really hate liberals, don't you, Ben. Not dislike—hate."

"I didn't used to, Cec. I used to think they were amusing. Then that feeling of amusement vanished when they became dangerous, a real threat to law and order and morals and values. I don't hate the average liberal, Cec. I'm just filled with indifference toward them. I don't care what happens to them. The colleges and universities— some departments—began preaching liberalism, social- ism, Big Brother-is-wonderfulism, whatever you want to call it, years before the collapse and the Great War fell on us all. And some were not subtle about it. Thousands of young minds were corrupted by that crap. Some studios in Holly- wood got into the act and so did the TV networks. If it feels good, do it. No limits." Ben paused, a frown on his face. He waved a hand. "I'm preaching to the choir, Cec. You know all this. Forgive me."

Cec smiled at his friend. "You're forgiven, Ben. Some- times I need reminding about things. And you always man- age to do just that. Ben, I don't trust Osterman or most of the people around her. You don't have to worry about that. However, there are a few in her inner circle who want peace, and if they have to depose her in order to achieve it, they will."

"They'll try, Cec. And they'll fail. She'll have them killed, bet on it."

"Or they'll kill her."

Ben shook his head. "Don't count on that, ole' buddy. Claire Osterman is a survivor. I hate the woman, but I'll give credit where it's due." Ben stood up and started toward the door. He paused and turned back to Cecil. "Don't leave the SUSA for any meetings with Osterman's people. That would be very unwise on your part."

"I'll keep that in mind."

"You do that, Cec."

Ben sat in his Hummer in the parking lot for several moments, deep in thought. He did his best to ignore the security people who were assigned to protect him . . . and, he thought with a smile, to keep a eye on him.

He knew that Cecil wasn't buying the garbage Osterman's people were handing out. However, Cecil wanted peace between the USA and the SUSA. Because of that, Ben's old friend might get lulled into a false sense of security, get careless and let his guard down. If he did that, Osterman's people would kill him.

Ben knew from years of dealing with Osterman types they would stop at nothing in order to get their way. All for the good of the people, of course.

Ben wondered just what the hell Osterman was up to. All fighting between the Federals and the Rebels had abruptly ceased. In the thirty-six hours since Ben had been ordered back to the SUSA, not one shot had been fired along the several thousand mile long front. Something was up, and Ben didn't think it was the Federals' overwhelming desire for peace.

To say that Ben didn't trust the USA's federal government was a gross understatement.

Ben cranked the engine and dropped the HumVee into gear. As he did so he was thinking: *Cecil had better be damned careful.*

Ben was awakened by the ringing of the telephone. He fumbled for the receiver and swung his legs out of bed, almost stepping on Mal, who had been sleeping on the rug beside his bed.

"Yeah?" Ben said, glancing at the clock on the nightstand. 0200 hours.

"Ben?" Cecil said in a tired voice. "Get down to the command center's war room. We've got a building situation."

"On my way." Ben didn't waste time asking what the situation was. That would be explained when he got to the war room.

Ben took a quick shower and dressed in BDUs. Fifteen minutes after Cecil's call, Ben was pulling out of his driveway. Mal sat in the front seat of the Hummer beside him, looking out at the night.

"Something big is brewing, Mal," Ben said. "Osterman has pulled something. You can bet on that."

The dog gave her deep, Malamute reply.

"I'm still working on a name for you, girl," Ben told the dog. "Don't worry. I'll come up with something."

"Woowoowoowoo!"

"Right. I know we're being followed. Better get used to it." There were several Rebel security vehicles trailing Ben though the quiet early morning hours.

Ben's team met him in the parking lot of the command center. Ben handed Mal's leash to Anna. "Take care of her, Kiddo."

"Will do, Pops. Come on, Jodie."

Ben stopped and turned around. "What 'd you call her?"

"Jodie. You like it?"

"Yeah. Yeah, I do. OK. Jodie it is."

Ben passed through several checkpoints, then was admitted to the elevator that would take him down to the presidential command center. There, he passed through another checkpoint and was admitted to the war room.

A very tired-looking Cecil smiled at him. "I just hung up

the phone after speaking with Madam President Osterman, Ben. She has given us an ultimatum.''

Ben poured a mug of coffee. He glanced up at the Defense Posture Board. The top light was slowly blinking a dull red—the next to highest defense alert. When it changed to a constant bright red, the SUSA was on a full alert and on a war status for possible missiles coming at them.

"What is the ultimatum, Cec?"

"Immediate surrender."

"And if we don't comply, which of course we won't?"

"She will order the launch of missiles against us."

"Oh? Nuclear?"

"She didn't say."

"I rather doubt they'll be nucs. Probably germ warheads. Kill all us nasty ole' conservatives and keep the buildings for use by the occupying troops." Ben laughed. "Socialist carpetbaggers. Now that's funny, Cec."

"I truly wish I could find something amusing about this situation, Ben."

"What's her deadline for launch?"

"0600. I have our air defenses on alert."

Ben walked over to a red telephone and picked it up. He was answered immediately. "This is General Raines. All air defenses are to go on full alert nationwide . . . immediately. We're going to have missiles to intercept, and we don't want any to strike SUSA soil. OK. Good shooting."

Ben slowly hung up the phone just as Cec was opening his mouth to object. He managed a "Ben—"

Ben shook his head. "My show now, Cec. You know our constitution better than I."

"You're right, of course. Do we warn our citizens about the possibility of a strike?"

"Not just yet. An hour's time is all many will need. A few minutes is all most will need."

"I've told Osterman that her demands are ridiculous."

"I would have told her a lot more than that," Ben replied.

The men drank coffee and chatted for a half hour until Ben told Cecil to go take a nap, get some rest. He would man the command center until Cec woke up.

Ben told the security people to get his team into the war room. While that was going on, he got Ike on the horn.

"I think you should be here, Ike."

"I'll stay with my troops," the ex-Navy SEAL said.

"I thought you'd say that, Ike, but I wanted to try. Intel says they're ninety-nine percent certain the warheads are germ. But they aren't sure what type of bugs they contain."

"We have the vaccines for every type of bug we know Osterman has," Ike replied. "The troops are ready."

"You know that some of the missiles are going to get through."

"I know."

"We're probably going to lose several hundred thousand people."

"If that rotten bitch uncorks those missiles, Ben . . ." Ike let that trail off.

"There will be precious little left of the USA. That is a promise."

"Will you use our missiles?"

"Will I have a choice?"

Another long moment of silence. "No, I reckon not. God help us all."

"Osterman and her followers don't believe in God."

"Oh, yeah, I forgot. They're too intelligent to believe in God. Then God help the SUSA."

"That's more like it."

"Keep your head down and your ass covered, Ben."

"I will, Ike. Luck to you, ole' buddy."

"OK, partner."

Ben spent the next few minutes in a conference hookup, talking with all his brigade commanders. They were as ready as they could possibly be. Cecil had ordered additional vaccines flown in to all Rebel locations as soon as Osterman had issued her threat. But, as General Georgi Striganov pointed out, if the missiles carried nuclear warheads there was very little the Rebels could do except ask for heavenly intervention.

Ben sat at a desk in the war room, talking with his team and petting Jodie.

And waiting.

Corrie was handling the communications now. Every so often Ben looked over at her and shook her head.

Nothing.

At 0500 hours Corrie stiffened in her chair. Ben heard her say "Are you sure?"

Ben smiled knowingly. "Goddamn socialist democrats. I knew it. You can't trust those two-faced bastards."

"Birds are in the air!" Corrie said. "Just launched."

"Cooper, get President Jefferys, please."

Cec had awakened a few minutes earlier and had been washing his face in cold water. He walked in the door just as Ben was speaking to Coop.

"It's only 0500, Ben," Cecil said, glancing at the clock on the wall. "President Osterman gave us until 0600. What the hell happened?"

"I warned you about trusting that bitch. She jumped the gun on us."

"Our missiles have intercepted most of the first wave," Corrie said. "Two got through. First one carried a germ warhead and struck in North Texas."

"Goddamnit!" Cecil flared.

"Right on the border with New Mexico, just north of Interstate Twenty."

"Very lightly populated," Cecil said. "Thank God."

"Second bird struck in Eastern Tennessee. In the mountains."

"Ready all silos and surface based facilities," Ben said quietly. "Prepare to launch on my orders. Repeat. On my orders!"

"Right, Boss."

"Miserable no-good lying bunch of assholes!" Ben said.

"I will certainly agree with that," Cecil said, pouring himself a mug of coffee.

"Second wave of Federal missiles launched and on the way," Corrie said.

"Any ground troops taking part in this so far?" Ben asked.

"Negative, Boss."

Anna had filled a container with water and was sitting on the floor beside Jodie while the dog drank. Malamutes are not the most delicate animals when they drink, and Anna got water all over her.

"I should have warned you," Ben said with a smile.

"Shit!" Ben's daughter muttered, wiping her pants legs with a handkerchief.

"One got through, Boss," Corrie called. "It struck in Central Arkansas."

"Damn! Which way are the winds blowing?" Cecil asked.

"West to east," Beth told him. She was handling secondary communications.

Ben walked over to Corrie and motioned for her to give him the mic.

"This is General Raines speaking from the war room of Base Camp One. Launch the first wave of our missiles. Wait ten minutes and launch the second wave. Ten minutes later, launch the third wave." He paused for a few seconds. "And may God look with mercy on our souls."

The Wingman Series
By Mack Maloney